LIVING COLOR:
ANGIE RUBIO STORIES

By Donna Miscolta

Published by Jaded Ibis Press.
www.jadedibispress.com

 JADED IBIS PRESS

For my smart girls, now smart women,
Natalie and Ana

CONTENTS

Welcome To Kindergarten

In the morning welcome circle, Angie could see all the faces of her classmates, all of them pink, pale, or freckled. Then there was hers—toast, well-done—not unlike the Hawaiians she had expected to see at Charles W. Nimitz Elementary, her new school with an un-Hawaiian name and no Hawaiians in the classroom. There was the teacher whose skin was neither brown nor white, but the beige of cake batter. Everything else about her though shrilled with color—her purple dress and green high heels, the yellow beads at her neck, the orange powder on her cheeks and the candy-red lips. Her hair was construction paper black. She looked like she lived in a comic book. She said her name was Mrs. Pai, and the children laughed, but she didn't smile, and for some reason this made Angie long for Hawaiians in the classroom.

At recess she found Eva, a second-grader, playing hopscotch with a girl with muddy blond hair and three moles on her cheek. "Where are the Hawaiians?" Angie asked her sister.

Eva, who knew everything, told her coldly, "Hawaiians are extinct."

Angie knew the term extinct, having heard it from Eva's lips before in reference to dinosaurs, dodo birds, and jitterbugs. Angie didn't believe that Hawaiians were extinct. She had seen them herself and so had Eva when they stood on the deck of their docking ship. Their father had taken pictures with his movie camera. Their mother held thumb-sucking Letty in one arm and pointed with the other. "Look at the hula dancers."

It's true that she hadn't called them Hawaiians. So now Angie asked Eva, "What about the hula dancers?"

The girl with the moles whipped her skinny hair around. "Those are just shows. I'm taking hula lessons and I'm going to be in a show." She jerked her hips and made wiggly motions with her arms, which made Angie want to change the subject. "Guess what my teacher's name is?"

"Mrs. Pai," said Eva, who knew everything.

"She's mean," said the girl with the moles. "And she's Chinese." The girl pulled at the corners of her eyes.

While the girl with the moles was busy making Chinese eyes, Angie watched Eva nudge the girl's hopscotch marker back a square.

In the afternoon, Mrs. Pai announced it was large motor skills time, and she clapped her hands and trotted around on her high, green shoes urging the children into a circle. Then she set the record on the phonograph spinning. "Skip to My Lou," she ordered. Angie obeyed along with the other children, their heads earnestly bobbing as their arms swung and their legs kicked. Except rather than alternate her kicks, Angie canted along, her right foot never surrendering the lead to her left.

Suddenly the music stopped, and Mrs. Pai clip-clopped her way through the children frozen in mid-skip until she came to Angie whose stubborn right foot remained flagrantly ahead of her left.

Mrs. Pai said, "If you can't skip, you shouldn't be in kindergarten."

She set the record playing again and as the other children skipped even more earnestly now, Angie stood at Mrs. Pai's desk watching her write a note of harsh scribbles. Up this close, Angie could smell the powder on Mrs. Pai's face, see the furriness of her black, black eyebrows and the wrinkles at the edges of her lollipop mouth.

"I hate to do this," Mrs. Pai said as she finished her note and folded it three times. "Nevertheless." She pinned it to Angie's dress.

After school Eva unpinned the note but couldn't make out the scrawl. Still, she pronounced to Angie, "You're in trouble," and she handed the note to her.

Angie said she was quitting kindergarten.

"You can't quit. It's against the law." And Eva, who knew everything, told how in Hawaiian jails they only gave you coconuts to eat and drink and there were no toilets. Just the scooped-out coconut husks to pee in.

Angie began to cry. Eva put her arm around her, a rare gesture that made Angie cry harder and made Eva impatient. "Don't be a kindergarten baby," she said, and then she huffed away down the street toward their row of Navy housing. Angie watched her sister move farther and farther away, furiously wishing her extinct.

She clutched at the note in her hand, squeezing it into a clump. She hurled it in front of her, but it landed at her feet and a lady yelled from a passing car for her to *pick up that trash*. Instead, she kicked at it with her right foot and took a step and kicked with her left and took another step to kick with her right again. Back and forth she went, step right, kick left, step left, kick right, *skip to my lou*.

* * *

9

"Clean your plate," her mother said. "Children are starving in Timbuktu."

"Where's Timbuktu?" Angie asked, wondering if it was part of Hawaii, still pondering the whereabouts of Hawaiians.

Her mother frowned, hands on hips even though she was slouched deeply into sofa cushions. "It's far across the ocean."

Angie's whole family associated the ocean with seasickness and vomit, their voyage to Hawaii having taken place on a vast, gray ship whose long, slow movements churned their stomachs up into their throats. Her father had trained his movie camera on all of them as they lay lined up in deck chairs, wrapped in blankets, heads lolling to the side, dull-eyed and baggy-mouthed.

Nevertheless, Angie thought, using Mrs. Pai's word. She would suffer an ocean crossing to take her unwanted food herself to the starving Timbuktu children.

Everyone had left the table and Angie sat alone with her cold peas and carrots, soggy as snots. She scooted them around with her fork as if acts of eating and swallowing would somehow naturally follow. Scattering the vegetables across her plate did nothing to make them disappear or diminish their number. She squinted at them. If anything, they seemed to have multiplied. Angie threw her paper napkin across her plate and smothered the living daylights out of the peas and carrots. She squished the napkin in her fist and stuffed it in her shorts. Her heart beat with disgust at the feel of the flattened bits, all smashed together like swatted tropical insects.

"I cleaned my plate," she announced. Her parents were on the sofa watching TV, her father's hand resting on her mother's belly that was fat with what her parents were hoping was a brother for Angie and her sisters.

Her mother glanced at Angie's plate, unbelieving, but weary, too. "Your milk," she said, sighing, turning her attention back to the TV.

Every so often, her mother poured glasses of milk for them at dinner the way the mothers on TV did, except her mother wore curlers and house slippers, not pearls and high heels. Angie knew the appearance of milk at the table was related to her mother's big belly, which made Angie look spitefully upon the bulge. They all hated milk, even her parents, though they bravely drank theirs. While Eva, holding her nose, gulped hers down, then belched in protest, and Letty, though three now, was given a baby cup with an easily swallowed baby portion, Angie had reduced her full-size serving by one tepid, stomach-turning sip.

Eva and Letty were outside playing. "Can I drink my milk outside?" Angie asked, hoping her father would answer this time. Even her mother prodded him. "Henry?"

But he was concentrating on *What's My Line?* He liked guessing at other people's lives, liked revealing the truth right there in his own living room. He didn't take his eyes from the screen, though he did speak, if absentmindedly, with the same questioning inflection— "Delia?" —to acknowledge her utterance of his name.

Her mother's face was puffy with irritation even before she turned to glare at Angie. Sometimes, when faced with that look of her mother's, Angie yielded. "Never mind," she would say. But Angie would not take back this question, and so they waited for rescue or intervention, but none came. Finally, her mother huffed another sigh, removed Angie's father's hand from her belly and said, "Go ahead," in the way that meant she didn't really want Angie to go ahead.

Nevertheless, Angie thought, and she went ahead.

She sat on the back porch and watched Eva and Letty play tag with the Gorski sisters and their awful little brother. Jan and Lou Ann were the first children the Rubio sisters met when they moved in at 833 Seventeenth Street.

"We're from Wisconsin," they said, making it sound better than California where the Rubios were from. "Our name is Polish," they said.

"Ours is Mexican," Eva said.

"Do you speak Mexican?" Jan asked.

"Do you speak Polish?" Eva countered.

The standoff ended when Lou Ann said, "I can speak Hawaiian" and they all shouted *aloha* at each other.

The Gorski sisters wore identical hairdos, straight brown hair that flapped at their cheeks and bangs that made a straight line above their yellow-flecked brown eyes. They went to the Catholic school and knew the mass by heart. They could do cartwheels and they were doing them now even as Letty chased them. Having recently learned to skip, Angie thought, *I must learn to cartwheel.*

Angie blew bubbles into her milk, and some of the milk escaped down her throat. She gagged, a half-fake strangulation that jerked her body and made her milk tip onto the grass. She made an *oh no* gesture, her hand to her mouth. She caught her breath, righted the empty glass and then ran to join the game, her insides bloating with guilt, her limbs light with triumph, itching to do a cartwheel, but overruled by her brain's refusal to turn itself upside down, to risk falling. Confusion and panic. Utter embarrassment.

* * *

In the morning after breakfast—Tang and toast and soft-boiled eggs—their mother yanked their hair into braids, the big lump of her stomach intruding on their behinds, her thick-fingered hands gripping their hair and pulling scalp and eyebrows upward. Eva arched her back dramatically around the curve of their mother's belly. Their mother looped and snapped the rubber band into place and let the taut braid slap Eva's spine. Eva staggered across the room.

"Basta," their mother warned, using her Spanish that no one in Hawaii had any use for. Back home in California, her sister Nelda and her parents spoke it. "That's enough of that," their mother said, though Angie and her sisters had understood her the first time. Just as they understood that their mother missed California and that the Spanish words that escaped her were mostly scolding and faultfinding.

So, Angie was required to plant her feet and resist the impulse to sway with each tug at her hair. When her braid was done, Angie still felt as if her mother's hands were there at the back of her skull.

Their mother handed them their metal lunch boxes. "Don't talk to strangers," she said. "And eat all your lunch."

She didn't say "don't dawdle" because Eva never did. And if Eva didn't, Angie couldn't. Even when the walk was new to them and they were easily confused by the look-alike Navy housing, Eva charged ahead as if she knew exactly where she was going, though Angie suspected more than once they walked the same block twice.

She had asked her father why they didn't live where the Hawaiians lived.

"We're Navy," he told her. "We're all Navy," he said, gesturing to take in the rows of pink and gray housing up and down the block.

"What about Cani?" she said of the boy next door whose house and occupants always smelled of cooking even when nothing was being stirred on the stove. He was in her class at school and she thought they should be friends, except she didn't like saying his name, so she called him what she'd heard his mother call him.

"You mean Canuto?" her father said, and Angie squirmed at the correction, her tongue balking at the pronunciation. She nodded.

"They're Navy, too."

"Not Hawaiian?"

"They're Filipino," he said, and Angie wasn't any closer to understanding who or where the Hawaiians were.

She skipped to stay up with Eva's bloodhound pace, and her lunch box rattled and sloshed. She hoped her mother hadn't put milk in her thermos.

"I don't think I want a brother," she said to Eva.

"Jan and Lou Ann have one," Eva said.

Angie didn't think that was a good reason to have a brother. Anyway, they already had Letty—not a brother, but an extra child, which is how she thought of Letty.

"He's a brat," Angie said of Jan and Lou Ann's brother, who had once banged his toy hammer on her head.

"Ours will be better," said Eva, who knew everything.

They were at the corner where the patrol boys in their yellow helmets and red vests were holding their long poles horizontally to bar anyone from stepping into the traffic. The patrol boys were sixth-graders, practically grown-ups, important with their uniforms and sticks and whistles, their freckled faces serious with the job of keeping schoolchildren from being run over.

In the duck-and-cover drills they had in class, Angie imagined the patrol boys were somehow involved in protecting them from the bombs that might drop any minute on the playground, holding up their stop signs against the exploding chunks of blacktop and shattered hopscotch squares.

Eva marched to within inches of the patrol boy's pole and stood straight as a pole herself. Angie pulled up just behind, not even with, Eva's shoulder. But as they waited for the traffic to slow and for the patrol boy in charge to blow his whistle, Angie decided to break with the unspoken understanding that the oldest was always first. She leaned forward on her toes and as soon as the whistle blew, the traffic stopped, and the pole was lifted, Angie shot past Eva, launching herself off the curb and into the crosswalk.

Halfway across the street she was leading not only Eva, but all the rest of the children who had lined up behind them. She swung her arms as she increased her pace even more and swung her lunch box right out of her hand. It reeled in front of her above her head and its flight spun her stomach with panic. She lunged and held out both her hands, but the lunch box bounced off them and clattered open on the asphalt.

Other kids, their lunch boxes safely in hand, laughed and bumped past her as she fumbled to reach hers, its lid flung open, the contents exposed. Soon the patrol boys would withdraw their stop sign, the cars would move through the crosswalk and her lunch would be smashed, a possibility that part of her wished for fervently. But then Eva was there, bending down quickly and snapping the lunch box shut as if she, too, could not bear to have it open in the street.

Angie ran to the curb after Eva, who shoved the lunch box into her ribs.

"Next time I'll leave it for a car to run over."

"And then I'll starve like the children in Timbuktu," Angie said, defiant. There were times when she just wanted to run to her mother, wanted to bang her head into her belly.

* * *

Mrs. Pai sat in a chair and the children sat at her feet on the floor as she read them *Ping the Duck*. Her eyebrows dipped toward her nose and the growl of her voice made Angie believe that Mrs. Pai herself would carry out the warning that the last duck on the boat would be spanked.

Mrs. Pai turned the book open toward the class to show the picture of Ping waking up all alone after hiding in the reeds to avoid punishment. Her eyebrows slid deeper into their dip and her nose began to twitch, the wide nostrils swelling. Her face, which was lifted in the air, turned dark as she sniffed. She held the book crookedly, her fingers blotting out Ping in the reeds. Angie and the other children shifted, impatient, but then they too sniffed the air, smelled the smell, which was displacing the scent of crayons, paste, chalk, and mayonnaise-steeped lunch boxes.

Mrs. Pai clapped the book closed. "Who has made an accident in their pants?"

The children were silent. They looked around, searching for a safe place to settle their unblinking eyes.

Mrs. Pai stood up and lay *Ping* on the chair. She gave the children one long last glare. "Well, then, line up," she said.

It wasn't at all clear what they were lining up for, but Angie never wanted to be first in line for anything. Today, though, neither did a lot of the children so after all the shifting and shuffling, Angie found herself in the middle.

Mrs. Pai began her inspection. She peeked down the pants of the boys and underneath the dresses of the girls. Even though Angie knew she had not made an accident in her pants, she feared that somehow Mrs. Pai's very act of looking would produce a smudge.

Angie did not want to feel fear. Even though Mrs. Pai was mean, even though she never smiled, and her voice was always bossy, Angie still thought there was something they shared in the same way that she thought she and Canuto had something in common.

In this land of Hawaii where she had yet to see any Hawaiians, Angie was aware that in the classroom, the three of them were somehow the same. Nevertheless, Mrs. Pai gave it no notice. Cold-blooded, Eva would say. Like the unmoving lizards that stuck to their walls at home or splayed themselves droopy-eyed on the windowsill.

Still, after Mrs. Pai snapped the panties back into place on the girl ahead of her, Angie looked Mrs. Pai directly in the face, something she seldom did with grown-ups. For a moment, she thought she saw a flicker of understanding in the hard, black marbles of her teacher's eyes. But it may have been the blink of Angie's own eyes that caused the glimmer because Mrs. Pai went about the business of eying Angie's backside. Angie held her breath. Though Mrs. Pai found nothing, and Angie could join the ranks of the innocent on the other side of the room, Angie felt that Mrs. Pai had wanted her to be the culprit, or at least expected her to be.

When Mrs. Pai found the accident in Polly Dodson's polka-dot panties, there was relief all around. Even Polly's sobs were welcomed. She was sent off to the principal's office. They watched her waddle away, but the nasty smell lingered and tainted the story of *Ping*. Mrs. Pai put the book away without finishing it.

They did animal flash cards. They went around the circle, each child naming the animal on the card that Mrs. Pai held up between her colored nails. Mallard, catfish, ladybug.

Mrs. Pai held up a card for Angie and even though her long painted fingernail was strangling it, Angie recognized the animal.

"Platypus," she said, nearly rising to her knees.

"No need to shout," Mrs. Pai said.

"Platypus," Angie said again, softer this time, sinking back onto the floor, but Mrs. Pai was already holding up a new card for the next student.

* * *

Angie ate her cream cheese sandwich, celery sticks, and graham crackers, and sluiced it all with the grape juice in her thermos, but an apple still bulged red and large in the middle of her lunch box. She knew she couldn't fit its terrible size inside her stomach. She held it in her hand, wondering how she could make it disappear, when Candace Martin marched passed her table with an apple cradled in her hands and her lunch box dangling empty and light from her wrist. She went straight up to Mrs. Pai and extended her offering, "Here's an apple for you, Mrs. Pai."

"Well, thank you, Candace. You may put it on my desk."

Candace opened her lunch box for Mrs. Pai's inspection.

"Very good. You may go to recess."

Angie noticed her apple had a bruise from having been dropped in the crosswalk that morning. She turned the bruise to rest against her palm and approached Mrs. Pai, who looked at her with an unwelcoming eye.

"Angie, I can't accept an apple from every child. You'll have to eat that."

Angie returned to her seat. She bit into her apple and her stomach spasmed. The flesh was mush. It camped out on her tongue until saliva pooled and she swallowed hard. She held her breath, waiting to see if it would come back up. When she was sure she would not see that bite of apple again, she relaxed a little, only to be gripped with a sudden need for the lavatory. But the rest of the apple sat fat and unfriendly in her hand.

She wrapped her fist around it and with her other hand, held her now empty lunch box like a shield as she sidled toward the nearest waste can, empty because Mrs. Pai allowed no waste in her classroom. Fearful of the thunk a falling apple would make inside an empty waste can, Angie bent her knees, stretched her arm and lowered the apple into its bottom with a soft thud that was lost amid the chatter of her classmates. Angie went again to Mrs. Pai where she stood like a traffic signal in a yellow blouse and red skirt. She opened her lunch box to the inky eyes of Mrs. Pai, who dismissed her to recess with a nod.

Angie scuttled out of the room, dashed to the lavatory, slammed herself inside a stall and sank onto the toilet seat. As her bowels released a mad torrent, she thought about Polly Dodson's accident and Ping the Duck and Candace Martin and rotten apples. Then as her stomach began to feel lightened from its burden, voices echoed off the bathroom walls and penetrated her locked stall where she sat bent over, her Keds gripping the base of the toilet.

"She's in there," someone squealed.

"Mrs. Pai wants you."

"You threw away your apple."

Angie considered what would happen if she refused to leave her stall. Would they call the police? Would her mother come to save her? Maybe, she answered to the first. Maybe, she wanted to believe of the second. But she knew it was useless to delay. She stood, wiped herself, hitched up her panties, and flushed the toilet. When she exited the stall, the girls, whose voices had been ricocheting around the bathroom, stood watching her, pressing their lips together against their giggles. Angie walked back to the classroom where most of the children had finished eating, so only a few were left to watch Mrs. Pai hold the garbage can to Angie's nose and ask, "Angie, is this your apple?"

"Yes," Angie said into the garbage can, which made a faint echo back at her, affirming her guilt.

"Go get your mat and lie still during recess."

After Angie had laid her mat on the floor and herself on top of her mat, Mrs. Pai shooed the rest of the children out to recess.

A fly buzzed in the empty classroom.

"Food in the waste can attracts flies," Mrs. Pai said as she wiped down tables, her high heels making unforgiving clacks on the floor.

Angie, who had been concentrating on staying motionless, felt the fly land on her leg. She jiggled it slightly, but the fly didn't budge, so she gave a small kick and shed the fly.

"Angie, you're to lie still on your mat."

"The fly," Angie said, but Mrs. Pai held up her hand to shush her. *I must learn to cartwheel*, she thought and imagined herself airborne.

The next time the fly landed on the same spot of the same leg, Angie gritted her teeth until finally the quivering on her skin forced her leg up in the air, which once again brought the clacking of Mrs. Pai's shoes. Angie dropped her leg back onto the mat just in time to feel Mrs. Pai's hands on the spot where the fly had been. When Mrs. Pai's footsteps reached the other end of the room, Angie peeked at her leg. Mrs. Pai had put a Band-Aid on it. On a place where there was no wound.

At the end of the day, Mrs. Pai called Angie to her desk and pinned a note to her dress. When Angie met Eva at the front of the school for their walk home together, Eva crossed her arms in exasperation.

"Otra note?" she asked, sounding like their mother, unpinning it from Angie's chest as if she *were* their mother.

Eva unfolded the note and squinted at it. "Looks serious," she said.

Angie tore the note from her sister's hand. She looked at the black scrawl, put a corner of the paper to her mouth and began to chew. Eva watched her with her arms folded, tapping her foot, frowning. Angie chewed and chewed until the pieces slid down her throat.

*   *   *

Each day after recess, Mrs. Pai asked, "Who wants to play with the blocks? Who wants to play in the doll corner? Who wants to play on the farm?"

With each question, she plucked children from their seats and sent them to their assigned play area. Angie always raised her hand for the doll corner but was almost always dispatched to the farm. Canuto often ended up there too, even though he always raised his hand for the blocks. Angie hated the farm. There were too many boys playing there and they never played right. Instead of setting the cows out to graze or corralling the horses, they tossed them like grenades and exploded the barn onto its side.

"Cani, let's race our horses," Angie said one afternoon, hoping for some realistic imaginary play.

"Don't call me Cani," he said and moved to the other side of the farm so that Angie was left to trot her horse alone.

When she got home from school, her mother was lying on the couch, her stomach rising in the air like a mountain. Her feet rested on pillows and she was reading a magazine. Angie went to stand near the couch, resisting the urge to press down on her mother's belly. Her mother looked up from her magazine. "¿Qué quieres, Angie?"

"Can I take my doll for show-and-tell?"

"Which doll?"

"My grown-up doll."

"That's not to play with."

"I know. Just to show and tell."

Her mother patted her belly as if comforting its bigness. Finally, she said to Angie, "Go ahead."

The previous Christmas, their mother had given Eva and Angie grown-up dolls. They came in display boxes, which is where they remained. "They're to look at, not to touch," their mother had said. This didn't bother Eva at all. She had not been thrilled by the high-heeled, page-boy brunette in the black satin dress made poufy by petticoats. Pearl earrings dangled at her plastic lobes and a strand of pearls circled her neck. She had brown eyes and lids that blinked with mechanical clicks.

Angie did want to play with *her* doll. It had a blond ponytail tied with a blue ribbon that matched the blue eyes and also the blue skirt of the dress, its black bodice plushy as the eyelashes. It had black high heels and silver earrings that, though they didn't dangle, sparkled like tiny stars.

The doll stood atop the dresser, trapped in its box, a clear plastic hood protecting the perfect ponytail. Angie had to ask permission to hold it, which her mother was granting with more frequency lately due to her belly.

*   *   *

Smug and shy, Angie entered the classroom. She held her doll, encased in its cardboard and plastic wrapping, face out to her classmates. Canuto stared at her. "What did you bring that for?"

Angie teetered momentarily off balance, her doll a strange weight against her chest. Suddenly, she was surrounded by the girls in the class, and even though Angie knew it was the doll and not herself that drew their attention, she felt what it was like to be admired.

The doll did not fit in her cubbyhole, so Mrs. Pai stood it in its cardboard box on top of the dresser in the doll corner. Behind her plastic veil, she shimmered and drew the eyes of the girls in the classroom.

When it was time for show-and-tell, Angie sat in the meeting circle with the doll in her lap. Bobby Reese brought a picture of his dog, since he wasn't allowed to bring the real thing. Becky Hooper brought a bean plant in a coffee can. Ricky Smith brought his front tooth, though it had been a full week since it had detached. The other children were required to ask three questions of the show-and-tell children.

When it was Angie's turn, she said she got her doll for Christmas, it was a grown-up doll, and it was wearing a party dress. Then the hand of every girl in the room shot in the air and Angie had to decide who to call on to ask a question. They were all straining toward her, their arms wiggling, their mouths open. She couldn't remember anyone's name, so she nodded at the girls closest to her. *Can she stand up by herself?* No, she has to be leaned against something. *What's her dress made of?* The top is like velvet and the bottom is like silk. *Can you take the plastic bag off?* It's not recommended, Angie said, repeating a line she'd heard on TV about cough medicine.

Three more children had their turn for show-and-tell, but Angie's doll had stolen the show.

Later, when Angie raised her hand for the doll corner, Mrs. Pai chose her along with three other girls. At first, the other girls busied themselves with the regular dolls, washing their faces, changing their clothes, brushing their hair, getting them ready for a tea party. Angie sat in one of the chairs at the tea table holding her high-heeled, grown-up doll inside her plastic-covered box. One of the girls, Iris, brought her freshly groomed doll to the table. She looked at Angie's doll. "How will she drink tea if she has plastic across her face?"

"I'm going to pretend," Angie said.

The other girls gathered with their dolls at the table. "You could pretend that she has a disease and has to wear a plastic veil to keep her germs from spreading," said one of the girls.

"Well, maybe I could just take off the plastic," Angie said, and she slowly lifted it off her doll. The girls crowded in for a better view.

"Hey, she looks like Iris," one of the girls said.

It was true. Angie's blue-eyed, blond doll looked exactly like Iris.

You should let Iris hold her for a minute, they said, so Angie handed over her doll.

It began with one girl touching the dress, another the curly bangs, and another a sparkly earring. Suddenly, the hands had removed the doll from its box and they swarmed over her, removing her hair ribbon, rearranging her ponytail, stripping off her high heels, yanking at her petticoats.

Stop, Angie thought. *Basta*, she wanted to shout. She tried to get the word out of her mouth, but it jumped around in her throat. Even though the girls saw her trying to tell them something, they carried on as if they didn't.

Angie closed her eyes and took a deep breath. Her mother had warned her and her sisters often enough. *Don't make a scene.* Not that she was inclined to anyway. It was Angie's own terror of public shame, not her mother's warning frown that kept her in check. And yet it was the thought of her mother that made Angie exhale not a controlled breath, but a robust screaming of *basta*, though the second syllable was lost in the gape of her mouth and Angie instead bleated like a tortured lamb.

Her cry silenced the room and Angie for a very brief moment felt what it was like to be in command. Mrs. Pai clomped her high heels over to the doll corner and said, "Angie, we do not scream in class."

Mute once again, Angie pointed at her disheveled doll with a convulsive finger.

"Girls, give Angie back her doll." She turned to Angie. "It was really not a good idea to bring such a special toy to school."

The girls threw everything at Angie and went back to the regular dolls. Angie tried to put her doll back to her original state, but nothing was the same—the hair, the ribbon, the shoes. Everything was off, awry, no longer perfect. She held herself stiff as Mrs. Pai pinned another note to her dress. She feared what her mother would say.

Even Eva feared it because she didn't say a word on the way home, except once to offer an idea as they passed a dumpster. "You could say your doll was stolen."

It was true that a missing doll would be far better than a doll that was forever rumpled. She could cartwheel her doll into the big, wide opening. The high-heeled feet would scissor, the blue fabric of the dress would lift like a parasol, her wild ponytail would spread and cushion her fall. She would rest in peace. Instead, Angie threw Mrs. Pai's note in the dumpster.

Despite its rumples, Angie wanted her doll. They had endured something together that day. There was another reason Angie wanted to keep her. She held the tiniest hope that her mother would take them both in her arms and tell them that everything was fine, everything was going to be all right.

But when they got home everything was wrong. Their mother wasn't home. No one was home. Just a note in large block letters on the door. Eva read the note which said for them to go next door. Canuto answered their knock. He glanced pitifully at the doll as he let them in. Letty was sitting on Canuto's mother's lap.

"Mama's at the hospital having our brother," Letty said.

Later their father came to take them to the hospital. They stared through the glass at their squishy-faced brother. "There he is," said their father. "Our little Hawaiian."

Angie opened her mouth to protest, but Letty was already cooing *aloha*.

Monster

Angie sat on the front porch, a cement ribbon that connected the units of Navy housing. She fiddled with the Kodak Brownie her parents had given her recently for Christmas, though her joy at getting a camera had long dissolved since she realized hers was practically a toy. It was a clunky plastic box, and even though real film could be threaded into it, it didn't look like the real thing. Even the click of the shutter sounded pretend.

Angie was peering through the viewfinder, trying to decide what to take a picture of when a truck heaped with furniture pulled up at the curb and behind it a shiny lime-green car. She didn't know cars came in that color. She thought she should take a picture of it even though the color wouldn't show up on the black and white film.

Don't waste film, her mother was always saying. *Film costs money.*

Before she could decide whether to ignore her mother's nagging in her head, the car doors opened. Angie lowered her camera to her lap, partly because her mother had warned her about intruding on other people's lives—*Mind your own business!*—but all too often other people's business was more interesting than hers. Angie lowered her camera not to mind her own business, but to marvel at what she saw. A little girl in a bride's dress. The girl had cottony yellow hair that made a halo around her head. Her look-alike mother might have been a movie star with her red lips, blue eyelids and high-heeled sandals, but there was something hard about her face and voice that made you think she could only ever belong in scary movies, like the ones Angie watched on *Science Fiction Safari* every Saturday afternoon. The mother wore clingy shorts and a halter top, the kind of clothes Angie's mother called *beachwear,* meant only for the beach. Both mother and daughter lugged bulging paper bags up the short walkway to their front door just a few feet from where Angie sat.

"Look, Susie, there's a little girl."

"I know. I already saw her."

Angie fiddled with her camera some more.

Two men had jumped out of the truck and were unloading a couch. They had the short sleeves of their T-shirts rolled up to show tattoos that flexed with their muscles. Cigarettes hung from their lips. One man was blond, and the other had dark hair. She knew they were sailors by their haircuts. The tattoos, too. All the men in the Navy housing had them.

As the men carried the couch onto the cement porch, the dark-haired man paused, held onto his end of the couch with one hand, removed his cigarette, and called into the house, "Hey, Susie, there's a little girl here."

From inside the house, Susie bellowed, "I know, Daddy."

It surprised Angie that the dark-haired man, not the blond one, was Susie's father. She had become used to seeing people grouped by color—skin color, that is. But it made her want to arrange people by hair color too, to package them together in sets. The way she and her sisters had long, black braids and the Gorski sisters had hair the color of peanut butter.

Susie's father was named Mick and her mother was Marla. Sometimes they called each other by their names and sometimes they said *babe* or *hon*. Sometimes they said *idiot*.

While Angie pretended deep absorption in her camera, she watched from the corner of her eye all the back and forth movement from car or truck to porch—the transfer of chairs, mattresses, tables, lamps, suitcases, boxes and bags. And a toy chest! Marked with Susie's name. It rode on Mick's back, empty, its lid open, the latch flapping and clanging against the wood. Susie was swishing the skirt of her bride's dress from side to side above her bare feet and prancing as she followed the progress of the toy chest. The size of it made Angie wonder about the number of toys that could fit inside. Susie caught her staring and stopped in the middle of her sashaying and stared back. Angie looked down at the camera in her lap and twirled its plastic strap with her fingers until she no longer felt the stab of Susie's eyes.

There were no more things to unload, but the door to Susie's unit remained open. Angie could hear her new neighbors moving things around inside, giving orders to each other, calling out each other's real name along with the *babes* and *hons* and *idiots*. They were a smaller family than Angie's, half the number, and yet their voices made them seem bigger. It was their loudness, the way they owned their words, and yet tossed them about so easily.

There was some rustling out on the porch and the soft slap of bare feet on cement. Things were being dragged and arranged and rearranged and finally Angie could no longer not look. She turned her head to see Susie at her shoulder peering down at her. Angie jerked backward and chirped a nonsense syllable through her nose.

"Can't you talk, girl?" Susie demanded.

Angie stood up to measure herself against this girl whom she was sure was younger than herself, despite her bossiness. Angie was definitely taller.

Susie aimed her pert nose up into Angie's face. "Are you Hawaiian?"

Angie took a step back. "No, Mexican," she said, eying the toys Susie had arranged on her porch, weighing her chances of playing with them.

"Say something in Mexican."

Angie sighed. She didn't know many Spanish words. She knew how to say *hello* and *goodbye*, could count, and sing parts of "El Barquito Chiquitito." She knew colors and names of some fruits. She knew that her last name meant blond. Like Susie's hair, being tossed impatiently at the moment as Angie considered a response.

"Hola," she said.

"Ha," Susie snorted. "That's not Mexican. That's Hawaiian, and you said it wrong. It's *aloha*."

Before Angie could untie her tongue, Susie lobbed another question at her. "What's your name?" she asked, sticking a finger up her nose on a search mission.

Angie was so startled by the nose-picking, which was so completely forbidden in her household, that she gave up her name without a thought. Susie seized it and made a rhyme.

"Angie Bangie," she sang. She ran to her throng of toys, fished out her play high heels, and slipped them on her dirty feet. She tottered back to Angie.

"I'm Susie Wren. Can I play with your camera?"

"It's not a toy," Angie said, glancing at the hoard on Susie's porch—stuffed animals, a play oven, a rocking horse, plastic golf clubs, cowgirl boots, and a miniature guitar. "But you can hold it."

Susie grabbed the camera and put her eye to the viewfinder and began shooting picture after picture until it stopped clicking.

Susie handed the camera back to her. "I think your camera's broken."

"No," Angie said, cradling it as if were some wounded animal. "You used up all the film."

"Why don't you get some more?"

Just then Susie's mother leaned out the door. Angie could see up close her blue eyelids and her lips red as jam. "What's your friend's name, Susie?"

"Angie Bangie."

"Well, Angie Bangie, Susie has to come inside now." Susie's mother smiled a big, red smile that teetered to the wrong side of cheerful.

"Bring your toys in and put them away," Susie's mother said as she went back inside, a flutter of blond hair the last of her to disappear from the doorway.

Susie took tiny, quick steps in her high heels and began dragging and shoving toys through the doorway until the porch was empty. She went inside and slammed the door.

Angie took her camera with its used-up film and went inside her own house. Eva had already turned on *Science Fiction Safari* and Angie sprawled on the floor beside her to watch a movie about giant African vines that strangled hunters who stalked lions.

That evening after Angie and her sisters had had their baths and their wet hair hung long and damp against their nightgowns, their mother called them to her, scissors in her hand clicking the air.

"I don't have time to braid so much hair," she told them. Their baby brother Anthony made her tired all the time.

She cut Letty's the shortest—to her ears like the Gorski sisters. She cut Angie's and Eva's chin-length, not even long enough for a ponytail anymore. Eva pretended to like hers. Angie cried. Her mother scolded. "Do you want the neighbors to hear you?"

But it was they who heard the neighbors. Susie Wren and her mother Marla and dad Mick could be heard through the walls.

"Did you tell Mrs. Wren your last name was Bangie?" her mother asked.

"No," Angie said, shaking her head so that her shortened hair spanked her face.

"Well, she called me Mrs. Bangie. Why would she do that?"

"Susie said it."

The voices next door banged like firecrackers. Talking, shouting, calling names. *And saying things that weren't true*, Angie thought.

"You need to learn to speak up and correct people when they make a mistake. Really, it was so embarrassing to be called Mrs. Bangie."

Her mother was cradling Anthony and holding a bottle to his mouth. She bent over him and talked in a baby voice, "What kind of silly name is Bangie? ¡Qué tontería! Anthony did spastic baby kicks and her mother laughed as his foot kissed her chin.

* * *

Susie didn't walk to school. Marla drove her. Angie referred to Susie's parents by their first names. Not out loud. In her mind, they were Marla and Mick, *babe* and *hon*, *stupid* and *idiot*.

While Angie and Eva were waiting for the patrol boys to let them cross the street, they saw Marla's lime-green car pull up in front of the school. It was a convertible and the top was down, and both Marla and Susie wore scarves tied over their blond hair. Marla wore movie star sunglasses and Susie had on a pair of flimsy plastic children's sunglasses. They untied their scarves and shook their hair, and then walked to the school office, Susie's little hips swaying like Marla's.

"There's the little princess," Eva said.

"You mean bride," Angie said, thinking Eva had mistaken Susie's costume the other day for a ball gown like Cinderella's.

Eva rolled her eyes and snorted.

When they reached the school entrance, Marla was coming out of the office. She stopped in front of Angie and Eva. "Well, hello, there, Angie Rubio. Hello, there, Eva Rubio." She put great emphasis on their last name.

"Hello, Mrs. Wren," Eva said, smiling what Angie knew to be her fake smile.

"Well, you girls have a nice day at school."

They watched her walk away in her tight pedal pushers and high-heeled sandals. Other children were watching too. No one else had a mother like Marla.

Angie saw Susie at recess surrounded by other girls. When Angie had been the new girl, no one had crowded around her. Susie spied her through the thicket of her sudden friends and shouted, "Hi, Angie Bangie!"

"Qué tontería," Angie muttered.

Later as Angie and Eva walked home from school, the lime-green convertible drove past and Susie turned around to wave, her sunglasses like giant, green insect eyes on her face.

When they got home, Susie was on her front porch where she had again dragged out an assortment of toys. She was wearing a red cape and was putting toys in and out of the hands of Jan and Lou Ann who were already home from their Catholic school just blocks away.

"What's that you're wearing, Susie?" Eva asked.

"A cape." Susie twirled and the cape wrapped and unwrapped around her.

"I think she's Red Riding Hood," Jan said.

Susie shook her head, scattering blond wisps around her face. "It's not a fairy tale cape. It's like a real cape from the olden days."

Jan snickered. "C'mon Eva, let's go ride our bikes."

"Okay, but I want to change into my hula skirt first," Eva said.

"Hey, I have a hula skirt!" Susie said.

Eva and Jan left, laughing.

"I do have a hula skirt," Susie said, and she ran inside her house. She ran back out, shaking the hula skirt in front of her as she swayed her hips. "See."

Angie was about to ask Lou Ann if she wanted to go ride bikes too, but Susie piped up first. "You want to play house?"

"Okay," Lou Ann said.

"I'll be the mother," Susie said, pulling the hula skirt on underneath the cape. She pointed at Lou Ann. "You can be the father."

"I'll be the daughter," Angie said.

"No," Susie said, "We're newlyweds. We don't have any children yet."

"Then how can you be the mother if you don't have any kids," Angie said.

"It's just pretend," Susie chided, hands on her hula hips.

Angie looked to Lou Ann for support, but Lou Ann just shrugged.

"Then who will I be?"

"You can be the mailman."

Angie wasn't sure she wanted to be the mailman.

"Or the burglar," Susie said.

Angie decided to be the mailman. But it was soon clear how limited her role was. While Susie as the mother got to paint her toenails, drink coffee, go shopping, and tell her husband to get his feet off the furniture, and Lou Ann as the father got to shave, read the paper, go to work, and come home and ask his wife to get him his slippers, Angie as the mailman had only the mail to deliver, which was just folded strips of paper in an old cloth purse. Once, Angie tried to deliver the mail twice, but Susie told her the real mail only came once a day. Angie had to wait until Susie the mother and Lou Ann the father had dinner, watched TV, went to bed, and got up the next morning before she could deliver the mail again.

"Can we play a different game?"

To Angie's surprise, Susie agreed. In fact, she was enthusiastic. She started clapping her hands and bouncing in her pretend high heels. "I know what we can play!" She clattered into her house and came back with her bride's dress flapping behind her.

"This game is called Prettiest Girl."

Angie didn't like the sound of it—hated it, in fact. And yet she asked, "How do you play that game, Susie?"

"Let's pretend I'm the prettiest girl in the world." She pointed at Lou Ann. "You can be the handsome prince who saves me."

"Saves you from what?" Angie asked.

"The ugly monster."

"I don't think I want to play," Angie said.

Susie had already stripped off her hula skirt and cape and was stepping into the bride's dress. Her face went pouty and hard for a moment, her eyes mean, and Angie was fascinated by this transformation. Angie and her sisters were always being admonished not to make a scene. Angie couldn't help but stare at this display of real feelings. Lou Ann was looking on disapprovingly.

"No one's making you play. It's a free country. It's the United States of America where we live, you know. We went to the Hawaii's-a-State celebration. I wore a pink muumuu and a lei with red, white, and blue flowers."

Angie wanted to clap her hands over her ears, but instead just turned to go home.

But Susie pulled her back, her face changed again, brilliant with aggressive goodwill. "Here," she said, thrusting the cape at Angie. "You can wear the cape!"

Seduced by the cape, Angie agreed to be the monster. She tied the cape around her shoulders, enjoying the way it fell and spread down her back. She swung her torso so that the cape wrapped itself around her hips and legs. She took some running steps and felt it fly out behind her. Even as she made scary monster growling sounds as she chased Susie, the prettiest girl in the world, and was fended off by Lou Ann, the handsome prince, Angie made believe she was special in her red cape, that she was loved and adored. Even that she was Miss America.

That Saturday on *Science Fiction Safari*, a mad professor set up a lab in the jungle to experiment on ways to harness the energy of ants. He accidentally created a giant ant the size of a gazelle. The ant terrorized the nearby villagers who threw their spears at it and the safari adventurers who blasted their guns at it. While scary in appearance, the ant was really docile and harmless, but the scientist was forced to destroy it to calm the natives and the great white hunters. He concocted a goop and set a trap. The ant became mired in it. The breathing holes in its body clogged up and the ant writhed and collapsed. Angie turned off the TV, sighing at the injustice.

*   *   *

Most of the time Marla made Susie drag her toys out to the front porch, but sometimes she let Susie invite Angie and Lou Ann to play in her room where her toy box beckoned with its secrets. But while Susie's toys had their appeal, the toy box itself was an even bigger lure. Empty, it was big enough for all three of them to sit inside, knees huddled to their ears. If just two of them were inside, they could face each other and stretch their legs out with only a small bend in them. With just one of them in the box, it was a bed, a bathtub, a coffin.

Susie's name was carved on the lid, a reminder to Angie and Lou Ann that the toy box belonged to her and she was the boss of any game they played in it. The scenario never changed though. Susie was the princess or the most beautiful girl in the world, Lou Ann was the prince or the husband, and Angie the mailman, burglar, or monster.

That afternoon they played Snow White, and Susie wore her bride's gown. Lou Ann, who was the prince, wore the red cape, and Angie, who was the wicked stepmother, wore Susie's hula skirt on her head. Angie didn't mind this particular role, and in fact liked cackling and handing Snow White a poisoned apple. Still, her role wasn't as good as Susie's, which required her to swoon and stagger and collapse into the toy box where she clasped both hands over her chest. And then after the prince kissed her—really, just smacked the air above Susie—she got to flutter her eyes open and slowly and miraculously wake from the evil spell. Sometimes she insisted that the prince lift her out of the toy box, but Lou Ann couldn't lift Susie by herself, so Angie had to abandon her hula skirt hair and pretend to be the prince's helper.

Every so often Marla would call up the stairs, "You're not playing inside that toy box, are you?" Angie and Lou Ann would look at each other, while Susie put her finger to her lips and then shouted down the stairs, "No!"

"C'mon, let's play mummy," Susie said. She tore the sheet from her unmade bed. "Who wants to be the mummy?"

"Why don't you be the mummy, Susie?" Angie said.

"I can't. I'm the princess."

"I'll be the mummy," Lou Ann offered.

"Good," said Susie. "You can be buried with my best toys."

"Okay, what should I be?" Angie asked.

"You can be the grave robber," Susie said.

This time Angie accepted the role without argument. Stealing Susie's toys, if only in play, was not a bad deal.

Susie and Angie wrapped Lou Ann in the sheet and helped her into the toy box where she lay with her knees bent. Then Susie dressed in her bridal gown and veil. Angie holstered the gun from Susie's cowgirl outfit and tied a kerchief over her mouth.

"Okay, go to your robber hideout," Susie instructed Angie.

Angie scooted beneath Susie's canopy bed and watched as Susie trotted solemnly around the room collecting treasures for the mummy—a ballerina doll, an organ grinder monkey, a glittery magic wand, binoculars, Chinese checkers, puppets on strings. At first, she tucked them in neatly around the sheet-bound Lou Ann, bowing after each offering and chanting words from a Hawaiian song she'd learned from hula dance class. Then she started throwing the toys in, eliciting *ows* from Lou Ann.

"Oops," she called into the toy box before lowering the lid. Because of the overflow of toys and Lou Ann's bents knees, the lid didn't close all the way, the latch not quite fastening.

"Put your knees down," Susie yelled to Lou Ann as if she were deaf as a real mummy.

But Lou Ann yelled back. "Hurry up and rob the grave. I want to get out of here."

Angie crawled from her hideout, skipped the part she had planned about tiptoeing stealthily to the grave and made straightaway to loot the toy box, shoving the goods into a pillowcase from Susie's bed. She'd only begun her plunder when Lou Ann sat up and wriggled her shoulders free of the sheet.

"I'm not done," Angie protested.

"I don't like this game," Lou Ann said.

Angie thought of all the times she hadn't liked the games they'd played, but she'd done them, played along, been the bad guy or the boring guy or the mean person. Never had she quit the game early.

"You're a bad sport," she told Lou Ann.

"Am not."

"Are too."

They heard Marla's high heels on the stairs. "Girls, if you're fighting, I'm going to have to send you home."

Susie leaned out the doorway. "I'm not fighting, Mama. And I'm not playing in the toy box."

Lou Ann tumbled out of the toy box, her legs still entwined in the sheet which she kicked off as she sat on the floor. Angie tossed the pillowcase of toys on the bed. They listened to Marla's footsteps fade away down the stairs.

Susie brushed the veil from her face. "Want to play house?" she asked.

Angie waited for Lou Ann to say no, but Lou Ann was twirling the end of the sheet with her toe, so Angie said it for both of them. But in the end, she was the only one who left.

She watched another episode of *Science Fiction Safari*. In it a woman became separated from her safari group and wandered alone for hours, fending off dive-bombing birds, recoiling from snakes, and hiding from spear-wielding natives. A band of chimpanzees surrounded her protectively and eventually led her to safety. She adopted one of them and named it Ezra, which sounded like a girl's name even though the chimp was a boy.

* * *

Each Wednesday afternoon for fifteen minutes Mrs. Maloney put on a record, clapped the beat on a tambourine and called out commands—half-turn left, full-turn right—which always ended in collision since many of them, Angie included, still had not memorized the difference. While Angie dreaded putting her hands in the sweaty palms of a boy, what she dreaded more was being the last to be picked as a partner. There were a few girls who found themselves the object of multiple potential partners, while others, like Angie, were left stranded looking at their shoe buckles.

One Wednesday morning, after several weeks of playing monster or mailman or burglar to Susie's princess, bride, or Miss America, Angie opened her closet and surveyed her choice of dresses. Most of them were regular, everyday dresses that she'd worn time and again. But there in the back was her Easter dress—an itchy, frilly, silly thing. Pink and puffy.

"You'd better hurry up," Eva told her. Eva was wearing a blue plaid dress and was pulling on blue socks and blue Keds. "Beat ya." She ran downstairs for breakfast.

Angie took the Easter dress off the hanger and put it on, wrinkling her face at its stiffness. She put on lacy socks and slipped her feet inside her tight Sunday shoes. The squeak of them on the stairs made her tiptoe. She took her seat at the kitchen table as if nothing were out of the ordinary, even cooed at baby Anthony, who was mashing scrambled eggs in his fist and eating the ooze.

"Why are you wearing that?" her mother asked. "¿Qué estás pensando?"

Angie shrugged and frowned to convey that she didn't know what her mother was talking about, which was half true since she really wasn't sure what the Spanish words meant.

Eva hummed the Miss America song.

Letty whined that she wanted to wear her pretty dress, too.

Anthony threw eggs on the floor.

"My teacher said we had to wear our best dresses today," Angie said over the erupting chaos. She grew hot inside her ruffles.

Her mother gave her an unbelieving stare, but Angie concentrated on her toast, sipped her Tang, and waited as her mother considered the energy it would cost not to believe.

Her mother sighed. "Just don't get it dirty."

"I promise," Angie said, sitting straight and smoothing the dress over her lap, raking its scratchy fabric across her legs.

While Angie made a show of catching toast crumbs over her plate, Eva made an equal show of pulling a napkin across her mouth, folding her arms across her chest, and tapping her foot.

Finally, their mother said, "Well, go on, you'd better get to school now." She dabbed a blot of egg from Anthony's cheek and pushed it between his lips.

Since Anthony's appearance in the family, Angie sometimes felt as if she were being dismissed from home the same way she was dismissed from school. She followed Eva who walked especially fast, knowing that Angie's shoes pinched and her dress itched. But Angie gladly suffered because she was wearing a pretty dress, the effect marred only by the plaid lunch box she carried.

When she got to her classroom, several girls stood around her to ask why she was dressed like that. "Is it your birthday?" one of them asked.

Angie, embarrassed by the attention, shrugged, which they took as a yes.

"Where are the cupcakes?" The mother of the birthday child was expected to send treats to school.

"I forgot them."

"No fair."

They headed off in a posse to tell Mrs. Maloney.

Mrs. Maloney thumbed through her index cards on which she wrote information about each child in the class.

Angie sat at her desk relieved to take the pressure off her pinched feet, though sitting did nothing to ease the disturbance in her ribcage as she watched Mrs. Maloney slide her eyebrows together above her jeweled glasses while studying the card that had all the numbers of Angie's life—telephone, address, birthdate.

"Angie, can you come here, please?"

Even though the bell hadn't rung yet, most of the children were in their seats, attuned to the potential for spectacle or disaster. Angie rustled and squeaked to the front of the room to Mrs. Maloney's desk where her fingernail made an indentation underneath Angie's birthdate. Mrs. Maloney turned her toothy smile to her and, though she spoke in almost a whisper, Angie felt as if the words were visible, pounding things.

"It appears, Angie, that there might be a mistake. The card says your birthday isn't for another two months."

Angie took a shallow breath since a deeper one would've caused friction between her skin and her frilly dress. "Yes," she said. "There's a mistake."

Mrs. Maloney waited for more, so Angie nodded, hoping that would settle things.

"So, your birthday is today?"

Angie wondered how she got here in this lie, in this dress. She lowered her voice as much as possible. "I'm sort of celebrating it today. But without cupcakes."

"I see," said Mrs. Maloney.

"Just a dress."

"And it's a very pretty one, too. Nice and twirly for dance period today."

So, after the Pledge of Allegiance, which Angie as the birthday girl got to lead, the class sang "Happy Birthday" to

43

her, though she could sense some reluctance in their voices, not to mention their faces.

But by the afternoon, the silent grievances about her questionable birthday and the lack of cupcakes had subsided, in fact, disappeared, which made Angie feel sad about the fleeting attention a birthday could bring, even a pretend one. But at least she had on a pretty dress.

When it was time for dance, the children pushed the desks against the walls and then milled in the middle of the room waiting for Mrs. Maloney's instruction—painful, cajoling words that Angie dreaded a little less today.

"Now gentlemen, choose a partner. Don't be shy. These young ladies won't bite."

The boys wandered in and around the huddle of girls and tapped a shoulder or nudged an elbow. Angie, often among the last to be chosen, kept her eyes on her Sunday shoes. As she stared at the smudges that had appeared since she had buckled them on that morning, a cluster of shoes surrounded hers. She looked up to stare now at three boys waiting to be her partner.

Mrs. Maloney swooped in to break up the staring contest, paired Angie with one of the boys and shuttled the others off to girls in less pretty dresses. *What a difference a dress makes,* Angie thought, hardly feeling the pinch in her shoes as she and her partner turned left and spun right, the twirl of her dress making her feel like a princess.

*   *   *

With Anthony commanding most of her attention, Angie's mother was less strict now about Angie and her sisters "lying around doing nothing but watching TV," which is how she complained of it to Mrs. Gorski over coffee one Saturday morning.

Mrs. Gorski agreed TV hours should be severely limited. "Of course, cartoons are harmless," she said.

"And sometimes a movie can take them places even their imaginations can't," Angie's mother said.

"Game shows," Mrs. Gorski noted, "could be educational."

The Gorski and Rubio children were crowded in front of the Rubio's slant-legged TV. "Philco in blond mahogany finish, ordered through Sears Roebuck," Angie's mother said to Mrs. Gorski, who had commented on the modern design.

Angie thought Saturday morning cartoons would be much better without her mother and Mrs. Gorski talking right there at the kitchen table. Angie thought watching TV would be a whole lot better by herself.

Later that day, when Anthony, Letty, and her mother were down for naps, Eva was skating on the front sidewalk with Jan, and her father was washing the family car in the parking lot while sipping a beer, Angie turned on the TV to watch *Science Fiction Safari*. Angie's mother didn't approve of these movies set in the jungle with white adventurers (including, without fail, a beautiful woman) and natives with spears, voodoo, poisons, and sometimes huge cauldrons of boiling liquids meant to cook humans. But hadn't she said that very morning that TV was better than their imaginations?

Besides Angie didn't feel like playing with Susie and Lou Ann, didn't feel like being the monster or the mailman or the grave robber.

The movie that afternoon was called *Gorilla Magic*. It was about a white woman who, having spent the bloom of her youth in the African sun on safari with a band of great white hunters, seeks out a magic potion from the local voodoo medicine man to rid her face of the wrinkles that have made pleats at her eyes and nose and mouth. The medicine man warns her that the potion requires that a gorilla be killed for bits of its internal organs. The woman says haughtily, "Do it."

No, the medicine man tells her. It's necessary that the woman kill the gorilla. The woman is horrified at the idea, not because she can't slaughter an animal. No, she'd been doing that for years, firing her rifle expertly into herds of elephants or gazelles or into trees to spill monkeys. She feels it's beneath her to do the work of the medicine man.

It's the only way the medicine will work, he tells her. So, she dons her safari clothes and with a hunting party treks to the highlands, locates a gorilla sitting in a clearing chewing on a stick like some after-dinner mint, aims for the forehead and topples the ape. The camera closes in on the woman's face that is steely with resolve, though there is a slight tremble of her lower lip. Her expression deepens the wrinkles on her face. She turns on the heel of her safari boot and heads back to camp, leaving the medicine man and his helpers to slice open the gorilla for its magic guts while drums pound, chants fill the air, and dancing swishes the tall grass.

When the medicine man comes to her tent, the woman greedily eyes the potion in his hand. "Give it to me," she commands and lunges for it.

The medicine man hugs the potion to his chest. "You must only take one small sip. When the effects begin to wear off, you take another small sip. But only then. Understood?"

"Of course," she says, grabbing the potion. She takes one small sip and the medicine man nods in approval. He picks up a hand mirror lying on a trunk in the tent and holds it up to her face.

She gasps as she watches the lines on her face soften. She strokes her cheek with her fingers.

"Little by little, you will regain your beauty," the medicine man tells her.

The woman continues watching herself stroke her face. "You may leave now," she tells him, without taking her eyes away from the mirror.

The medicine man leaves, the bangles at his neck, wrists, and ankles making an ominous sound as he exits.

"Little by little," the woman purrs to herself. The camera closes in on her reflection, which shows her eyebrows arching with a notion. She uncorks the potion, eyes it like a lover, and drains the flask in several big gulps, a drop or two spilling on her chin, which she wipes with the back of her hand.

It's the change in her hand she notices first. How young and lovely the skin. She grabs the mirror again and sees how taut and smooth her neck is, even the tiniest lines gone from her face. Her beauty moves her to tears. Overcome with emotion, she covers her face with her hands.

But something terrible is happening. There is evil-sounding background music, shadows flicker outside the tent, the camera holds steady on the woman's hands which still cover her face. There is hair growing on her hands, her fingers are changing shape, growing longer, turning dark. She feels something is wrong, her body stiffens. She slowly pulls her hands away from her face and stares in horror at her gorilla hands. She looks in the mirror at her face, just minutes ago that of a beautiful woman and now rapidly on its way to a flat-nosed, heavy-browed monster. She drops the mirror and screams, but it comes out as a roar. She is now completely transformed, and the silly gown has been exploded to shreds as her gorilla body expands to its full size and power. She shakes her massive head from side to side, beats her hairy chest, and bursts through the tent to where her safari companions, guides, and porters are gathered around the campfire. You know she is trying to say, "Help me!" But the only thing the safari companions, guides, and porters see is a gorilla coming at them, arms waving wildly, face contorted, so they run for their rifles, their machetes, their spears. Only the medicine man watches calmly, smoking a long pipe as the gorilla is felled by several shots, its body writhing, anguished animal cries issuing from its mouth before it goes completely and forever still.

But wait, what's happening? The gorilla's hair and all of its animal bulk are disappearing. The face and figure of a woman is emerging, the woman they recognize as their safari companion, but younger and more beautiful than they'd remembered. A magical transformation! But more incredible is that the process is now reversing. Before their eyes, the woman ages until finally she is old and wrinkled, and they turn away in disgust and even a little fear.

Angie had just turned off the TV, a swift trembling twist of the dial, when a knock on the door made her jump. "Who is it?" she yelled, louder than she meant to, spooked a little by the thought of a gorilla on the other side of the door.

When Lou Ann announced herself, Angie opened the door. "Yes?" she inquired.

"You want to play?"

"I thought you were busy playing with Susie."

Lou Ann shrugged. "Sometimes her games are boring."

"Sometimes her games are stupid." Angie wondered who played the monster when she wasn't around.

Lou Ann tossed her short hair around. "Pretend I'm the prettiest girl in the world."

"Pretend I'm the mother, but I don't have kids yet," Angie said.

"I'm a princess," Lou Ann said, walking on her tiptoes as if her feet were in high-heeled shoes.

They imitated Susie, exaggerating her walk and talk, her smile, the toss of her blond halo until they were rolling on the floor giggling. Angie's mother hushed them from upstairs.

"You want to play checkers?" Angie asked.

"You can be red," Lou Ann said.

They had barely begun when there was a knock at the door. Angie peeked through the window. It was Susie in her bride's dress. Angie opened the door wide enough to make sure that Susie saw that Lou Ann was playing with her now.

"What are you doing?" Susie asked, though it was plain for anyone to see.

Lou Ann plucked two checker pieces from the board and held the black disks to her eyes.

Susie sniffed, "That's boring."

"You're boring," Angie shot back.

Susie called to Lou Ann, "You want to come and play with the toys in my toy box?"

"N-O spells no."

Susie's face went all rumply, the way it did when she pretended to eat the poisoned apple from the wicked witch or when she fainted at the sight of the ugly monster. She stomped away as hard as her bare feet would allow. Minutes later she was at the door again, knocking importantly.

Angie opened the door wide again. "Yes, may I help you?"

"My mother said I can't play with you two ever again. I have a good imagination and can play perfectly well by myself."

"Then do it," Lou Ann jeered.

"And don't ever come back," Angie added, letting the door shut in Susie's face, feeling a bit breathless with her command.

* * *

Angie was setting the table for dinner when the sound seemed to make the fork she was holding quiver. Her mother stopped stirring the pot on the stove and her father turned the volume low on the TV. At first, they thought it was an animal, its howling burning with hurt, but then they recognized it was Marla. The whole family ran out the kitchen door and other families were coming out of theirs. Angie's father rushed to knock on the Wren's door, but before his fist reached the wood, the door burst open and Marla, horror and panic twisting her face, carried a limp Susie, her face blue as a bruise, the bride's dress wound around her knees, her bare feet floppy as fish. Angie's mother gasped and pushed Angie and her sisters back inside the house. She made them sit at the dinner table and eat as if nothing was the matter even as the sirens screeched right outside their door.

Later Angie's father came home and told them that Marla had found Susie trapped in her toy box. Susie wasn't dead, but she would never be the same. Their mother cried and sent them all to bed. Angie couldn't sleep. She lay awake and stared at the shadows on the ceiling, her heart beating with the fear of a monster.

FIRST CONFESSION

"You are at the age of reason," Sister said, "ready to understand the mystery of transubstantiation." She cued them with her ruler.

"Tran-sub-stan-ti-a-tion," the children repeated. Angie spoke it softly, enjoying the roominess of the word, its multiple, mysterious syllables that would teach her how to be good.

They were in second grade, preparing for their First Communion. They were seven years old.

It was catechism hour, and Sister Patrick Marie swept up and down the aisles of the classroom, impossibly quiet in her heavy, black shoes and voluminous, black drapes. She called out questions, and Angie mouthed the words inside the murmurings of the other children.

Who made me?

God made me.

Then Father Mulligan, who had the habit of dropping in without warning, stood at the door, and the children scrambled to attention beside their desks and greeted him. But they were not in unison. Their voices were low, their syllables staggered, and everything sounded like scuffling feet. Sister Patrick gave a closed-mouth smile to Father with one side of her face and scowled at the children with the other side. They had failed her in front of Father. Sister signaled for them to atone by reciting more of their catechism, which they delivered in the perfect singsong of their playground chants.

Where is God?

God is everywhere.

Father asked them to pray for John F. Kennedy who was running for President of the United States. They all obeyed fervently, lifting their brown faces heavenward, since everyone knew that if Nixon became president, he would make them go to school on Saturdays, and that was un-American.

Before Father left, he told them to make room on their chair for their guardian angel who was always at their side. They all scooted to the edge of their narrow wooden seats as they resumed their lesson. Angie's thigh and shoulder soon ached from scrunching herself up. She didn't dare move, though. With Sister Patrick patrolling the aisles and Father Mulligan making surprise visits, her guardian angel taking up part of her desk space, and God everywhere, Angie was surrounded and under watch.

It was the same at home, which was not really their home. They were staying with her grandparents. It was the home their mother Delia grew up in along with her sister Nelda. They had shared a bedroom and fought and told each other secrets. Now the three Rubio sisters shared a room with Nelda who said and did surprising things. Sometimes, after taking off her bra and before slipping on her nightgown, she would hold one of her breasts in her hand and say, "Want some teta?" And she would laugh a wicked, cackling laugh.

Her son was Little Eddie, even though there seemed to be no Big Eddie from whom to distinguish him. Little Eddie slept in the dining room on a cot now that the Rubios had moved in. Angie's grandparents snored in their twin beds in the bedroom just off the living room. Angie's parents slept in the living room on the fold-out couch which creaked when they tossed and turned. Baby Anthony slept between them. They had left his crib behind in Hawaii.

They had left other things behind in Hawaii. Some toys, most of their comic books, their skates, their plastic pool, boxes of clothing, and their hula hoops. And Angie felt like she had left something of herself behind. They had crossed the ocean, this time not by ship in a three-day seasick journey, but by plane. The close-up view of clouds and the long drop to earth made Angie think of how much space there would be between their life in Hawaii and their life back here in California.

Crossing an ocean made Angie sense the importance of being seven. They were all bigger now—Eva was nine and Letty five. And there was the extra fact of Anthony. It was crowded in her grandparents' house, and Angie felt they could absorb each other's sweat during the day and hear each other breathe at night. The bathroom offered no escape, nor did the porch or backyard. There was always someone else there or someone waiting their turn. Nelda and their mother sat on the front porch until it was dark and the moths flattened themselves around the porch light. Anthony would sit and babble in his playpen in the living room soothed by their grandfather's growls as he argued with the TV and their grandmother clicked her crochet needle against a fingernail. They watched the Spanish-language station which their mother and Nelda understood, but their father didn't. He would walk around the block over and over for fresh air until their mother called out to him to come inside.

Angie and her sisters did their homework on the dining room table, played a few rounds of Crazy Eights, and then ran their own bath. The sisters were required to take a bath together to save water, then Eva ran one for Little Eddie who was four and still sucked his thumb and ate his snots. The Rubio sisters stayed in the bathroom with him, sometimes lathering and scrubbing him as if he were the family dog.

One evening, instead of taking a walk around the block, Angie's father got in the car and came back with a small portable TV, which he hooked up in the dining room. Now after dinner each evening, he would watch the news and then *Perry Mason* or *Gunsmoke* while the TV in the living room jabbered in Spanish, and Angie's mother and Nelda shared movie magazines on the porch. Angie and her sisters crowded at the small kitchen table to do their homework, a move they accepted without protest as it placed them within arm's reach of their grandfather's stash of Vanilla Wafers. Sometimes Angie peeked into the dining room from her perch at the kitchen table to watch her father watching TV. One night she went to sit with him while the news was on.

"Daddy," she asked, her cheek harboring part of a Vanilla Wafer. "Do you know what transubstantiation is?"

"Ask your mother."

"I know what it is."

"Then why are you asking me?"

Angie decided to ask her father a question that he could answer.

"Daddy, what's the Cold War?"

"It's when people aren't fighting each other, even though they really want to."

Gunsmoke had come on and her father raised the volume to drown out the Spanish-dubbed *I Spy* in the adjoining room.

* * *

Sister Patrick stood at the front of the classroom, grimmer than usual and with the disconcerting appearance of a tear in one eye, its glisten magnified by her glasses.

"Our beloved Sister Paul Anna has taken ill."

Some of the girls started crying. Angie felt a pang inside her ribcage, as if a rock had lodged there, and felt her face go hot at the thoughts she had recently had about Sister Paul Anna. Since she had seen Nelda's breasts, Angie had wondered about her mother's, even her grandmother's. At school, she had wondered about the nuns. Did they have them? But really, it was Sister Paul she had been curious about. Kind Sister Paul with her young, movie-star face that her mother said was the image of Elizabeth Taylor.

"We must all pray for her," Sister Patrick said.

Angie closed her eyes and imagined Sister Paul in her bed beneath the blanket pulled to her chin, her head and body encased in the big black robes of her habit, her face pale and sweaty. Angie concentrated so hard on the image, she could summon no words of prayer. Sister Patrick ended the silence with a loud *Amen*, and Angie held herself rigid, certain that Sister could read her thoughts or know her lack of prayer.

Sister told them to take out a sheet of paper. "You will each write Sister Paul Anna a heartfelt get-well letter."

Sister Patrick lay her hand over her heart to demonstrate the expected source of their words. Angie copied Sister Patrick's gesture, her fingers hanging off her left collar bone. She felt her heart thump into the corner of her palm.

Angie listened to other people's conversations a lot and because she lived in a house with so many people and two TVs, she had a lot of conversations to listen to and, therefore, lots of words and sentences hovering in the spaces of her brain. She was a careful writer, both in forming her letters and her thoughts, even if not all of them were exactly her own.

> *Dear Sister Paul Anna,*
>
> *During this time of cold war in the world, you have always been a breath of fresh air. You are the favorite of girls and boys and for those who think young. My faith that you will get well soon keeps me going strong.*

Angie reread her words. She didn't think nuns watched TV so was pretty sure that Sister Paul wouldn't recognize the slogans from the Pepsi, Slinky, and Sugar Crisp commercials. It was a pretty good letter she thought, but not special. Sister Patrick was telling them to finish up their letters soon, so Angie wrote quickly.

> *When you come back, you will have a big surprise.*
> *Sincerely,*
> *Angie Rubio*

Angie didn't know what made her write such a thing. As Sister Patrick collected their letters, she wondered what exactly she had meant by that. What surprise could she, Angie, possibly invent? She watched Sister stack the letters on the corner of her desk and Angie felt relief to see that her letter blended in with the many.

The next day when she came in from recess, there was a familiar sheet of paper on her desk. It was her own letter to Sister Paul Anna. She panicked at the sight of her words that were exposed for all to see. She looked up to see Sister Patrick who was making a gesture at her, turning her open palm to face down, and finally Angie understood to flip over the letter. On the back was a letter from Sister Paul.

Dear Angie,

Thank you for such a lovely letter. It cheered me up greatly. I look forward to the day when I can return to the classroom.

Yours,

Sister Paul Anna

No one else had received a letter from Sister Paul. But then probably no one else had promised her a big surprise.

Angie knew Sister Patrick had read her letter and she knew Sister Patrick had read the response from Sister Paul. It was a terrible thing to know.

* * *

It was her mother who had insisted they go to the Catholic school, though her father argued they couldn't afford it. "I'm on a seaman's salary."

"What's the alternative?" her mother demanded. "The public school, all rowdy with bullies?"

"You think there are no bullies in Catholic school?"

"Bullies are everywhere," Angie said, amending a line from her catechism.

Her mother would not budge. The money they might have spent on renting a house went instead to paying Catholic school tuition for three kids. Anyway, her mother reasoned, Catholic school made more sense now that Angie was to make her First Communion.

But when Angie came home with homework to memorize the Ten Commandments, the Seven Sacraments, the names of the Apostles, plus learn all her prayers, there was no one to help her. Her father liked to watch the news and *Perry Mason*, and her mother was always busy rocking Anthony.

Angie followed her mother into the bedroom where she lay Anthony on the bed to change his diaper. Angie thought her mother might have some ideas about what kind of a big surprise a nun might want. She handed her mother a wet cloth, the baby powder, and a fresh diaper. Her mother cooed to Anthony as she wiped and changed his fidgety butt. Angie cooed with her. "You're a good boy, aren't you, little Anthony?"

There were just the plastic pants to slip on, but Nelda was calling Angie's mother to come listen to Doris Day on the radio. "Cantemos con la Doris."

"I'll be right back," her mother told her. "Watch Anthony. Make sure he doesn't fall off the bed."

Angie watched her little brother squirm, his arms and legs like fat thrashing worms.

"You're a good boy, aren't you, little Anthony?" Angie said again, though this time it didn't come out as a coo or as sweet encouragement. It sounded mocking, and Anthony started to cry as if he understood her taunt.

"I'll be right there, mijo," her mother called, interrupting for a moment her sing-along to "Que Será, Será."

Angie decided to deliver Anthony to her mother to save her the trouble of coming back to the bedroom. "Okay, mijo," she told him as he observed her with wide eyes and a spit bubble at his mouth.

She lifted Anthony off the bed, her arms wrapped around his bottom. She expected his torso to follow the momentum of his butt against her body, but Anthony lurched backward, and Angie did a dance with him as she tried to get her balance underneath his arching body. He was trying to launch himself out of her grasp and she knew the only hope she had was to make sure the bed was beneath him when he forced himself out of her arms and became airborne. But she was too late.

The thud of his head on the floor stunned him into silence for a long moment during which Angie wondered if she might've killed her brother. But then he opened his mouth in a tragic scream. Angie gathered him quickly and practically threw him on the bed, which seemed to mollify him as his screams petered out to hiccups just as her mother rushed to the bedside. She picked Anthony up and patted his head, his back, his diapered butt, and sent soothing whispers into his neck. She looked at Angie. "Did you let him fall?"

She hesitated. The answer was technically no. She had not *let* him fall.

"Don't you lie to me," her mother warned. "Did you let him fall?"

"No," Angie said.

Her mother appeared to fume. "I sincerely hope not," she said, whisking Anthony out of the room.

* * *

"Bless me, Father, for I have sinned. This is my first confession." They were the words Angie had been practicing in catechism class, words she would say to the priest the first time she stepped inside the confessional. They were to be followed by a recitation of her sins. So far, Angie's list was short, which worried her. She was sure that much was expected of second-graders in terms of sin. Should she lie about her sins? No, that would be a sin. But then at least she would have something to confess. She was undecided about whether dropping Anthony was a sin.

"You're not afraid of the dark, are you?" Aunt Nelda said as Angie kneeled at the bedside practicing her lines. "Because it's dark in the confessional, you know."

In fact, Angie *was* afraid of the dark, though she seldom had to worry about being alone in it at her grandparents' house. There were so many of them living there under one roof. Anyway, there were lights constantly turned on as one or another of them made their way to the bathroom for a pee or the kitchen for a glass of water in the middle of the night.

Letty was in Nelda's bed and Eva was next to Angie, and Nelda as usual was in her underwear as she sat at her dresser, wiping makeup from her face with cotton balls dipped in baby oil from the same bottle used for Anthony's butt. When she was finished, she shrugged the straps of her bra off her shoulders and reached around the back to undo the clasp and said what she always said. "Want some teta?"

They had always shaken their heads, not really knowing what they were being offered. For once though, tonight Letty asked, "What's teta?"

Nelda laughed. "I'm just teasing."

Then she explained she used to feed Little Eddie with milk from her breasts.

"Our mother uses bottles," Angie said.

"Not with me," Eva said. "I was breastfed."

"You were not," Angie said, though she had no way of knowing. She just felt it shouldn't be true. But Nelda confirmed it.

"What about me?"

Nelda wagged her finger at her as if she had committed a wrong. "It's just too much to ask of a woman to do it with more than one child. It makes a saggy bust," she said, cupping her breasts in her hands, lifting them up and then letting them go. "They wouldn't look this good if I'd had another baby to feed."

Angie didn't like having Nelda wag her finger at her. She didn't like Nelda reminding her that the confessional was dark. She didn't like when Nelda would tease and ask them to do the hula just because they'd lived in Hawaii.

Before Hawaii, Angie had not thought to question the absence of a father for Little Eddie or a husband for Aunt Nelda. But now, after Hawaii, now that she was seven, these things occurred to her and she formed her own conclusions. That you didn't have to be married to have children. That somehow just being a grown-up caused you to have a child. Of course, this conclusion was soundly refuted by Eva. It doesn't just happen automatically, she snorted. There has to be a kiss. And there's a seed in the kiss. And the woman swallows it and it grows into a baby in her belly.

Who kissed Aunt Nelda, Angie wanted to know. She said it out loud, "Who kissed you and gave you a baby, Aunt Nelda?"

Nelda looked stunned, and her lashes batted wildly. It made them all go silent.

"I'm telling Mama," Letty said, and she slid from the bed and backed out of the room like the policemen on TV.

Within seconds, their mother stalked into the room with Letty trailing behind. "What's going on here?"

"Angie wanted to know who kissed Aunt Nelda and gave her a baby," Eva said.

Their mother pursed her lips and folded her arms. "Nelda had a husband, but he died." She looked sternly at Angie as if she might have been responsible for killing him.

"Now no more discussion," her mother said, and Angie knew she was lying.

*   *   *

Angie felt the house filling up with her family's biting words and harsh silences. Her father was tired of being a sailor and tired of living in someone else's house. Her mother said to him that at least he wasn't the mother day in and day out to all these kids—at least he got to leave the house to go to work. Nelda was still looking tragic after Angie asked who kissed her. And Angie was still worried about the big surprise she had promised Sister Paul Anna. The grown-ups decided a drive to Marine Land to see the dolphins dance and the seals play polo would make them all smile. But they would have to get an early start and miss church.

"But I'm not supposed to miss church when I'm studying for my First Communion," Angie reminded them.

"Do you want to go to Marine Land or not?" her mother asked.

"On Mondays Sister Patrick makes us stand up and say why we didn't go to church."

"Ay, chica, just don't stand up," Nelda said, rolling her eyes.

Angie didn't want to stand up. But she knew she wouldn't have a choice. At least she could add not going to church to her list of sins to confess, along with asking Nelda who kissed her.

All of them squeezed together in the car, the one that had come back with them from Hawaii. The three grown-ups nudged up against each other in the front with baby Anthony on her mother's lap, and the sisters jostled for space in the back with Little Eddie around whose neck Nelda had tied a barf bag. There was no room for a guardian angel anywhere. No one complained about the lack of space, because it was better to be crammed in a car with a destination that wasn't home than it was to be home, which wasn't really their home.

They were scarcely out of their own neighborhood when a fiercely loud but mostly minor collision sent them home after all. Angie's father had pulled to a stop behind another car at the traffic light. When the light turned green, and the car ahead failed to move, Angie's father honked the horn. "We don't have all day," he muttered. The car ahead of them had stalled, but its engine was doing its best to grind back to life as Angie and her family fumed impatiently in their cramped seats. The engine finally revived with a roar, but before the family could celebrate, their heads were flung against the dashboard, seatbacks, or each other. Angie ended up on the floor, knees at her chin. Little Eddie was splayed over her, his barf bag trapped beneath him. As Nelda screamed for her son, Angie held her hands up uselessly to ward off the puke from Little Eddie's mouth. Angie closed her eyes and waited for rescue, listening to her mother's low wailing of something vague and garbled, which she slowly recognized as prayer.

The car ahead of them had, after revving its newly recharged engine, thundered into reverse and taken out the front grill of the Rubio car. Once they were all extricated from the dented vehicle, and Angie's hands hosed off at the corner gas station, they sat on the curb as a police officer asked questions, wrote in his notepad, and talked into his two-way radio, after which they were allowed, bruised and scraped, to climb back into their beaten car with its cracked windshield, buckled hood, and empty headlight sockets and limp home.

*　*　*

On Monday morning, Sister Patrick stood at the front of the room and asked which of them had failed to attend church on Sunday. Those who stood had to explain what had been more important than God. Angie stood bravely to face the humiliation. She stood partly out of her sense that

Sister Patrick, Father Mulligan, her guardian angel, and God already knew of her absence from church. But partly because she felt a little heroic, and she was disappointed that the bruise on her forehead that had seemed so robustly purple the previous day was already fading.

"We were in a car accident," Angie said, and she couldn't help raising her hand to her forehead where the bump was—or used to be.

Sister Patrick frowned and though it might have been concern, suspicion was also a possibility.

"My mother had stitches," Angie said.

"Well," Sister said, "thank God you are all safe." It was a command.

Angie bowed her head, wanting to thank God instead for saving her from the wrath of Sister Patrick.

During silent reading time, when thirty sets of lips were moving soundlessly, including Angie's even as her mind wandered to the problem of inventing a big surprise for Sister Paul Anna, Sister Patrick called Angie to her desk.

Angie, shaky with guilt about her inattention to her reading, made her way slowly to Sister Patrick sitting large as a monument at the front of the room.

"Yes, Sister Patrick?" she whispered, aware that many of the lips in the room had ceased moving.

"Angie," Sister Patrick said in a low, deep voice, "what is this big surprise you have in store for Sister Paul?"

Angie could not swallow, could not force words from her throat. She shrugged, not quite meeting Sister Patrick's small, gray eyes behind the rimless glasses.

"Do you mean to say that what you wrote is not quite true?"

Angie coughed to test her vocal cords. "I wanted it to be true. I meant for it to be true."

"You know that's not the same thing."

There was a long pause, during which Angie considered running from the room. Some of the other students had stopped pretending to read and were watching the scene before them.

"What made you write such a thing?" Sister Patrick asked.

Angie heard Sister's voice trying to be kind but saw that her eyes were not. Angie's impulse to flee left her. She stood rooted and faced Sister's unfriendly gaze. "I wanted to make her happy. Because I love her."

Angie wasn't at all sure this was true. She only knew that she didn't love Sister Patrick, whose pursed lips parted with a slight quiver.

"That will do. Please sit down now."

Sister Patrick stood up. "And now for phonics."

After their phonics lesson at which they all did poorly since no one understood what phonics meant and Sister Patrick's chalky jowls spasmed with displeasure at their failings, she instructed them all to put their heads face down on their desks. They did this whenever they played Heads Up, Seven Up on rainy days, but today it wasn't raining.

"Heads down, no peeking," Sister Patrick said.

Angie watched little orange blobs float behind her closed eyelids. She could hear the restlessness of the children around her—the chafing of thighs, the skimming of saddle shoes against linoleum, the friction of sweater sleeves against grainy desktops. Angie was about to lift her eyes for a tiny peek when she felt a hand covering her head, guiding it back to its down position, holding it there. Finally, letting go. And the severe whisper of black moving past.

"Heads down, no peeking," Sister repeated. Her voice came from the front of the room again, and it hovered over their bowed heads as she gave her next instruction. "If you hate me, raise your hand."

There was a moment when the restlessness ceased, like the moment after a door slams and smothers everything to a hush when no one breathes. Then the fidgeting began again, the chafing thighs, shuffling shoes, rasping woolly sweaters, but Angie held herself still, her legs, her arms, especially her arms. It was hot with her face pressed upon her desk. It was hard to breathe. Her head pounded with voices. *It's a sin to hate. It's a sin to lie. Raise your hand if you hate me.* It was a single voice and then it was a chorus and though her eyes were closed and her head down and she could see nothing except tiny orange blots, couldn't they all see her? Sister Patrick, Father Mulligan, her guardian angel, God. Angie needed air. She lifted her face, took a deep breath and raised both hands high in surrender.

BROWNIE

"How now, brown cows."

Angie and her sisters went silent as they halted at the top of the stairs at the main entrance of Paradise Grove Elementary. They found their way blocked by a boy with mean red hair. Next to him was a girl with reddish blond curls, green eyes, and perfect little teeth that glinted like shiny, hard candies.

Angie, taken aback by the unexpected unwelcome, twisted a strand of her hair until her scalp hurt. Then Eva straightened her shoulders, lifted her chin and mooed at the boy, practically in his face. He recoiled with pretend fear, and Eva sallied past him and the polished-toothed girl, pulling along a rubbernecking Letty. Angie slunk behind, skirting the stucco wall like a shadow.

They were back in public school because their mother said there were no gangs and bullies in Paradise Grove. Their rental house had two bedrooms, one shared by Angie and her sisters, and the other by her parents and baby Anthony, now a bona-fide, temper-throwing toddler. There was a tiny front yard covered in ivy and a sloping backyard wild with weeds. They hadn't met many of their neighbors, who seemed only interested in them from their porches or their passing cars. The school they would attend was at the bottom of the hill. Whenever they drove by it in the family station wagon, their mother would say, "There's your new school. Isn't it nice?" Angie wanted to believe that it was.

In Miss Wolf's third-grade class, Angie was assigned to a table at the back of the classroom. Across from her sat a large girl with red cheeks named Frances. Next to Frances was a boy who had spelled his name B-r-a-i-n on his name card. Next to Angie was the girl on the stairs that morning who seemed not to recognize her. When Miss Wolf called her name, she only said *Carol*. "It's Carol Elizabeth," the girl said.

"Take a few minutes to get to know your table partners," Miss Wolf said, adjusting her black-rimmed glasses on her sharp nose. "Ask them something about themselves and then each of you will introduce someone at your table to the rest of the class."

At first no one spoke at Angie's table and Angie worried about failing her first assignment in third grade. Finally, Frances said to the boy next to her, "Isn't your name Brian?"

The boy pointed to his name card. "That's what it says."

"No, it doesn't," Carol Elizabeth said. "It says Brain."

Brian shrugged.

"Well, I'm not introducing you to the class," Carol Elizabeth said. She turned to Frances. "What's your favorite food?"

"Sloppy Joes."

Carol Elizabeth pretended to gag. "Now ask me a question."

"What's your favorite color?"

"Fuchsia."

Brian snorted. "That's not a color."

Carol Elizabeth rolled her eyes. "Okay," she said now to Frances, "I'll introduce you and you introduce Brian the Brain."

"What about Angie?" Frances asked.

"Oh, Angie." Carol Elizabeth looked at her as if seeing her for the first time. "Well, we have to ask her a question first."

Angie was all ready to say that her favorite color was blue or that her favorite food was mashed potatoes or that her last name meant blond. But Carol Elizabeth leaned forward and peered at her. "Angie Rubio, where are you from?"

While Angie was trying to ponder whether this was a trick question (was she expected to say her mother's stomach? Or was it a matter of religion? *God made me*), Carol Elizabeth huffed, "Oh, never mind."

Miss Wolf rang a little bell on her desk and said it was time to do the introductions. Frances nudged Angie and whispered, "What's your favorite TV show?"

"I Love Lucy," Angie whispered back.

Mine, too, Frances mouthed.

When Miss Wolf called on their table, Frances blurted an introduction of Angie before Carol Elizabeth could utter a syllable. Angie introduced Frances, and they were sudden best friends. This left Brian and Carol Elizabeth to introduce each other, which did not sit well with Carol Elizabeth since Brian mispronounced "fuchsia."

Angie was relieved to have someone to play with at recess and to sit with at lunch time. But she couldn't help noticing that as she twisted her body to avoid the tetherball Frances smacked in her direction, or as she averted her eyes from the sight of Frances slurping soup from her thermos lid, that many of the other girls from Miss Wolf's class were clumped together like vines. Whether waiting their turn in line at dodge ball or eating their baloney sandwiches on a bench, they were a thicket of chumminess, arms draped around each other's necks.

"Why don't we eat with them?" Angie asked Frances, who had a piece of noodle clinging to her chin.

"You can if you want."

But Angie didn't know how.

Frances peeled the noodle from her chin and put it in her mouth. "You can join the Brownies. Almost all of them are in the Brownies."

Angie did want to be in the Brownies. She'd seen the brochure in the welcome packet Miss Wolf had passed out that morning. There were photos of uniformed Brownies busy in various agreeable pursuits. *Fun, friendship, and community. Be a part of it!*

Angie wanted to be a part of it. She wanted to earn badges. She wanted to wear a uniform with a sash and a beanie.

"Why aren't you a Brownie?" she asked Frances.

Frances shrugged. "I don't think they have uniforms in my size."

After school, Angie showed her mother the brochure. "Can I join the Brownies?"

Her mother, who was folding laundry, glanced at the paper in Angie's hand. "Absolutely not."

Angie wasn't convinced that her mother was actually seeing all the good things about being a Brownie.

"Why can't I? I can make new friends. I can be a good citizen. I can learn to be a leader." Angie pointed at the brochure.

Eva snorted into her math homework.

"Those things always cost money," her mother said.

"You can take the dues out of her allowance," Eva, the math whiz, offered.

Angie was not pleased with the suggestion but decided not to protest. And though she knew better, she could not resist another appeal.

"And I need a uniform."

"Oh, no, you don't."

Oh, yes, I do, Angie thought, but this time knew to hold her tongue.

*   *   *

During the rest of that first week of school, Angie and Frances solidified their friendship, sharing pencils, trading sandwiches, and playing unevenly matched games of tetherball. Neither of them was a good fit for dodge ball, since Frances was too large to dodge quickly enough, and Angie was too skinny to heave the ball very far or with any accuracy. Angie still looked with longing at the group of girls whom she knew now to be Brownies. They wore their uniforms to school on Thursday and then at the last bell at the end of the day, they strode with purpose to Carol Elizabeth's house. Carol Elizabeth's mother was the troop leader and had been a Brownie herself when she was a girl.

"It's hereditary," Carol Elizabeth had declared loudly to her group of friends at lunch regarding the Brownies tradition in her family.

That night at dinner, Angie asked her father what hereditary meant.

"It's something that's passed on by parents to their children."

"Like being a Brownie?"

Eva scoffed, ejecting rice grains through her nose and prompting Letty and Anthony to demand an encore. Eva made a ceremony of dabbing at her nose with her napkin, then turning to Angie and with a British accent informing her, "Being brown is hereditary. Being a Brownie is not."

"Is snot!" Anthony yelled.

"This is not dinner table talk," their mother yelled even louder.

* * *

On Saturday night, Angie's family piled into the station wagon and headed to the drive-in movie. Because being trapped in a car with four kids jockeying to see the Disney movie on the screen was not Angie's father's favorite way to spend a Saturday night, he always splurged on a pizza from the concession stand. Her mother passed around Cokes from the cooler at her feet. The food and drink increased the bump and tangle of elbows, producing the inevitable spill, a brief tantrum by Anthony, her mother's tortured sighs, Eva's complaint that she couldn't hear the movie with all the commotion in the car, and then her father's threat to start the engine and drive them all home. Oh, how Angie wished she were an only child at times like these. But this time she wished she had a twin sister, like Hayley Mills in *The Parent Trap*, the movie they were watching now about identical twins separated at birth and reunited at summer camp, their initial meanness replaced by sisterly love and a plot to reunite their divorced parents—a plan that first required Sharon to cut Susan's long, wavy hair to match her own short, wavy bob.

Angie wished her parents would send her to camp. She wished her parents were divorced so she could reunite them. She wished her parents were movie stars. She wished she had round, blue eyes and wavy, blond hair like Hayley.

On the way home, Angie sang softly, "Let's get together, yeah, yeah, yeah," until Eva told her to shut up and their father told them both to shut up and their mother told them all to be quiet and not to say shut up. They were being bad examples for Letty and Anthony.

"They're asleep," Eva pointed out.

"Please, everyone just shut up," her mother said, and finally they were all silent.

*   *   *

On Sunday morning, Nelda and Little Eddie came over as usual. Nelda's handbag bulged and as she slipped it off her arm, it slumped with the weight of whatever was inside. Instead of Nelda and Angie's mother sitting down for coffee while Little Eddie showed the Rubio kids his latest tap-dancing moves, Angie's father rounded up Little Eddie, Letty, and Anthony for a drive to the park. Now that he was away in the evenings at night school, he was giving Angie's mother time on the weekend to pursue creative projects with Nelda. Optimistically, he had tucked a couple of baseball mitts inside his arm, but Little Eddie refused Nelda's suggestion to change into his play shoes and shuffle-ball-changed out the door.

Eva and Angie, who were sprawled in front of the TV, watched their father herd the younger children out of sight. "Ambush," Eva warned, just as their mother and Nelda called them into the kitchen.

"We have a surprise for you," Nelda said. Their mother held something behind her back.

"What is it?" Angie asked, holding back her enthusiasm because Eva, arms folded and foot tapping, was looking sideways at the grown-ups.

Their mother swung both arms out in front of her. In each hand was a box that Angie recognized from TV commercials.

Toni Home Permanents. "We're going to give you a brand-new look! Won't it be fun?"

Angie perked up at the idea of a brand-new look. Eva took one of the boxes and was examining the photo on the front of a pretty young woman with perfect curls.

"You sure you know how to do this?"

"Of course, we do," her mother said, taking the box away from Eva.

"The directions are easy," Nelda said. "Besides, your mother and me, we're creative. You think our only talent is raising kids?"

Angie thought it was a joke and laughed but stopped when she saw that neither Nelda nor her mother was smiling.

"What if it doesn't work?" Eva asked.

"I'm an Avon lady. I know all about beauty," their mother insisted. "Don't you want to have curly hair?"

"No," Eva said, "I want to have wavy hair. Like Hayley Mills in *The Parent Trap*."

"Me, too," Angie said, and even though she had yet to have her mother agree to a Brownie uniform, she wondered how a Brownie beanie would look on her hair once it was graceful with waves.

"Then have a seat," Nelda said. "You can thank us later."

With bath towels draped around their necks, Angie and Eva sat side by side at the kitchen table. Nelda had brought some of her movie magazines for them to thumb through. "Just like at a real beauty salon," Nelda said.

Angie hoped her mother would do her hair, but her mother took her comb to Eva's head, so Nelda started on Angie's. Nelda leaned around to face Angie. "I'm going to make you look like a million dollars, mija."

Angie smiled. Nelda could be fun. And Angie liked it when she called her "mija."

It was cozy in the kitchen with the four of them. They weren't just playing beauty salon. They *were* a beauty salon. Their mother, the Avon lady whose heavily fragranced bottles and tubes and jars bulged from a red vinyl carrying case at her bedside, did know about beauty! Their mother and Nelda chatted and hummed as they worked, and Eva and Angie, giddy from the scent leaching from the open Toni Home Permanent boxes, traded information about movie stars.

But even after Eva and Angie had turned every single page in *Movie Screen* and *Photoplay*, their mother and Nelda still had not finished putting the plastic rods in their hair.

"When are you going to be done?" Eva asked.

"Soon," their mother snapped.

"Yeah, don't rush us," Nelda said. "You want us to make a mistake?"

"No," Angie said. "Don't make a mistake." She wished there was a mirror in front of her so she could see what she looked like—not her hair, but her face. If she didn't look as worried as she felt, she might be reassured. But her mother had earlier nixed any mirrors. "We want this to be a complete surprise," she had said.

"Don't distract us," her mother said now.

Nelda held a handful of Angie's hair while she conferred with Angie's mother. They spoke in Spanish the way they always did when they wanted to keep their conversation private. But their occasional lapses into English, along with the tone and pitch of their voices, allowed Angie and Eva to glean the predicament. Apparently, there was more hair on Angie's head than there were rods to roll it up in. Nelda was trying to negotiate for more rods, but Eva protested, gathering up the remainder from her box and clamping them in her fist.

"We don't need your rods, Eva," Nelda said. "I have a simple solution. Simple, but brilliant."

"What?" Angie wanted to know, wishing she were brave enough to flee.

"I merely put a little more hair on each of the remaining rods and then take that into account when applying the lotion and in deciding how long it stays on compared to the rest of the hair. Muy científico." Then she added, as if remembering the stated reason for their endeavor, "And creative."

"Nothing to worry about," her mother said, as she finished rolling rods into Eva's hair.

Then they all waited as Nelda wrestled with thick strands of hair, wrapping them onto skinny plastic rods and squeezing them shut again each time they snapped open.

"There," Nelda breathed as she wound the last rod onto Angie's head. "Okay, now, no te muevas."

So, Angie stayed still to keep the rods from popping off her head. Nelda applied the lotion to each row of rods and Angie felt it trickle down her scalp and onto her neck like an invasion of insects bitter with chemicals. She stiffened at the slow crawl, wrinkled her face at the smell.

"Keep still," Nelda warned. She set a timer.

Her mother's timer had already gone off and she was rinsing Eva's head of rods at the sink. When Nelda's timer went off, she positioned Angie to bend sideways over the sink. The idea was to rinse all but the rods she had rolled last, the ones that were bursting with chunks of hair. These she would leave alone so the lotion could work doubly long to account for the doubled amount of hair on the rod.

But Nelda's calculations were off. When she finally unfurled the hair from the rods, one side curled tight as tiny fists and the other sprung open like lank new blossoms. Though Angie couldn't see the lopsidedness, she could feel it.

"It's ruined," Angie said. "My hair is ruined."

"Don't be dramatic," her mother said.

Angie looked at Eva, whose curls were elastic and even. Eva mouthed with big, silent, sympathetic loops of her lips, your hair is ruined.

"Of course, it's not ruined," Nelda said. "Don't you want to be different? Don't you want to be special?"

Angie shook her head no. She shook her head yes. The curls on the left side of her head waggled. The ones on the right were unmoved. Tears swamped her eyes and though they blurred her view of Nelda, her mother, and Eva, she could tell there was regret in their faces. She ran to the bedroom and slammed the door and waited for her mother to yell at her for that, but all she heard were snappish murmurings from the kitchen. She heard more voices and she knew her father had brought the other kids home from the park. She heard her name mentioned, her father's questioning tone, Nelda and her mother's high-pitched explanations, and the uninvited chirps of Letty and Little Eddie who were playing a rhyming game with the word "perm." The last voice she heard was Nelda's, flinging an injured goodbye.

With Nelda's departure, Angie wept some more. While Nelda had still been in the next room, Angie held out hope that what had happened to her hair could somehow be undone. Now she knew such a possibility never existed.

The bedroom door opened, and Eva, Letty, and Anthony trooped in. Angie lay on her bed with a pillow over her head. There was no place to be alone when you shared a room in a small house that your parents didn't even own. "What do you want?" she cried.

"Your hair doesn't look stupid," Letty said.

"How do you know? You haven't even seen it."

"I just know it."

Even though Angie knew that Letty was just saying what she was being told to say, trying to be nice, trying to be good, Angie was angry. She ripped the pillow from her head. "Now?" she asked. "Now do you just know it?"

Letty gaped at Angie's hair and Angie took a strange satisfaction in her ability to render Letty's words useless and wrong.

"I'm telling Mama you're being mean to me."

"See if I care," Angie said, wishing she could tell someone that her mother and Nelda had been mean to her.

After Letty huffed out of the room, Eva said, "It really doesn't look that bad."

Angie glared at her sister whose own hair rippled in even waves around her head.

"See," Eva said, "Anthony likes it."

Their little brother had climbed onto the bed next to Angie and was pulling at a curl and watching it spring back into its insistent coil. Angie sat morosely as Anthony looped his fingers experimentally through first the kinked and then the slack curls, as if her head were one of his touch-and-learn educational toys.

"It's not so bad," Eva said again as she left the room.

The phone rang and soon her mother was telling her to come out, saying the call was for her. It was rare that anyone but the grown-ups received a phone call at their house. She wondered if it was Nelda, calling to apologize for ruining her life. She knew she would be expected to forgive her. She emerged from her room still aggrieved, but inwardly smug that she had a phone call. She answered with an injured sniff, but it was not Nelda. It was Frances wanting to know if she could go to the beach. Her teenage sister was being allowed to drive the family convertible on the condition that Frances and a friend go along too.

Angie tugged at a curl. It was only now that it really struck her that she would have to walk out into the world with her lopsided perm. At least she would get to go to the beach. "Just a minute," she told Frances and put her hand over the receiver.

She turned to her mother who was reading a magazine, one of the ones that Nelda had brought over for the home perm salon. "Can I go to the beach with Frances?"

"What about your hair?"

"What about it?" Angie asked, defiant.

Her mother put down her magazine. "I don't know why we even bothered with that perm."

Words throttled in Angie's throat, fighting to get out, producing only a gargle.

Her father appeared in the doorway from the kitchen, leaning on the jamb, scratching his head, perplexed by this tragedy. "Go ahead. Go to the beach."

Her mother looked at neither of them, just raised the magazine to her face. "Don't go too far into the water," she said into its pages.

"I'll be right over," Angie said into the receiver to Frances. Then she went to change into her bathing suit and pack a beach bag, a thrill passing through her about going to the beach, about riding in a convertible with teenagers—a detail she omitted telling her mother. She ran out the door, the curls bobbing on one side of her head like tiny slaps and on the other side like whips.

*   *   *

They were waiting for her, already sitting in the car, the top down on this warm September day. Frances's sister was at the wheel and her friend was in the front passenger seat, their faces obscured by movie-star-large sunglasses. They barely gave Angie a glance until Frances said, "What happened to your hair?"

The teenagers, with their smooth ponytails, turned around and lowered their sunglasses at Angie.

Angie was determined not to cry. *I'm going to the beach,* she told herself. *I'm riding in a convertible.*

"It's a home permanent," she said.

They all stared a moment and then the girl who wasn't Frances's sister turned around, saying under her breath but still loud enough for Angie to hear, "You better hope it's not permanent."

"Oh," Frances said, "I forgot to introduce you. That's my sister, Patty, driving and that's her friend, Darlene." The girls didn't turn around, just each waved a hand. "Twistin' the Night Away" came on the radio, and Patty and Darlene shrieked "Sam Cooke" and started singing.

The wind blew Angie's curls around her head and into her face, the tight, springy ones vibrating, the loose ones thrashing her scalp. Whenever they came to a stop, Angie restrained herself from touching her hair, not wanting to call attention to it, even as she watched the teenagers in the front seat smoothing back the strands that had escaped from their wind-blown ponytails that still looked perky and attractive. Frances's hair was a straight bob and all the hairs seemed to settle into their original places when the car ceased moving.

By the time they arrived at the beach, Angie's hair was a riot. Patty and Darlene donned hats and Angie wished she owned a floppy beach hat, too. Maybe she should've brought a scarf or a bathing cap, though she didn't see anyone else wearing a bathing cap except a few old ladies. There were so many people at the beach, maybe nobody would notice her.

"Why don't you two lay your towels over there," Patty said, pointing to a spot away from the blanket she and Darlene had anchored against the breeze with the cooler of drinks and the basket of snacks. They were rubbing suntan lotion all over themselves.

"They want to talk about teenager stuff," Frances explained.

"Yuck," Angie said, as if she believed that was the real reason, as if she didn't care about being banished. She hated Nelda for ruining the perm. She hated her mother for letting it happen.

Angie watched as Frances lathered herself with Coppertone. The bottle showed the picture from the commercial and the billboards—the dog pulling the underpants from the little blond girl and exposing her white butt. Angie avoided looking at her own skin, which she knew gleamed even darker under the hot sun and bright sky.

Frances finished applying the Coppertone, hesitated, and then offered the bottle to Angie.

"No, thanks. I put some on at home," Angie lied.

"That was smart," Frances said.

"I know," Angie said.

"Should we go in the water, now?"

They ran into the waves and splashed each other. They sat down in the shallow surf and let the waves slap over them. Angie's curls became heavy with saltwater, and a shred of seaweed clung to one side of her head. She removed it and flung it away, thinking there were other things she would like to so easily toss in the ocean. All of her hair was wet and limp now, though one side hung limper than the other, the tight curls on her left side resolute as ever.

Frances's hair was plastered to her head. Her dark blond hair was lit by the sun and gleamed against the blue sky.

"Want to hear something funny, Frances?" Angie asked, moving her gaze out to the ocean that stretched far away to forever.

"Yes," Frances said, and Angie liked her eagerness, her friendly acceptance.

"My last name means blond."

"Rubio?"

Angie nodded, squinted up at a lone cloud.

"Angie Blond," Frances said. "That *is* funny."

"I know."

"Hey," Frances said, "My last name is Carpenter and I'm not a carpenter. Funny, right?"

Angie didn't say so, but she didn't think it was quite the same thing.

When they went back to dry off, Patty had left a pair of sodas and sandwiches on their towels. They sat shivering in the breeze while they drank their root beers and ate their baloney sandwiches with mayonnaise. Angie didn't like mayonnaise. Nelda always made comments about white people and mayonnaise. Angie didn't like that either, and she didn't like being reminded of Nelda and her ruined perm. And now that it was satisfyingly drenched, it was hard to picture a Brownie beanie on top of it.

She watched Frances lick mayonnaise that had leaked from her sandwich onto her wrist. She glanced behind them at Patty and Darlene who were also consuming mayonnaise-laden bread.

She liked Frances and she was glad to be at the beach with her. And yet, she wanted to be a Brownie, which Frances was not.

After lunch they buried their legs in the sand so that only their feet were exposed, and Angie wondered what it would be like if her skin were the color of sand.

"Race you to the water," Frances said, who had already freed her legs and was on her haunches.

Angie burst through the sand and sprinted ahead of Frances, and though she didn't know how to swim, she threw herself into an oncoming wave, her eyes shut tight and her breath closed up inside her. She thrashed her legs and reached her arms out, feeling the water spill through her fingers. Her knees bumped against the bottom and she staggered to her feet, her arms still outstretched, and when she opened her eyes she saw seaweed dangling from a wrist, but beyond that the sun glimmering on the ocean that stretched out to faraway and forever, and she glimpsed, in the largeness of the world, possibility. She shivered off the seaweed and shook the water from her face. Her hair was slicked against her scalp and neck and though she knew as it dried, the ringlets would form again, she took pleasure in these small moments of freedom. She splashed herself with water, dousing Frances, who had come up beside her. They splashed each other, screaming and giggling, until Angie sucked water up her nose and she found herself coughing as she flung handfuls of salt water and seaweed at Frances's face.

They didn't notice Patty yelling at them to cut it out and get their butts dried off and in the car until she was at the water's edge flapping her arms. Angie's throat stung and France's face blazed from exertion as they watched Patty beat the air.

"Come on," Frances said. "Run."

They dashed past Patty to gather their things and Angie reached over to peel a shred of seaweed from Frances's shoulder. "Thanks for inviting me to the beach," Angie said.

"It's okay," Frances said.

In the car, their towels were wrapped around their bottoms to protect the upholstery, though their hair still shed tiny droplets of water on the back seat. Darlene kept changing radio stations, hoping to hit on Sam Cooke again so they could sing along. But they settled for Peter, Paul, and Mary, and Darlene came up with hand motions for "If I Had a Hammer," which Angie didn't feel like doing, but which Frances did with much enthusiasm until finally with the last chorus, Angie raised her fist and pounded it into her palm, which she had to admit felt good.

When they pulled up to the curb, Angie's hair was thoroughly dry, the only visible effects of the outing on her hair were the tangles wrought by the wind, which Angie was sure her mother would overlook. Angie thanked Patty for driving her home. Patty shrugged, popped her gum, and tossed her ponytail.

"See you at school tomorrow," Frances said. "And don't worry about your hair. It'll look much better in a few days."

And though Darlene snickered, Angie did feel encouraged by Frances's words.

As it turned out, Angie's perm was upstaged by Brian the Brain's broken arm and the rush to sign his cast. Of course, there were the initial stares, whispered comments and outright giggles at Angie's asymmetric hairdo, but in the end a broken arm trumped a flawed perm.

Angie saw no reason to reveal this reprieve to her family who still treated her with the deference due an invalid. It took more than a few days for her hair to look better, and even then, the two sides were still conspicuously mismatched. Each morning her mother tried to make them harmonize by pinning the lanky curls against her head with a barrette. Each day Angie was silently tragic. Finally, her mother sighed.

"So, you really want to be a Brownie?"

Angie nodded. "With a uniform," she said.

Her mother sighed again. "Okay. Fine."

*　　*　　*

Angie and her assigned partner, Carol Elizabeth, were drawing a Navajo village with Navajo people in it. They were both meticulous drawers and Carol Elizabeth, important in her Brownie Scout uniform and new pageboy hairdo, was working on the rungs of a ladder that led to the second story of a Navajo duplex apartment. She blew her blond bangs to flutter up her forehead as she heaved a sigh of concentration.

Angie gripped her brown crayon as she traced the edges of a hogan. She sighed too, but her sigh did not lift her bangs because of her permanent. Nelda who had resumed her Sunday visits never did apologize, insisting that she had invented a new hairdo that everyone would want to copy. Why, Angie wanted to ask, would anyone want this muddle of tight, frightened curls and feebly flappy ones that made you feel all uneven?

Carol Elizabeth was starting to color in some of the Navajo people they had drawn. Angie watched as Carol Elizabeth gave her Indian woman blond hair. Frances who was working with Brian on a drawing of Hopi Kachina spirits, looked over and said, "Um, I don't think that's right."

Carol Elizabeth looked up from her work without lifting her crayon from the page. "Haven't you ever seen a blond Indian?"

"No," Frances said. Angie didn't think she had either. But Carol Elizabeth, whose house Angie would go to after school for her first Brownie meeting, seemed not only confident in her work but furious at being questioned about it. So, Angie picked up another yellow crayon and joined Carol Elizabeth in coloring the hair of the Indian women. They worked in silence until the page was populated with a tribe of blond Navajos.

Miss Wolf came by and looked through her cat-eye glasses at their work, so carefully drawn and neatly colored inside the lines. "Girls," she said, "Indians have black hair. Not blond. I'm sure you must know that."

Carol Elizabeth glared at Angie, who tugged at her own wretched hair and for some reason glared at Frances. Carol Elizabeth grabbed a black crayon and began scribbling over the yellow until the smooth Navajo pageboy hairdos were globs of wax on the paper.

*   *   *

After school, Eva and Letty started the walk home without Angie. Eva gave Angie a mocking salute, which she then twirled into a crazy-person motion above her ear and then into a pretend gun, which she discharged at her temple. Angie ignored her and turned in the direction of Carol Elizabeth's house. She had twelve dollars in a sealed envelope pinned to the inside of her sweater. Money for a second-hand uniform derived from her mother's guilt at the bad perm inflicted by Nelda.

Though she didn't want to be late, she walked slowly. She was finally going to be a Brownie, one with a uniform. One also with black hair in a horrible home perm. A girl that Carol Elizabeth didn't like. But Angie believed the brochure. *Fun, friendship, and community.* She wanted to be part of it. She picked up her pace, rounded the corner, and saw Frances lumbering slowly up her driveway, past the family convertible Angie had ridden in recently. She stopped in her tracks, fearing any motion would cause Frances to turn around. But it was as if Frances knew she was there, standing there long enough to make Angie impatient, finally pivoting to face her.

"Want to come over and play?" Frances asked.

"My Brownies meeting is today," Angie said, aware of her use of *my*, a tiny word that seemed to echo throughout the neighborhood.

"I know," Frances said, standing, waiting, and finally turning to go into her house.

Angie hurried on, not wanting to hear the door close.

When Angie arrived, Mrs. Rogers pulled the old uniform from a paper bag and led her to the bathroom to change. Coming toward them in the hallway was the red-haired boy Eva had mooed at on the first day of school. Mrs. Rogers stopped him. "Kenny, say hello to Angie Rubio, our new Brownie."

Kenny grinned and widened his eyes as if he'd never seen her before. "Hello, Angie Rubio, our new Brownie."

Mrs. Rogers gave her son a playful tweak of the ear. "He's being silly," she told Angie. She put the uniform in Angie's hands and Angie gave her the envelope. The transaction nearly made her tremble.

"When you're dressed, come join the rest of the troop in the rec room," Mrs. Rogers said.

In the bathroom, Angie stood on tiptoe to see as much of her uniformed self as possible in the mirror. It hardly mattered that the belt was missing, that the dress sagged at the shoulders, that an ink stain marred its pocket. And, of course, there were no badges yet. Still, it was an official uniform. She held up her fingers in the scout salute.

She joined the other girls in the rec room, a cheery place with gingham curtains and pictures of kittens on the wall. The girls were sitting around a table already engrossed in the week's craft project. They looked up from stringing beads as Angie took the one empty seat.

"Let's welcome Angie to our troop with the Brownie Smile song," Mrs. Rogers said.

The girls dropped their beads and stood up. Angie didn't know if she should also stand so she was grateful when Mrs. Rogers pointed her chin upward at Angie's half-way-off-the-chair dithering. The other girls sang with great gusto and big gestures and ended by pointing to their "great big Brownie smile."

Even though Angie suspected that they sang more for the sake of singing than to welcome her to the troop, she did feel more at ease there in Carol Elizabeth's rec room.

Carol Elizabeth must have felt more at ease about Angie being there since she volunteered to explain the bead project they were working on. "Well, it was kind of my idea," she began, but then corrected herself when there were little sounds of protest from some of the other troop members. "A lot of us came up with the same idea when we saw this news story about an orphanage in Mexico. We wanted to brighten up their lives by making these goodwill bracelets. I've already made two."

She started gathering beads and string for Angie. "Here's some stuff to get you started."

Then Carol Elizabeth took her seat, flushed with importance, but also, Angie thought, a sense of generosity, and she smiled at the beads in front of her as if they were old friends.

"Thanks," she said.

She strung her beads quickly. Her fingers were fast and despite her nearsightedness, her eyes were unerring. She was sure she could finish a bracelet that afternoon. She worked without joining the talk at the table, which was about school and church and TV shows and movie stars, and when Mrs. Rogers went upstairs to prepare snacks, it turned to badges and who might be the next to earn one.

"Angie," one girl said, "aren't you going to get a sash?"

Angie looked around. All the girls wore the dark brown sash on which their badges were sewn.

"Yes," Angie said. "Pretty soon."

"Your uniform is kind of loose," another girl observed.

"And there's no belt," said another.

"Well, one thing's for sure," Carol Elizabeth said. "You sure are a *brownie*."

There was laughter and Angie, her scalp tightening, her skin prickling inside the musty uniform, laughed, too, at this joke. As she waited for the amusement to die down, she helped herself to more beads and concentrated closely on stringing them faster than anyone else in the room.

* * *

Later, she ran all the way home, the uniform chafing with each slap of her feet on the sidewalk. Alone in the bedroom, she stripped off the uniform and stuffed it at the back of the closet. She stomped around the room, head in hands, and then fell backward onto her bed and closed her eyes and felt her deepest wish—to be Hayley Mills—pulse in her thumbs that pinned themselves at her temples. Angie scrambled off the bed and switched on her record player and imagined she was strumming a guitar next to her identical blond twin, harmonizing on "Let's Get Together, Yeah, Yeah, Yeah."

Then she played Side B which was "Jeepers Creepers" and she crooned softly to that while she looked in the mirror. When she came to the line, "Where'd you get those eyes?" she widened her own to try to make them round like Hayley's. But even if she could make them round, they would never be blue. And her hair, kinked with a Toni Home Permanent, would, despite her last name, never be blond. Angie flung herself on the bed at the injustice.

Eva came in and plopped onto the opposite bed. "What is it now?" she asked.

Angie sat up and hiccupped an account of what had happened at the Brownie meeting.

"Well," Eva said, "we *are* brown, you know."

"I know that," Angie snapped and flung herself down again. "But, Eva?"

Eva was turning the record over on the record player. "What?"

"I don't want to be a Brownie anymore."

"What are you going to do?" Eva switched on the record and Hayley Mills's bubbliness filled the room. *Let's get together.*

Angie thought about how her hair was such a far cry from the graceful waves of Hayley Mills.

"Eva, remember in the movie when Sharon cuts Susan's hair so they could look alike?"

"Yeah, so?"

"We could cut each other's hair."

Eva's hand went to her head of evenly distributed curl. "I don't think so."

Angie went to the bureau drawer and withdrew a pair of scissors. "Then watch me cut mine."

She stretched out a curl and sheared it off. She looked at the curl in her hand. No longer attached to her head, no longer a part of her, the curl was useless, without purpose, a throwaway from Nelda and her mother's efforts to be creative, of her own desire to be someone else.

Angie sheared off more curl from both sides of her head until only the back curls remained. She reached behind her head and snipped, her scissors angling blindly.

"Here, give me those," Eva said.

Angie handed over the scissors and Eva slipped her fingers around a strand of hair. The bite of the scissors was even and steady. She closed her eyes and waited for the sound of her mother's footsteps, the door opening, her mother coming to ask about the Brownies.

Social Studies

"You know this is the dumb class, don't you?" Wanda Garcia said to Angie at recess, right after Angie had won the California History Bee that Miss Leake had said would be the most challenging test so far in their social studies unit. They would have to stand up, think on their feet, and say their answer out loud. It would be a measure of their preparation. It would test their poise. It would strengthen their character.

Miss Leake referred to character a lot, the meaning of which rather stumped even Angie, who had established herself as the smartest one in the class. She was always the first to raise her hand, she sped through the reading levels, and she always scored a hundred percent in spelling with hardly any effort, even breezing through the word "squirrel," which everyone else got wrong. So, Wanda's question, which was given without malice, but in the sympathetic, helpful way someone would inform another that a booger dangled from her nose or she had food in her braces, dismayed Angie. Because she didn't want to be told something she didn't already know, Angie answered, "I know that."

There were three fourth-grade classes at Kimball Park Elementary. Angie, who was standing in the four-square line next to Wanda, looked over at the four-square game in front of Mrs. Dewey's class, and then beyond that to the children playing in front of Mrs. Wright's class. Angie's next-door neighbor and sometimes best friend, Silvia Rico, was there and so was bashful, ever-smiling Teddy Mendoza who could do long division in his head. But the rest of the kids in Mrs. Wright's class were white. Mrs. Dewey's class was a mixture of white and brown students like some swirled dessert. Then there was Miss Leake's class, which was nearly all brown, and except for the unwanted attentions from the horrible Armando Cornejo, it was a class in which Angie had felt at ease and essential—until Wanda Garcia's question.

After school, as she walked home with Eva, she reported this news. "Of course, that's how they do it," Eva said. "They put people together who are alike. Otherwise, you have bedlam and mayhem and anarchy."

Angie was afraid to ask what all those words meant. Besides, she couldn't tell if Eva was joking. Because they were new to Kimball Park Elementary, Angie asked, "How did they know what I'm like?"

Eva shrugged. "It's in the records."

Angie wondered if know-it-all Eva knew what she was talking about. When Angie tried to imagine such records, all that came to mind was the stack of 45s on her dresser at home—the Shirelles, Martha and the Vandellas, Leslie Gore. She would buy the new Beatles record with her next allowance, she decided. While Angie's mind had wandered to records, she fell a few steps behind Eva's slightly pigeon-toed, but purposeful stride.

Suddenly, it occurred to Angie that if the fourth-grade classes were split into dumb, smart, and in-between, the sixth-grade classes had to be too. She caught up to Eva. "What are you in?"

Eva looked at her as if she were stupid. "I'm in the smart class."

* * *

Angie's family had moved into the neighborhood in the summer, one of the first to occupy the new housing tract where Angie hoped she would finally have a best friend. Before Kimball Park, their frequent moves meant attending a school no more than a year before leaving for another. But when they moved to Kimball Park, Angie's father, recently discharged from the Navy, dug his Pumas into the hard soil of their as yet un-landscaped yard and announced, "We're here to stay." He had finished his night school classes and had started a job with the city reading water meters. She knew he had hoped for a different job, one with a desk and a calculator, but his voice was resolute, and there was also relief. Angie felt it too—a chance to belong somewhere.

When Silvia Rico moved in next door, Angie believed her life in this new house in this new neighborhood had finally begun. Over the summer, she and Silvia rode their bikes, cooled off in the sprinklers in the park across the street, played hide-and-seek with the other kids in the neighborhood, and danced and sang to Neil Sedaka's "Breaking Up Is Hard to Do." They speculated on what school would be like and hoped they would not have a mean teacher. Angie had not thought to hope not to be in the dumb class.

A week before school started, they went to the main office where the room assignments were posted in the window. Angie crossed her fingers that she would be in the same class as Silvia. "Then we could do homework together," she said, and Silvia smiled at her. When Silvia found her name listed under Mrs. Wright, Angie scanned the names again and again hoping to find hers there too.

"Here you are," Eva said, stabbing the windowpane with her index finger at a list other than the one Angie had been staring at, hoping she could blink her name into existence. "You're in Miss Leake's class."

Eva proceeded to examine the other lists for Letty's class, while Angie stood glumly in front of the list that had her name on it. She had wanted to find her own name. It was her name. Her class. Even if it wasn't the same as Silvia's. She remained in front of Miss Leake's list, wondering who she was and what she looked like.

As if she were reading Angie's mind, a girl with a perfect ponytail said, "She's the new teacher." The girl also managed to report that her mother was the PTA president.

There was a moment of polite appreciation for this news and then the chatter resumed about the new teacher. "Miss," someone said. "That means she's not married."

"She's probably young," someone else said.

"Or an old maid," a boy said, which Angie thought was rude.

"She's from Alabama," said the girl whose mother was PTA president.

With all the talk about her teacher, Angie began to feel important, until the PTA girl turned to Silvia and said, "Hi, my name's Judy. We're going to be in the same class. We should be friends. Do you know the words to 'Breaking Up Is Hard to Do'?"

At home Eva, as the oldest, was the first to report the name of her teacher to their mother, who was watching a soap opera with a dust cloth in her lap. "Mr. Grayson," Eva said, business-like, when the commercial came on.

"A man teacher," their mother noted, nodding at the rarity, as if it signaled something extraordinary about her first-born.

Normally, as the second oldest, Angie would give her news next, but she said, "Letty, you go."

Letty frowned at the break in protocol, but their mother, who often seemed to forget that Letty was well past kindergarten, coaxed her with the sweet smile she normally used for other people's children.

After Letty named her teacher and their mother had applauded the news, Angie broke in breathlessly with hers. "My teacher is Miss Leake, and she's new and not married so she's probably young, and she's from Alabama."

"Alabama?" Her mother looked alarmed. "You know what they're like in the South, don't you?"

Angie turned to Eva to see if she knew what their mother was talking about, but Eva had on her pretend look of understanding, so it was up to Angie to ask the question. "What are they like?"

Their mother lowered her voice as if what she was about to say was forbidden. "They don't like black people."

"But we're not black," Angie said, looking at her sisters and then back at her mother as if this were something that required corroboration. But the commercial was over and their mother went back to the soap opera.

Angie was, nevertheless, about to pursue her point when a news announcer interrupted the soap opera, to which her mother objected with a sigh that was deeper than annoyance. "What is it now?" she asked, not of Angie, but of the newscaster whose voice vibrated with a grim vocabulary: missiles, threat, Cuba.

Angie's mother swatted the TV off in the same squeamish way she slapped at spiders with a rolled-up newspaper. Then she turned on them all. "What are you doing standing around in your school clothes. Go change."

Her sudden shrillness woke Anthony prematurely from his nap down the hall. A slow, wakening whine soon grew to a wide-awake wail, and Angie and her sisters scurried for cover to other parts of the house.

After Anthony's mouth had been plugged with a popsicle, Angie could hear her mother all jittery-voiced on the phone with Nelda. They spoke in Spanish and Angie tried to isolate recognizable sounds in her mother's mad, jumpy syllables. *Hysterical,* Angie thought, putting to use her new vocabulary, another reason why she belonged in the smart class. She had learned the word from the TV, another time when her mother's soap opera was interrupted by a news bulletin. She had found it in the dictionary after much trial and error when her mother declined to spell it for her. "You don't need to know that word," she'd said.

Angie closed her eyes to concentrate on her mother's half of the phone call. Coo-ba, she heard her mother say again and again.

"What's coo-ba?" Angie asked Eva.

Eva looked at her coolly. "In America, we say Q-ba. It's an island. En el Caribe," she said, adopting an Eydie Gorme and Trio Los Panchos accent.

* * *

Miss Leake was not yet old enough to be called an old maid, but neither was she particularly young. She was thin and long-faced with big teeth that her upper lip worked hard to close over. Her short, brown hair was combed neatly against her small head. When she sat down, ankles touching, in front of the class to read, her skirt lay just above her knees, the bones of which gleamed like polished rocks through her nylon stockings. She wore flat, red shoes.

"She's prim," Eva said when Angie described her.

"I think her red shoes are nice," Angie said.

"Does she speak with a Southern accent?" Eva asked.

"She sounds like the people on *Petticoat Junction*," Angie told her, remembering Miss Leake's *y'alls* whenever she addressed the class.

"That's Southern," Eva confirmed.

But Angie liked Miss Leake, and it was clear that Miss Leake liked Angie back. Brown Angie, who had always worked hard to please in school, had at last found a teacher who noticed and rewarded her efforts. Her homework came back with stick-on gold stars and *Good work!* in Miss Leake's pretty penmanship. Angie always answered correctly whenever called on in class and once she even caught a spelling error by Miss Leake who had written "histerical" on the board. Angie's hand shot up so she could say politely, but oh, so helpfully, "Shouldn't that be a *y*?"

Based on the evidence of her abilities, Angie was voted president of her classroom. Her duties included standing at the front of the class to lead the Pledge of Allegiance each morning, sharpening Miss Leake's pencils after school, pinning the daily attendance report outside the classroom for the office assistant to collect, and, most importantly, every two weeks choosing the new classroom monitors—ball monitor, blackboard monitor, paper monitor, and girls' and boys' line leaders. Angie was judicious in her picks, choosing as many girls as boys, as many kids she considered her friends as those she knew less well. She could not be swayed by someone offering her candy at recess or a Twinkie at lunchtime. She did not let her own likes and dislikes get in the way of her judgment. Which is why after a few weeks, she had to pick

Armando Cornejo for ball monitor. She didn't like Armando because it was plain to everyone that he liked her and she did not want to be liked by a boy who was a poor reader, couldn't spell, and had been the first one eliminated during the California History Bee. When she called his name, she pretended not to notice the dumb smile he gave her. He was just a dumb boy. In the dumb class! And Angie was in it with him.

* * *

In Silvia's bedroom, they looked through hair-do magazines for groovy styles that they could experiment with each other on. Judy Wiekamp had brought her styling kit—a collection of hair rollers, bobby pins, barrettes, rat-tail combs and a large jar of Dippity Do. Judy was one of the "old kids" who lived in the older houses in the neighborhood—small, flat-roofed dwellings that did not all look alike the way the ones did on Silvia and Angie's street. Judy claimed her house had character, and Angie looked up with interest at the word, but Judy offered nothing else that would clarify its meaning. Mentally, Angie constructed a sentence: *Judy lives in a house of character.*

Judy had attended Kimball Park Elementary since kindergarten. She had hair that reached her waist. Her mother was president of the PTA. All this gave her authority, which she wielded like a stun gun.

Judy held up a picture of a model with an up-do complicated with weaves and twists of hair. "This would look fab on you, Silvia. Your hair is just the right length and texture. Angie knew that her hair was similar to Silvia's. She filed away the word *texture* for her own future use.

"My hair could probably do that too," she said.

"Maybe," Judy said, "but it wouldn't match your glasses and braces."

"You wear glasses sometimes," Angie pointed out.

"Yes, but only sometimes." She smiled to show her teeth that had no braces.

While Judy combed Silvia's hair in preparation for the elaborate up-do that Judy said was a snap, Angie wondered if there were other words besides *texture* that Judy and Silvia learned in Mrs. Wright's class.

"What are you guys learning in your class?" she asked.

"We're not guys," Judy said, and Silvia giggled.

"Well, if you must know," Judy said, "it's all the standard stuff."

"Yeah, standard," Silvia agreed.

"Us, too," Angie said. "Standard."

When she got home, Angie looked up *standard* in the dictionary. It meant regular, normal, typical. She opened her special notebook where she'd been tracking her new vocabulary, which she had used in complete sentences.

> *Sometimes the world is a hysterical place.*
> *The measurement of character is probably not done with a ruler.*
> *School is no place for bedlam, mayhem, and anarchy.*

Now she added, *Angie Rubio is a standard girl.*

*   *   *

Maybe Wanda Garcia was wrong. If they were doing the same work as Mrs. Wright's class, why would one be the smart class and the other the dumb class? She pointed this out the next day to Wanda at recess in the four-square line. "Yeah, but we don't get as many right answers as the kids in Mrs. Wright's class. Wanda lit up at the homonyms, a topic they had discussed in class last week. But the word play only aggravated Angie.

Angie didn't think it would be polite to point out to Wanda that she, Angie, did get the answers right almost all the time, which is why she won the California History Bee. "That was a fun bee we had about California history, wasn't it?"

"I guess."

They had moved up in line and Wanda was next for a square. "At least it wasn't as hard as a paper test. Do you want me to get your boyfriend out?"

"He's not my boyfriend," she protested. "But get him out."

"Oh, and if you don't believe me that this is the dumb class," Wanda said, stretching on her toes to make herself limber for her turn, "ask Miss Leake."

Wanda stepped into her square and served the ball into Armando's chin, but Angie was too distracted to care.

A bee is as hard as a paper test, Angie thought. Harder. You had to know the answers and say them out loud. But then she thought of all the kids who had given the wrong answer on their first turn and returned to their desks to sit the rest of the bee out, not having to answer another question. Angie had drilled herself on the four main geographical regions of the state, the origin of the name California, the first settlers to arrive, the mission period and the rancho period, Sutter's Mill and the Gold Rush, and the Transcontinental Railroad. She had stood the longest until it was clear that no one could stump her, and she was declared the winner. But none of it mattered, because she was in the dumb class.

After school she went to her mother who was on her knees in the kitchen, stacking canned goods. Anthony was on the floor next to her, building his own tower of cans. Angie noticed with half-interest the unappealing stockpile: Spam, creamed corn, beets.

"Can you ask the principal to move me into Mrs. Wright's class?"

Her mother didn't look up from her can-stacking. "Why do you want to move?"

Her mother hated change, which is why she should've been in a better mood these days now that they weren't going to change houses anymore. She'd been collecting flashlights and batteries and now canned foods with the frenzy of a squirrel. Angie spelled s-q-u-i-r-r-e-l in her head to keep things fresh up there.

"I need to be in the same class as Silvia. It's hard to be best friends when we're in different classes."

"If you're really best friends, it shouldn't matter if you're in different classes."

"I think I need to be in a smarter class."

Angie's mother glared at a can of Boston baked beans in her hand, then turned her glare on Angie. "Now, don't go acting like you're better than everyone else."

"I'm not acting."

"Don't get smart with me." Her mother sighed, her shoulders shook, and her voice rose and trembled, startling Anthony into knocking down his tower.

The words boxed Angie's ears and her eyes welled with the impact.

"Honestly, Angie, it's not the end of the world," she shouted over Anthony's rising wails.

Angie trembled too as she tried to untangle sentences from her tied-up tongue. Unable to expel more than a few useless yaps, she stomped off to her room and flopped on her bed.

Eva looked up from her homework, which she insisted on calling her New Math homework. "Maybe next year they'll put you in a higher class—if not the smart class, then the next-to-smart class."

"You mean the next-to-dumb class?"

"They probably didn't have any room for you in the other classes," Eva said.

Angie thought a moment. "But why did they have room for Silvia?" Or Judy Wiekamp for that matter? There was a big difference between acting like you knew stuff and really knowing it.

Eva slapped her forehead in exasperation. "Do you mind? I have to do my New Math."

Angie heaved herself from her bed and huffed past Eva. In the living room, her father was nodding off in front of the evening newscast. She sat down near him just as Walter Cronkite was finishing a report on the president. Footage of a troubled Kennedy conferring with a knot of other serious-faced men filled the screen to Walter's right. As Walter signed off, Angie's father snorted awake.

He looked at Angie. "What are you doing here? You don't need to be watching the news."

"I wasn't," Angie said, wondering at his scolding, startled at the heat in her denial.

Her father closed his eyes, but Angie didn't believe it was to sleep. She waited, shifted in her space of the couch. He opened his eyes. "Need something?"

Her father wore the same brow-furrowing look as the men on the news these days.

"I need to be in a smarter class at school."

"Your class is too easy?"

Angie nodded.

"Let's just wait and see," her father said. "Things will work themselves out."

But his sigh and teeth-clenching grin gave her no hope and she left the room without a word, tears blurring her way as she veered off the hallway to the bathroom, wanting with all her might to shriek with the same thrilling, bloodcurdling zeal as Anthony in his tantrums.

* * *

Angie decided to ask Miss Leake. After school one day, she lingered at the pencil sharpener after grinding a dozen Number 2s to pinpoints. She practiced in her head her opening line: *It has come to my attention…* Or maybe: *Rumor has it…*

Miss Leake was putting on her sweater and pulling her purse out of her desk drawer.

"Thank you, Angie, you can put the pencils in the box. I'm locking up now."

Angie followed Miss Leake to the door and said to the spot between her shoulder blades, "Am I in the dumb class?"

The words escaped her and in the empty classroom they bounced like beach balls, huge and airy and waiting to be punched.

Miss Leake turned around. Her small eyes went hard. Her flat-cheeked face sagged with disapproval. "Angie Rubio, I don't ever want to hear you use that word in this class again."

That was proof enough. They were the dumb class. Miss Leake was too embarrassed to even speak the word. Angie was still holding the pencils, their sharpened tips aimed at Miss Leake's red shoes. She wanted to let them loose on the floor and watch them roll uncontrollably in every direction, or toss them in the air to stab the ceiling or rain down on Miss Leake's head.

"The pencils, Angie," Miss Leake said, pointing to the empty box.

Angie dropped the pencils into the box and covered them with the lid. She spun around and walked quickly out the door, which Miss Leake was holding open. Angie kept walking, her stride fast and fierce. As soon as she was off school grounds where it was against the rules to run, she raced home, rounding the corner to take the downhill at a pace that made her eyes blur behind her glasses.

The next day Angie refused to raise her hand in class, even when no one else came up with the right answer. It was a California History question. Sometimes Miss Leake popped a question on something they'd already covered just to keep them on their toes so the learning wouldn't go stale.

She pretended not to see the other students turn to look at her, tried not to see Miss Leake's neutral, unblinking expression, yet forced herself to match it.

Wanda Garcia whispered to her "What's the answer?"

Angie whispered back, "Junipero Serra."

Wanda's hand shot up. Wanda was allowed to be first in the lunch line for her correct answer.

"No fair," Blanca Terada said. Even though Blanca was only in the fourth grade, her mother let her tease her hair and spray it with Aqua Net. Even though she was short, her beehive made her seem big and hard, and Angie was a little afraid of her. So, to make up for helping Wanda, Angie gave

Blanca her homework answers. Word got around and pretty soon Angie was giving out turns, just as she gave out turns for ball and paper monitor and line leader.

Miss Leake asked Angie to stay in during recess. Only the bad students were ever denied recess. Angie was worried and a little pleased, but also determined to stand her ground so to speak. She sat at her desk and Miss Leake stood over her. Angie had to tilt her head back to see her and from this angle Miss Leake looked even longer and thinner and her face plainer and sterner, which made Angie more resolute.

"Angie, I'm disappointed in you."

Angie was surprised by the tears that sprang to her eyes. *I don't want to be in your class anymore*, she said in her head.

"Being a smart student is not just about knowledge. It's about character. Do you understand me, Angie?"

Angie nodded, though she didn't at all, not in the least—what she did understand was that she hated Miss Leake.

At lunchtime, Angie picked at half of her egg salad sandwich. Why didn't her mother remember that she hated egg salad? A squishy mouthful would surely make her gag. Resentful and cross, Angie shoved a hunk of sandwich in her mouth, thinking that she would willingly let the chips (or egg salad goo) fall where they may. But while the sensation was definitely unpleasant, the urge to upchuck did not materialize and now Angie was happy to suffer the slow torture of chewing and swallowing the gooey chaos that swamped her tongue. *Sometimes unhappiness has a texture.*

When Wanda Garcia offered to trade her barbecue potato chips for half of Angie's Twinkie, Angie declined the trade with a shake of her head and instead pushed the entire Twinkie package into Wanda's hands. Then like a nun ministering to the pitiable and the poor or a condemned soul shedding her worldly goods, she parceled out her remaining food. She bestowed her Red Delicious apple on Susie Caruso whose mother packed her raisins, but never fresh fruit. Then, her mouth still full of sandwich, she rose and went to the boys' table and, ignoring Armando, deposited the untouched half of her sandwich in front of big Mitchell Villalpando whose mother refused to pack him more than two sandwiches a day. Though she steadfastly refused to look at Armando, she knew he was looking at her and she was gripped with the impulse to open wide her mouth and show him the chewed-up glop there. But no, she was better than that. Having disposed of her lunch, except for the remnants of egg salad still testing the grinding and mincing powers of her teeth and tongue, she left the lunch table and headed for the library to seclude herself with the friendless during lunch recess. *There is no mayhem in the library.*

*   *   *

It was an unusually hot afternoon for that time of year and Angie, like the other students, was twitchy and peevish during silent reading time. She had checked out the fattest book she could find in the school library, a tiny room whose shelves consisted mainly of cast-offs from neighborhood garage sales. *The Agony and the Ecstasy* was a paperback, a grown-up's book, satisfyingly thick, and with a title that offered up both pain and jubilation like a natural pairing—bacon and eggs, field and stream, night and day. The looks she got from the other students when she pulled it out to read gave her a certain amount of pleasure. Though she tried to do more than appear to read her fat, impressive book, she was just as fidgety as the others. Even Miss Leake seemed to shuffle the papers she was correcting rather rudely. The grimness of the faces on the news, on her parents, and now on her teacher, made Angie want to either scream or hide.

Finally, Miss Leake rose from her desk, padded in her quiet, flat shoes to the light switch and clicked off the overhead fluorescents. "I think we deserve a little break," she said. "How about a game of Heads Up, Seven Up?"

It was usually a rainy-day game when they had to stay in during recess, so playing it on a hot, sweltering, cranky afternoon was special. Angie was relieved at the opportunity to put her head on her desk.

"Who would like to start?" Miss Leake asked.

Angie stared at the ceiling, still refusing to raise her hand, but regretted it when Armando was one of the seven to be picked. In fact, Miss Leake designated him as the leader. When the seven were assembled at the head of the room, Armando, told the rest of them at their desks, "Heads down!"

Angie put her head down, resting it on her forearms. She knew some kids cheated at the game, positioning their head and opening their eyes so that they could see the feet of whoever passed by and know for sure who tapped their head. Angie never cheated and now that Armando was it, she didn't have to. She felt a gentle, but insistent, tap on her head and she flinched a little. Moments later Armando said eagerly, "Heads Up, Seven Up."

Angie and the six others who had been tapped stood up, and Armando called on each of them in turn to guess who had tapped them. Angie was competitive and liked winning games and usually did if the game wasn't tetherball or kickball, or any kind of ball for that matter. If she guessed right, she could go to the front of the room and be a tapper, and if she tapped strategically, choosing the heads of those least likely to suspect her, no one would guess her as the tapper, and she would remain up front the longest. It was one of the reasons why she was considered the smartest in the class. Today, she knew who had tapped her, but she refused to say his name. "Wanda," she said.

Armando, mildly peeved, snorted. "No. Sit down."

When everyone standing had a chance to guess their tapper, and those who had done so successfully had replaced their tapper at the front of the room, Armando told them again, "Heads down."

Angie felt a tap again, firmer than the last. She stood up and this time said, "Mitchell." There was twittering around the room. "No," Armando said, his face sour with irritation. When the round was over and the new tappers joined Armando at the front of the room, Angie laid her head once again on her desk and waited for the tap on her head, which this time was a thwack. Her brain roiled from the jolt and she had to clamp her mouth shut to hold back the roar escalating inside her.

When Armando announced "heads up," she rose angrily to her feet, and even though this time, Armando called on her last and almost all the tappers had been eliminated, and everyone knew she would have been right to choose Armando, she said through gritted teeth, "Blanca." The classroom erupted with sniggers and chants.

Even after Miss Leake, who had been at her desk, stood up, the ruckus churned, faster and louder. Angie looked around her, fear and excitement pulsing at her neck. Her feet sweated inside her socks. Her knees wobbled. *Mayhem*, she thought. Created by her. Tiny twin threads of satisfaction and dread wove themselves inside her limbs.

Miss Leake took two giant steps in her plain, flat red shoes. "This game is over," she said over the laughter which burbled down until the room went silent. The tappers at the front of the room returned to their seats. Things were nearly back to order. Angie remained standing a moment longer, not looking at Miss Leake or Armando or anyone, and ignoring Wanda's gentle pull on her sleeve.

It's not the end of the world, she remembered her mother saying. As she lowered herself back into her chair, Angie wanted to scream: What do *you* know?

CURRENT EVENTS

Three weeks into the fifth grade, Max Delgado said to Angie in the four-square line, "You're going into the smart class, aren't you?"

Max was tall and already showing traces of facial hair, through which a pimple or two erupted. It made him dangerous looking. His hair was wavy and a bit slick, his eyes hooded, his mouth mocking. He was known to get into fights after school. But when he spoke to Angie, his voice was quiet, a near mumble, and yet something like music, low and deep as a Righteous Brothers song.

Angie nodded, her vocal cords suddenly out of commission.

"You like four-square?" Max asked, looking briefly in the general direction of her face.

By the time Angie nodded again, Max's eyes had drifted somewhere beyond the four-square game, so Angie cleared her throat and said, "Yes," a puny, strangulated sound.

Max didn't ask another question, but when it was Angie's turn to take a square, he said, "Good luck."

She immediately missed the ball that came her way, her hands meeting air while the ball grazed her shoulder and she instinctively turned her face and closed her eyes.

"You're out," Lizzie Shortz yelled, just in case it wasn't obvious to the whole school.

Angie left her square and went to the end of the line to wait another turn. Max, who had been behind her in line, should've taken her square, but someone else was in the game instead. Angie looked around the schoolyard, trying not to be obvious about it. She finally spotted him at the far end of the grounds, his hands in his pockets as he leaned against the chain-link fence as if testing its give. He tilted his head back, observing the sky, and Angie wondered what he was thinking as he gazed at its limitless blue, wondered whether he pondered as she did the future and how to get there. More immediately, she wondered if he would ever speak to her again, and if he did, whether her mouth would manage to eke out something intelligible. Angie saw him shift his gaze toward the four-square game and she quickly spun her own attention to the ball, as if its zigzag were the most important thing in the world.

Angie had noticed at the beginning of the school year that in fifth grade fewer girls played four-square at recess than they had the year before. They preferred to stand in clumps on the asphalt playground, turning around to glare whenever a ball bounced its way into their circle. Sometimes, a ball was purposely thrown at the knot of girls, which splintered them like screaming bowling pins.

Angie thought they were silly. Yet she did wonder how one maneuvered herself inside such shoulder-to-shoulder alliance. Silvia Rico flitted easily between four-square and the cozy ring of girls. Whenever she came to stand with Angie in line for four-square, Angie tried hard not to say something stupid, wanting badly to keep Silvia at her side.

Now that she was moving into Mrs. O'Farrell's class where Silvia was, Angie was hopeful that she might find a place inside the circle. But the small bit of notice from Max Delgado almost made her want to stay in Mrs. Burnham's class, the in-between class. A safe place between dumb and smart.

Angie sat at the kitchen table putting the finishing touches on her last homework assignment for Mrs. Burnham's class—a page from the reading workbook that asked easy questions in a section called, "What Did You Learn?" to which Angie wanted to reply *nothing new.* Good thing she was going in the smart class. She closed her notebook on her last assignment for the not-so-smart class and considered joining her father in the living room to watch the news.

But it was Wednesday when her mother made enchiladas for dinner and Nelda came over to help, dragging Little Eddie with her. Angie liked to listen to her mother and Nelda talk as they cooked. Quiet, thorny-faced Little Eddie always shuffled his Gumby-limbed body in the door, nodding his hellos before seeking Eva out, with whom he had developed a rapport over their matching sullen personalities. Nelda called them the Moody Club.

Angie felt a bit jealous at being excluded from their twosome. She could be just as moody as they were. She also envied Little Eddie his looks. He had fair skin, a straight nose, and curly hair. He would be a beauty when he grew up. There was more to envy—that mysterious other part of him that clearly wasn't Mexican, his only-child status, and only one parent to boss him around, his ability to understand Spanish when it was spoken to him and respond haltingly in kind—something none of the Rubio kids could do.

Angie's mother almost never spoke to them in Spanish, only around or through them as a way of talking about them without having to ensure they were out of the room. Angie tried to isolate the Spanish sounds into their separate word parts in the hope of looking them up later. But the sounds all ran together. Only the inflections were obvious. And, of course, the facial expressions—the elevated eyebrows, the pinched lips, the Lucille Ball eyes, which Angie caught only in profile at the moment since her mother and Nelda had their backs turned to her.

Angie watched Nelda's rear end shake as she mashed avocados. Nelda, who always seemed to sense an audience, wriggled her hips in a dance. With bowl and masher in hand, Nelda circled the kitchen, swiveling her hips.

"¿Quieres bailar conmigo, mija? Así se mueve el cuerpo."

Her lower body was a slow, sexy motor. Nelda was sexy. She had on her Avon lady smell that made Angie think of moonlight and soft breezes.

"Get up. I'll teach you," Nelda urged with slinky shoulders.

Angie shook her head and bent over her finished homework.

"Ay, Angie, you should join the Moody Club." Nelda sighed and sashayed back to the counter to join Angie's mother in whispered conversation.

"Hey, Angie, I hear you're moving to the smart class," Nelda called over her shoulder.

"Yeah," Angie said, casually, as if it were not a big deal, as if it weren't something that had been burning in the back of her brain for what seemed like a lifetime. She was going to join the Smart Club.

"Gonna get yourself a smart boyfriend, eh?" Nelda asked.

"No," Angie answered, immediately regretting responding at all. She knew it was okay to ignore certain questions Nelda asked. She just hadn't learned to do so.

"You don't want no dumb boyfriend. Not even no average one."

Angie winced at Nelda's grammar, blushed at the idea of a boyfriend. She erased an imaginary blot on her notebook with the end of her pencil.

In the living room, her father had turned the volume up on the news to compete with Nelda's chatter, and JFK's voice reached the kitchen. "El guapo presidente habla," Nelda said, and she and Angie's mother scurried to the living room. Angie put down her pencil and followed.

JFK was being interviewed by Walter Cronkite. They were sitting in beach chairs, the Atlantic Ocean behind them, the breeze fluttering their lapels. Even in black and white, Kennedy's handsome face appeared ruddy with health and his sun-lightened hair flashed like neon. He was talking about desegregation in Alabama schools, the March on Washington, equality for all Americans, and they all listened there in the living room, nodding. And though Angie understood only some of it, she knew it was something she believed in. She felt the future approaching, and she would be ready for it because she was going in the smart class.

* * *

In Mrs. O'Farrell's class, Angie was given a seat at the back of the room, which suited her just fine since it allowed her to see everyone else and get a clue as to how to behave in the smart class. On the other hand, she did feel a bit forgotten since it was hard to be seen behind Perry Wheeler, a big boy whose glasses were secured to his head with an elastic band that made a deep dent in the back of his neck. Angie was both repulsed and fascinated by the sight, having to resist an urge to pull at the elastic and let it snap back into place, perhaps displacing some of the brain matter that made Perry such a scary smart boy. Perry raised his hand a lot, always ready with the right answer and when he spoke, Angie watched the skin on the back of his neck move with the syllables.

Once a week, Mrs. O'Farrell assigned a couple of students to bring in a newspaper article to share for Current Events. She asked for volunteers and Perry's big arm shot up. Though Angie didn't raise her hand, Mrs. O'Farrell spied her beneath Perry's armpit and said, "Thank you for volunteering, Perry. Angie, this is an opportunity for you to become an active member of this class."

When Angie walked home with Silvia that afternoon, they were joined by Judy Wiekamp, who didn't even live in their direction. Angie asked what kind of article she should bring.

"Oh, you know, something current in the news," Silvia said.

"Something important to our lives," Judy added.

Like what, Angie wanted to ask, but now that she was in the smart class, she was afraid to ask questions about something she was already supposed to know.

When they got to Silvia's house, Silvia said goodbye to Angie and headed up her driveway with Judy beside her. From the sidewalk, Angie watched the two of them disappear into the Rico house.

Angie, grim with purpose, hurried to her own house next door to find a current event.

It turned out that the event currently in progress at her house was an argument between her parents amid the sounds of the TV. Eva was in the kitchen, her pencil poised above her homework, her head cocked to listen to the goings-on in the living room.

"What's happening?" Angie asked.

"Dad was bitten by a dog on his rounds today. His leg is all bandaged and he asked Mom to bring him a beer."

Angie knew that being bitten by a dog was one of her father's biggest fears about his job checking water meters. She also knew that drinking beer was supposed to be a weekend activity and that no matter how much he thought he deserved a beer to soothe the suffering of a dog bite, her mother was going to frown him into denying himself one.

Her mother came into the kitchen and, seeing Angie, immediately gave her some chores. "Go check on your sister and brother, and then set up the TV trays in the living room."

"I have homework," Angie said, wanting to remind her mother that she was in the smart class now.

Her mother put her hands on her hips. "Do I have to do everything around this house?"

Angie turned and stomped uselessly down the hall, the shag carpet muffling her resentment. Letty and Anthony were lying on her parents' bed watching cartoons. They didn't look up from Mr. Magoo, but aside from their unblinking fixation on the TV, they appeared to be alive, so Angie went to the hall closet and rattled the TV trays out of their closely packed storage.

"Keep it down!" The shouts overlapped from three parts of the house, and Angie quietly vowed they would all be sorry when she was famous, which she believed to be a possibility now that she was in the smart class.

She dragged the TV trays into the living room where her father was watching the *Dialing for Dollars* movie before the news came on. She set up the trays, trying not to block her father's view of Sal Mineo with a cigarette hanging from what her mother called his kissable lips. Seeing Sal Mineo reminded Angie of Max Delgado and her skin prickled.

"What's wrong with you?" her father asked.

Angie realized she had been staring at Sal Mineo, at the way he released words between his kissable lips while balancing the cigarette at the corner of his mouth.

"Nothing," Angie said. She looked at her father's leg propped up on the coffee table, an icepack draped over his bandaged shin. "Does it hurt?"

"Like heck."

Angie knew he wanted to say "hell," but her mother frowned at that too.

She watched him take a sip of his iced tea. Her mother's one concession to her father's injured state was to have them all eat dinner in front of the TV. Angie was anxious to find her current event, so she asked her father for the paper that was on the other side of him on the couch.

"How's the smart class working out for you?"

"This is my first assignment," Angie told him. "I want to get it right."

Angie scanned the headlines on the front page. She wondered which article Perry Wheeler was going to bring. She wanted hers to be better. Angie turned the page of the newspaper and a photo caught her eye. She read the article and her pulse hammered with indignation.

Later, when the whole family was eating their chicken and rice off TV trays in front of Walter Cronkite intoning the news, Angie yelped, "That's my current event story. That's what I'm going to talk about in my class."

"I have an idea," her mother said. "Why don't you talk about President Kennedy's thousandth day in office that's coming up? It's been on the news and in the papers. It's an important event."

"But I've already chosen my topic," Angie said.

"Well," her mother said, "do what you want."

Angie followed her mother's glance to the side table where the *LIFE* magazine covers of both the president and Jackie were displayed amid the family photographs, including the most recent school pictures of Angie and her sisters slouching frameless against each other.

"It's her assignment," her father said. "Let her decide."

"I know that," her mother said. "Didn't I just say so?"

"Well, I've got homework, too," Eva declared and carried her dishes to the kitchen.

"Are we excused?" Letty asked.

"I don't know if I even have a say in this house anymore," her mother said as she started folding up the TV trays and everyone scattered from the living room, except for her father who raised the volume on a beer commercial.

*   *   *

Mrs. O'Farrell called on Perry Wheeler first during Current Events time. Perry talked about Hurricane Flora. He described the Intertropical Convergence Zone and held up a diagram he'd made that explained how a hurricane forms. He'd sketched a large map that showed all the affected countries in the Caribbean plus the tip of Florida. Over 7,000 people were killed by the hurricane. Luckily, only one of them in Florida. Perry then pointed out the custom of naming storms after girls because of their stormy natures. This last point, offered as just another fact, elicited a smug hilarity from the boys. There were some snorts of annoyance from the girls, but no outright refutation from anyone. Angie wondered if anyone else seethed silently with rage. Mrs. O'Farrell thanked Perry for bringing in a current event that gave them scientific, geographic, and historical information.

"Now, Angie, what have you got for us?"

Angie wished she had thought to draw a map for her current event. Since she had no visual aids, she jumped right in with the lead-in she'd practiced at home. "My article is about Sam Cooke, the singer and songwriter of hits like "Twisting the Night Away." He and his band—"

But Mrs. O'Farrell stopped her. "Angie, I'm sorry if the rules weren't explained to you, but we don't bring in news about celebrities. News about movie stars, singers, and athletes is not important to what we're learning in class.

"But he got arrested," Angie said.

"Angie, you'll get another chance for Current Events soon."

Angie shrank at the snickering of classmates, cringed at the embarrassed looks on her behalf. She tucked the newspaper clipping inside her notebook and pressed it closed on the article that told about Sam Cooke and his band being arrested for trying to check in at a whites-only motel in Shreveport, Louisiana.

She hoped she would see Max Delgado at recess. If he happened to speak to her, even if it was only about four-square, she would tell him about Sam Cooke. Maybe her eyes would well with indignation. Maybe Max would offer a sleeve.

But at recess, Judy Wiekamp shouted for all the girls in Mrs. O'Farrell's class to gather around her. Though Angie fit the category, she was still uncertain whether Judy meant to include her.

Judy handed round little white envelopes. But not to everyone. A few of the invitations had two names on them. Judy explained to the throng of girls around her that the person whose name came first was the primary invitee and the person whose name came second was invited because she was friends with the primary invitee. "It would've been rude to exclude you," Judy told the second-named, who in keeping with their status formed a second ring of girls around Judy. Angie stepped closer to Silvia, who turned and smiled at her from the inner circle. "Here," she said, handing Angie the envelope, "you can hold it until recess is over."

Her mother was skeptical when Angie announced she was invited to a slumber party, and when Angie could not produce an invitation as proof, her mother dismissed the matter altogether.

"But I *am* invited," Angie wailed. "Aren't I, Eva?" Angie had already explained to her the circumstances of the shared invitation.

Eva looked up from her homework. "It's true. Angie's invited," she said, making quotation marks with her fingers. Then she elaborated, "Only the popular girls got an invitation to take home. Like Silvia Rico."

"Popularity isn't everything," their mother said. She looked at Angie and then in the direction of the Rico house next door. "Well, if Silvia's going—" She left the room, her resignation trailing behind her.

Angie knew her mother wanted her to be more like Silvia. In fact, Angie was sure her mother wanted her to *be* Silvia, who was never awkward but shy in the way that charmed rather than aggravated people. She turned to Eva and repeated their mother's words, maybe for assurance, more likely for consolation, "Popularity isn't everything."

Eva scoffed. "That's what unpopular people say. And we," she said, "are not a popular family. FACT OF LIFE."

Eva said "fact of life" a lot, ever since she got her period. It was an irksome phrase and Angie often hid the box of Kotex to get back at her.

Junior high had hardened Eva. It was in P.E. class that the mortifications of adolescence were first laid bare to her. She had disclosed to Angie the horrors of changing her clothes side by side with other girls, of the gym monitors imposing demerits for showering without soaping, and the cruelly democratic policy of one girl, one towel. But what sent Eva to the precipice of despair and reckless sarcasm was one word in eighth-grade science—genetics. It wasn't as if she'd never heard the word before. It was just that only now had she really understood its implications. "It determines our lives," she said. "Hair color, eye color, skin color, bra size. Popularity."

Eva paused for breath and effect. "Fact of life: We're doomed."

That was Eva. But Eva had never been to a slumber party. Angie decided that this was where Eva's path and her own would differ.

*   *   *

In Judy Wiekamp's rumpus room, they ate frozen pizza, potato chips with onion dip from a plastic tub, and snickerdoodles. They burped indecently from root beer. They did each other's hair with Dippity-Doo and sprayed Aqua Net until they were faint from fumes. They danced to the Dave Clark Five and lip-synched to Gerry and the Pacemakers. They spoke to each other in English accents as they passed around the latest issue of *Tiger Beat*. Angie was always one step behind, miming the last note to "Ferry Cross the Mersey" when everyone else had begun to squeal over the pin-up of

Bobby Sherman. Then someone put Sam Cooke's "Another Saturday Night" on the record player and Angie's ears burned at the recollection of her Current Events failure, which would not have been a failure had she reported about JFK's thousandth day in office.

When the other girls sang at the top of their lungs, Angie only joined in at the end of the chorus, the part about *ain't got nobody* and being *in an awful way*.

Then they sat in a circle on their sleeping bags and told scary stories and then gossiped about their classmates. One girl, who apparently had forgotten that Angie was present at the party, exclaimed, "Did you see what Angie Rubio was wearing to school the other day?" For a minute, Angie wondered if there could possibly be another Angie Rubio. But no, there was only her. As she tried to recall what unforgivable thing she might have been wearing, Judy addressed her directly.

"Angie," she said, as if she'd just discovered her presence, "too bad about your current event."

"Yeah, too bad," Silvia said more gently.

"At least now you know the rules," Judy said in her PTA-president's-daughter voice.

While Angie, the part-time-cafeteria-worker's daughter, was trying to decide just how grateful she should be for Judy's assurance, the conversation turned to fashion and Jackie Kennedy's elegance, and Angie, eager to contribute to the discussion, announced, "My mother framed the *LIFE* magazine photos of Jackie and JFK."

But the topic had changed yet again. To boys. Judy first had everyone swear that anything said in that room (*her* rumpus room) that night would remain a secret. Then she revealed that she had a semi-crush on Max Delgado. Everyone gasped and gushed an opinion—that he looked like a sixth-grader, that his voice was already starting to change, that he hardly ever spoke to girls.

This time Angie knew better than to volunteer that Max had spoken to her.

"Of course, I would never kiss him," Judy said.

No one questioned this policy as there seemed to be a universal understanding of its logic, though it completely escaped Angie.

"I just need to walk on the wild side for a bit," Judy said, and the other girls nodded their agreement.

The conversation seemed to inspire the next slumber party activity. Strip poker. But after the cards were dealt, they discovered that none of them knew how to play poker. So, Judy ordered everyone to write down her name on a piece of paper. When pen and paper were passed to Angie, she hesitated, wondering what kind of disease she could claim that would exempt her from the game.

"What's the matter?" Judy asked. "Something wrong with you?"

"No," Angie replied quickly, wondering why she seemed to regularly invite such a question.

The pen was slippery in Angie's hand and her penmanship, normally sure and neat, wiggled out of the lines and it worried her to see her name so slouchy and untidy. She folded the paper tightly, her fingers, still greasy from chips and cookies, leaving stains along the crease. Judy collected the folded slips of paper in her cupped hands and then dropped them into the empty potato chip bowl.

The game was simple. Judy would draw a name and that girl would have to lose an item of clothing. There was nervous giggling all around except from Angie who feared any sound of protest that might escape from her constricted windpipe. Angie was grateful for one thing. Earlier, when they had all changed into their nightclothes, modestly taking turns behind a screen, Angie was made acutely aware that she was the only one not wearing a frilly nightgown. For once, she was happy for her departure from the norm. At least her pajama top and bottom gave her a two-to-one edge in pieces of clothing.

Judy swirled the names with her hand, making a show of it, raking the contents with her fingers, scooping a handful of names, letting them drift back down into the bowl, and increasing the drama of it all by humming the death march. At one point, Judy stopped swirling the names and raised her hand to tuck a strand of her Aqua-Net-stiffened hair behind her ear, and Angie caught a glimpse of a slip of paper stuck to the corner of her palm, saw it slide down the folds of Judy's rayon nightgown into the curly clumps of the shag carpet. From where she sat, even nearsighted Angie could see the telltale smudge that marked her name.

Surely someone saw it. Angie looked around her. Some of the girls had their eyes closed and their fingers crossed. But even those whose eyes were open seemed not to have noticed the stray slip of paper. Surely, she should say something. But then Judy leaned forward and buried the paper under her knee as she drew the first name and Angie felt a giddy relief at the knowledge that it wasn't hers.

She soon felt justified in her deceit. As numbers were drawn and clothing was gradually discarded, Angie was horrified to learn that under their nightgowns, everyone was wearing a bra. Even Silvia. Before long, a pile of nightgowns and a tangle of pink appliquéd training bras filled the middle of their circle, and the girls had wrapped themselves in blankets or burrowed like naked moles into their sleeping bags, all while something was happening—or not happening. Angie alone, though braless, remained fully clothed, sitting atop her sleeping bag, a creeping conspicuousness overtaking her.

"Why isn't Angie's name coming up?" someone asked from the depths of a quilt pulled to her chin.

Judy, suddenly suspicious, reached for the potato chip bowl and emptied the names onto the floor. Clutching a sheet around herself with one hand, she picked through each name with the other, taking roll call, each girl huffing a righteous "here." When Judy had called all the names from the bowl, only Angie had not responded. There was silence and accusing stares, and Judy's eyes narrowed as she searched for an explanation. Angie's eyes went to the floor, searching for her name, but it had become lost amid all the strewn clothes, which Judy was now flinging about with her one free arm. "Aha," she shouted, holding up the plastic dish of onion dip as if it were evidence in a crime. A little slip of paper, Angie's slip of paper, clung to the side of the dip.

"You were never even in the game," Judy said. The other girls in their covered-up nakedness glared at Angie, who without having shed a single piece of clothing, felt completely exposed.

Later when the lights were out and the last whispering and giggling around her had died and been replaced by soft breathing and snores, Angie remembered Eva's voice of doom, Judy humming the death march, Sam Cooke singing "I ain't got nobody."

* * *

On Monday, despite the oath of secrecy Judy had demanded of the girls at her slumber party, word circulated that there had been a game of strip poker, or a version of it, and that Angie had cheated. On Tuesday, Angie saw Judy talking to Max Delgado at recess, and on Wednesday she saw them walking home together. On Thursday, it was Silvia Rico's turn for Current Events, and she brought an article about the first push-button phone and Mrs. O'Farrell praised her for informing the class about the new technology. On Friday, Angie was ready for the world to end.

They heard the news while standing in the lunch line. At first no one believed it. It was just another piece of gossip or rumor that floated up somewhere in the line and twisted into something impossibly cruel and wrong. The lunch ladies cried as they ladled chicken and mashed potatoes onto plates. It was Angie's mother's day to spoon steamed vegetables into little shallow bowls. Usually, when they saw each other across the counter, Angie and her mother would exchange quick, little smiles. Today, Angie's face felt as if all the muscles had left it. She glanced at her mother, whose facial muscles seemed tied in knots. The teachers on cafeteria duty were red-eyed, their hands clenched around tissues. The children who were used to being told to eat their vegetables or finish their milk were left to their own devices. Some took advantage of the situation and tossed their green beans in the garbage. Others, affected by the gravity of the atmosphere, felt obliged to force their vegetables and milk on themselves. Angie was among the bewildered, dutifully swallowing milk and vegetables as if doing the right thing would somehow make up for the death of President Kennedy.

Back in the classroom after lunch, there were no more lessons that day. Mrs. O'Farrell sat at her desk and wept into her handkerchief. Most of the girls cried, too. Wads of tissue collected in fists and on desks, and floated to the floor like crushed, stemless carnations. Angie held back her tears.

The PA system crackled and then the principal's voice came somber and strained announcing that school would let out early on this day of tragedy.

Angie was among the last to shuffle out the door. She managed not to cry, but her eyes felt unfocused and unnaturally wide-open and she was glad to step into the sunlight which forced her to blink and shade her eyes. When her eyes adjusted to the brightness of the afternoon, which seemed rudely oblivious to the day's calamity, she spotted Max Delgado at the far end of the playground leaning into the fence, the way she'd seen him that day he first spoke to her. Except that he wasn't gazing skyward. He was looking at the ground, at his shoes, or the elongated shadows lobbed by the jungle gym. She wanted him to look up and see her, acknowledge her with a nod. She saw herself walking toward him, joining him in the concave bend in the fence, putting her hand in his, saying something wise and appropriate about the state of the world. Or maybe saying nothing at all. But Max didn't look up, and she remembered how he had walked Judy home the other day.

Angie bent down and picked up a rock—someone's abandoned marker in a hopscotch square. She heaved it, only meaning to hit the dirt at his feet. The thwack of the rock against the sleeve of Max's shirt made her gasp. Max turned a dark look in her direction. Angie was frozen in place. Max shifted his stance and Angie fled through the hallway to the front of the school where she threw herself in the bushes. There were still a few children making their way home and she watched their feet move past as she sobbed noiselessly. She waited until she saw Max's feet pass by. She waited some more until she knew he was gone.

When Angie got home, her mother had Letty on her knee while the TV carried the news of the assassination. "It's a terrible, terrible day," was all she said. Angie nodded, a burble in her throat refusing to expel itself into speech.

She sat on the floor in front of the TV and watched the somber newsman talk about the shocking national tragedy. "Just barely over a thousand days in office," the choked-up newsman said, and Angie felt accused and negligent, as if she might've saved JFK had she reported on him for Current Events.

Anthony woke up from his nap and dragged his innocent, cranky self and his blanket into the living room and displaced Letty. Eva came home on the junior high bus and sat grim-faced next to Angie. Their father came home next, still limping slightly, and her mother made room for him on the couch and leaned her head against his shoulder. Soon red-eyed Nelda and slump-shouldered Little Eddie came by too. They were all the Moody Club now.

Angie turned away from the footage on TV and looked at the side table. Amid the collection of Rubio family photos, President Kennedy looked into the distance at a future that would never come for him. Jackie gazed demurely at the world. Angie's fifth-grade school picture, not yet framed, threatened to nose-dive from its propped position.

HELP

Angie sprinted, slowed, veered left, then right, doubled back, the dust flying in her face, a pebble pinging off her glasses. On the blacktop now, she skirted the four-square games, jump-ropers, and tetherballers and ran onto the dirt field again, dodging dodge ball players, slashing through ordinary games of tag. She didn't need to be part of those games, because she had entered the chase. The breeze trapped her dress between her knees, clung to her legs as if to dissuade her. Her socks slipped off her heels and disappeared into her Hush Puppies. But still she ran.

After days of standing on the sidelines, she had joined the group, the small mob of sixth-grade girls in pursuit of Miles Jones—the boy with the English accent. He was not exactly from Liverpool, but that was a flaw easy enough to forgive. How someone with an English accent could find his way to Kimball Park was a miracle, one in a million, and no one should take it lightly. Certainly not this gang of girls, some of whom were already plotting to sneak Miles, a mere fourth-grader, into the sixth-grade dance on Saturday. The thought of the sixth-grade dance, that gateway event to junior high, made Angie want to run backward in time, rather than in circles as she was doing at the moment in this chase, mindless with Beatlemania.

And though she was a part of it now, she refused to scream or swoon at the sight of Miles's floppy brown hair or the sound of his Paul McCartney lilt, despite Jori-Page Schroeder.

Jori-Page Schroeder was the biggest screaming swooner of the pack, the tallest girl in the sixth grade and the most developed physically. She was not delicate and she lumbered when she ran, but she had a perfect, blond pageboy and blue eyes. Her name was really Debbie, but she had somehow managed to get everyone to call her Jori-Page—a name she had jigsawed together from the first two letters of the name of each of the Beatles. Jori-Page was smart and had a large vocabulary, she read fat books and spoke up in class, and even when she was wrong, she would give a smile that made you think she was really right after all and the teacher was a sorry idiot. Angie always made a mental note to work on her braces-hindered smile.

Jori-Page Schroeder made Angie feel small, not just because she *was* small and skinny to boot, but because Jori-Page used words as if they were baseball bats. Just yesterday in the girl's lavatory, Angie emerged from a stall only to be confronted by Jori-Page's blue eyes boring down on her.

"Don't you like The Beatles?"

"Yes, I love The Beatles." Angie had recently learned to gush by listening to Judy Wiekamp, whose status derived from the fact that her mother appeared to be PTA President for Life. Even Silvia Rico, her next-door neighbor and sometimes best friend, had become a gusher. Angie gave it another try. "I adoooooooore The Beatles."

"Then why aren't you chasing after Miles like the rest of us?"

Angie thought it best not to point out that Miles was not a Beatle.

"I have asthma or something," she lied. Her cousin Eddie was afflicted with all sorts of maladies, and Angie often borrowed one when it was convenient.

"I would sacrifice my life for something I believed in," Jori-Page said, narrowing her blue eyes at Angie before flouncing past her into the stall and slamming shut the door.

"But I think it might be under control soon—the asthma," Angie called through the door. "I have some medicine at home. I'll be fine tomorrow," she promised over the flush of the toilet.

Now tomorrow was today, and she was in the chase. So, she ran, and though a stitch in her side distorted her gait and one of her shoelaces had worked itself loose, she kept on running. Angie was normally not one to chase after boys, certainly in not so literal a manner, an all-out gallop through the playground in a posse of silly, shrieking girls. As she dashed breathlessly behind the others, she knew she was ridiculous. But at least she was not alone.

Still, she was not safe from reproof because there was Letty staring at her as she ran. Letty, the tattletale, always ready to share news about someone else's life at the dinner table when their mother asked them how their day was and Letty thought she was really supposed to answer.

Angie, trying to think of a bribe to keep Letty from tattling, suddenly realized she was running alone. There was just too much clutter with dodge ball and kickball games going on around her and kids running in and out of the sand box that held the monkey bars. She had lost the hunt and now trotted back and forth trying to locate the others. She stopped a moment to get her bearings when a stray ball bounced into her back, making her stumble and dislodging her glasses. She was adjusting them when she heard Jori-Page shout her name. Though she had her glasses on straight now, her vision was impaired by the cloud of dust kicked up by Miles as he shot passed her, followed soon by the panting posse. Jori-Page skidded to a stop in front of her, a scowl of incomprehension inflaming her face. "How could you just stand there and do nothing?" Then she was off, her rebuke trailing into a Beatlemania scream as she rejoined the chase.

The stitch in Angie's side seemed to have moved to her throat. She swallowed hard and stooped to retie the wayward shoelace. She would get back in Jori-Page's good graces, she vowed to herself. There was still lunch recess. Yesterday after school, Jori-Page had reminded the posse that they were all to know the words to "Help!"

So, Angie had gone home and played "Help!" on the record player over and over, closing her eyes, moving her lips to the words, fixing them in her head. But then Eva walked in. She was in junior high and wore a bra and black flats with nylon stockings and a touch of lipstick, all of which made her seem an imposter.

As she sang along to "Help!" Angie watched Eva take off her shoes and stockings and lipstick, watched her unmask herself, hoping to see the old Eva appear, the one who once showed her how to shuffle a deck of cards, ride a bike with no hands, track the arc of a fly ball so it landed smack in her glove.

"What are you staring at?" Eva snapped.

Angie moved her gaze to the ceiling and kept singing.

Eva turned off the record player.

"When did you get so mean?" Angie asked, but she knew the answer, knew that it was the junior high costume, its poor fit, the feeling of being trapped in those stockings.

Eva plopped onto her bed and opened her geography book and began reciting the main exports of Tunisia.

Angie, deprived of the record player, talked the words to the song.

"Shut up, Angie."

But Angie didn't.

The words drove Eva from the room and Angie sat alone to learn them by heart. Angie was good at memorizing and now she was consoled by the prospect of redeeming herself with the posse at lunch recess. Having tied her shoe and pulled up her socks, she stood and looked around.

She was sweaty from having run and she could feel a layer of dirt skimming her neck and clotting her scalp. If she stood where she was, other people might be convinced that she was part of one of the games around her, an outfielder for kickball or part of the ragged dodge ball circle, so there she stood. But she didn't know what to do with her arms, whether she should let them hang at her side or bend them at the elbows in readiness for something. She settled on the ready position, but finding a spot to fix her gaze other than her scuffed-up shoes was a problem. Shouldn't the bell have rung by now?

She squinted upward as if the answer was there in the sky, cloudless and blue, the sun beaming genially as if all life were fun and games. Orange spots were beginning to zip across her glasses, so she turned her head to the ground, too swiftly, though, for now she could see nothing. Just when the ground began to appear again, she heard the frantic shouts of her name, the command issuing from Jori-Page and Judy Wiekamp and Silvia Rico and the others. "Grab him, Angie!"

She looked up and saw Miles running her way, his John Lennon hair flapping. A breeze filled his shirt so that its ballooning fabric offered a handhold, but when she reached for it, the airy shirt fluttered from her grasp.

She made one last, heroic lunge and was rewarded with a fistful of sleeve, which she clutched triumphantly. Miles, slight fourth-grader that he was, still outmuscled her, and as he tried to continue his momentum, he pulled Angie after him. She staggered, fought for balance, finally gained both feet again, when he suddenly twisted sideways, away from the unyielding grip she had on his sleeve and the rip that followed seemed to slice through all the noise of the playground, seemed to bring all the games to a halt.

She was sure that everyone witnessed Miles staring at her, at the gap in his shirt, at the shred of fabric in her hand. He gaped in horror as if she'd torn off his arm rather than his sleeve. She stared back, unable to speak, and then he ran off in tears to the teacher on playground duty.

It was then that she understood, that despite all shouts of "catch Miles," it was never the intention that anyone really catch him, much less touch him, much less tear the sleeve off his shirt. It was all about the chase. Only the chase. Jori-Page, glassy-eyed and open-mouthed, sleepwalked toward her. Angie held the sleeve helplessly in front of her and she could see in Jori-Page's crushed expression, now that the chase was over forever, how much she wanted to grab the sleeve in Angie's hand, but couldn't, because even screaming, swooning Jori-Page Schroeder knew better—knew the rules of the game.

In the principal's office, Angie sat on the other side of Mr. Campbell's enormous desk. He was leaning back in his big swivel chair, waiting for Angie to explain why she tore the sleeve off Miles's shirt.

"It was a mistake," Angie said, her voice wobbly as her knees.

Mr. Campbell tilted his bald head to one side, waiting for more, but Angie could form no other words with her tongue trapped inside cheeks clenched to hold back tears. Mr. Campbell's face reddened at her silence, and he put paper and pencil in front of her to write letters of apology to Miles and to the whole Jones family. "Of course, I'll have to bench you," he said, shaking his head at her shameful self.

At lunch recess, Angie sat on the wooden bench outside the principal's office, a public display of the doers of bad deeds who were expected to ponder their crimes. But all Angie could think of was how she was missing her chance to give Jori-Page and the others a perfect recitation of the words to "Help!"

After school, she had to return to the bench for ten minutes, and she knew her life was really ruined. She was supposed to walk home with the other girls. They were all going to talk about what they would wear to the sixth-grade dance. But they left without her.

When Angie got home, her mother was in the kitchen on the phone with Nelda, the receiver pressed between her ear and her shoulder while she cut up onions and wept. Angie considered taking over at the cutting board since she could use a good cry. But she sensed from the pitch of her mother's words, which seesawed between English and Spanish, and the vigor with which she worked the knife that she did not want to be relieved of the chopping. Angie veered to the other side of the room divider and threw herself down on the sofa. Anthony was on the floor, his face inches from the TV, watching Huckleberry Hound botch another career, this time as dogcatcher. Angie envied the six-year-old mind, which seemed not to question why a blue dog with a gentlemanly Southern accent would be working as a dogcatcher. Letty was hunched over the coffee table doing multiplication problems.

Angie sat up. "Need any help," she asked Letty, whispering so as not to incite a riot from Anthony, who did not tolerate well sounds that did not come from the TV while he was immersed in its glare.

Letty frowned but didn't look up. "Nope," she whispered back, filling in an answer with a flourish. "Don't need your help."

Help, Angie thought, flopping back on the sofa with a sigh loud enough to warrant shushing from Anthony. The words from the song looped uselessly in her head and danced with the image of her hand letting the shred of Miles's shirt fall to the playground dirt.

At dinner, Letty had no opportunity to tell on Angie, since their mother never did ask them how their day was. She was too busy relaying Nelda's news that she was taking classes to become a real estate agent.

"Nelda? Real estate?" their father said.

"Yes, why not?" their mother said.

"Selling houses is a big leap from selling Avon."

"Nelda's a natural. She's going to be a success."

In her defense of Nelda was also a tiny hiss of jealousy in the way she said "success." Angie knew she wasn't the only one who heard it. It wasn't the first time family dinner talk was stalled into fierce silence, interrupted only by fierce chewing. Nelda was going to be a success and their mother was going to be stuck just being their mother and part-time cafeteria worker at their school. It was only a few hours a week and there was no glamour in spooning steamed carrots into little side bowls. Plus, she had to wear a hairnet and an apron.

"Huckleberry Hound sold houses once," Anthony said.

"No, he didn't," Letty said.

"Your Aunt Nelda is not a cartoon." Their mother let her fork rattle onto her plate, and they all stared at it in silence.

"I was sent to the principal's office today," Angie said.

"Really, Angie, not now," her mother said as she picked up her fork and stabbed at a piece of pork chop.

* * *

On Saturday, Angie stood in front of the mirror and practiced smiling without snagging the inside of her lip on her braces. There was still a chance she would go to the sixth-grade dance. She had called Silvia's house. Busy, said her mother. She had tried Judy Wiekamp's house. Not home, said Mrs. Wiekamp. They would call her back later, she was told. So, Angie practiced her smile.

"What are you doing?"

Angie whirled around to find Eva, arms folded beneath her padded bra.

Even though it was Saturday and Eva was minus the flats and stockings and lipstick, there was still that padded bra that made her a stranger.

Angie pushed passed her sister with her best retort, "Wouldn't you like to know?"

Eva followed her, demanding that their mother take Angie to a child psychiatrist. She emphasized the word *child*, and this somehow pierced Angie to the core of her skinny, undeveloped body. She fell to pieces, smearing her glasses with her sobs, and snagging her lip on her braces.

Their mother shushed them and delivered a single blow that shattered them both. "When are you two going to grow up?"

Eva stomped to her room to play Neil Sedaka and Angie escaped to the back yard and sat in one of the swings that even Anthony now shunned. She scraped the dirt with her heels as she thought about her mother's question, which was the wrong question. Angie knew the *when* of growing up was now. The real question was *how*.

She ran her finger across her braces as she considered this. Soon she was aware of other music drowning out the faint croon of Eva's Neil Sedaka. She climbed to the top of the old swing set, though her father had warned her plenty of times that she was getting too big for the flimsy structure. She could see across the fence to the Ricos' backyard and there was Silvia with Judy Wiekamp and Jori-Page Schroeder and some other girls from the sixth grade. They were playing records and dancing. Some of them had rollers in their hair. None of them noticed her.

She lifted herself higher on the swing set and as she waited to be seen, she realized that there was no Beatle music playing and there was a definite absence of swooning. Angie felt as if someone had suddenly switched TV channels on her.

"Hi," she finally called. "What are you doing?" She had to say it again louder to be heard over Bobby Boris Pickett's "Monster Mash." This time everyone stopped and stared at her and she expected someone to ask what *she* was doing, perched on top of an old swing set, spying on them. But apparently no one cared.

"Dancing," Jori-Page answered her, resuming her mashed potato.

"We're practicing for the sixth-grade dance," Silvia explained.

"Are you going?" Judy asked.

"Maybe," Angie said. "I might be busy."

"It's tonight," Judy said.

"I know."

No one seemed to hear her. They had changed the record and were practicing slow dancing with invisible partners.

Angie slithered down the leg of the swing set. When she touched down, she squatted on her haunches, elbows on knees, chin in hands. She listened to the talk sifting through the slats of the fence that separated Silvia Rico's backyard from hers.

"I'll die if a boy doesn't ask me to dance," Jori-Page said.

The other girls gushed reassurances. Angie twisted her face in a mock gush. She wanted and didn't want to be in Silvia Rico's backyard. She wanted and didn't want to go to the dance.

"Monster Mash" was playing again. Angie imagined a boy asking her to dance. Still in her squat, she shuffled her feet and bopped her shoulders back and forth, matching her movements to those of her own faceless, nameless partner.

She waddled in her squat to the back door. Inside, she straightened up and plodded heavily across the carpet past her father who was watching a baseball game on TV, past her mother who was scanning the classifieds in the newspaper, and past Eva in the bedroom who was playing Scrabble by herself. It was Angie's favorite board game, but she didn't ask to play, would not subject herself to more rejection. She lay on her bed and closed her eyes, trying to picture the dress she would wear to the dance, knowing it didn't exist in her closet.

At dinner, Angie's mother announced her intent to look for a real job. No more cafeteria work. No more chintzy hours with chintzy pay.

Angie's father shook his head. "As if our lives aren't complicated enough."

"Who's going to make our dinner?" Letty asked.

"I'll make it," Anthony said.

Letty snorted.

"You're all going to help," their mother said, and the way she said it made them all study their vegetables as if trying to glean the secret to cooking them.

After dinner, Angie went to the garage to contemplate a household in which the mother was not there when you came home from school. Angie had long ago decided that when she grew up, she would have a job—an important one. She just never imagined her mother doing anything other than being at home when they needed her, even though when they needed her, she was sometimes not really there. Like now, when Angie really would like her mother to know that she had done something embarrassingly, painfully stupid and she needed help. And a dress for the dance. And the courage to go.

The dance was at the community center and the girls would have to walk past her house to get there. She crouched behind the family station wagon to wait and watch without being seen. Soon though her legs began to ache, and she slumped to the cement floor next to a box of discarded toys and games. *Help, I need somebody.*

She pulled out Eva's baseball mitt, threw it back and found her own, and scrabbled through the jumble of things until her fingers grasped a ball. She played catch with herself, delighting in the weight of the ball in the perfect fit of her glove. But the space in the garage was too confining, so she went outside to the empty lot next door. She threw the ball high into the air and opened her glove to capture its simplicity, its soundness. She did it over and over. She didn't miss. She threw it higher this time, following its path in the pink light of dusk, never meaning to take her eyes off of it, but something made her turn and she felt the ball drop at her feet. *Help, not just anybody.*

There they were. They wore lipstick and nylon stockings with black flats. Their hair was styled like Annette Funicello's.

They carried purses. They didn't look at her and after a moment she stooped down to retrieve the ball, stayed there until they passed.

"What are you doing?"

Angie turned around to find Eva with her arms behind her back. Before Angie could muster an answer, Eva showed her hand—it had her baseball mitt on it.

They played catch in the empty lot until it was too dark to see.

DISAPPEARING ACTS

They weren't supposed to have opened the garage door, much less leave it agape. Stay inside and keep the doors locked, their parents said each day before they left for work, Angie's father to his old job reading water meters and her mother to her new, full-time job as a salesclerk at J.C. Penney. To pay for extra expenses, she said, by which she meant Angie's braces, a part of her anatomy since fourth grade. But also, Angie thought her mother wanted to escape them and their boring old house, which was Angie's wish for herself.

Her parents were even more adamant that they barricade themselves indoors when the TV blared the news of looting and arson in Watts. "Can it happen here?" Letty asked.

"Of course, not. This is Kimball Park," their mother said, though she did look out the window toward the end of their block, where beyond the aptly named Division Street was a mostly black community. On summer weekends, black families came from the other side of Division to picnic at the park across the street. In the fall, black boys in football gear and black girls in cheerleader skirts streamed past the house for the Pop Warner games. It was predictable, this back-and-forth migration, part of the life of the neighborhood and yet as separate from their lives as the riots on TV.

"Nothing happens in Kimball Park," her mother told Letty. There was relief in her voice. There was also disappointment—that life happened elsewhere.

*   *   *

The house was stifling. By unspoken agreement, Angie and her siblings trooped through the kitchen door to the dimness of the garage, where Angie took it upon herself to flout the house rules and open the garage door. The sunlight streamed in, and the outside air, though heavy and warm, freshened them. Angie welcomed the view of the street, which, though empty, reminded her that an outside world existed. They set up the card table and did jigsaw puzzles. They played records and practiced the frug. Letty tried to twirl her baton and Anthony, though years too big for his tricycle, pedaled it in mad circles. When they were done, they put everything away, again as if by unspoken agreement. Angie closed the garage door and followed her siblings inside to watch TV, mostly game shows interrupted every so often by news bulletins about Watts.

One afternoon, Angie was particularly cranky not just from the heat, but from the constant news bulletins. She wanted the riots to stop, the anger to stop, the problem to stop. And dignity. She wanted that too. Both Martin Luther King, Jr. and President Johnson said dignity was what the Watts people wanted. Yes, Angie agreed. Yes, her siblings agreed. But they agreed on little else.

Eva and Angie were playing chess, with Eva as usual winning. She had been the one to teach Angie the game and was dribbling out the rules with each game they played.

"Remember, I told you that," Eva would say.

"You never said that," Angie would retort.

When it happened again that afternoon, Angie fumed so hard she could barely think. She had a great urge to knock the pieces from the board.

"Your move," Eva said.

"I'm thinking."

Angie did try to think about her next move, but the heat of the day was melting her brain and Eva's glower was making her muscles tighten. She could only discern that her options were limited and there was no way she could win this game. Then Letty dropped her baton which clanged off the front fender of Anthony's old tricycle. Anthony proceeded to run over the baton, which tipped the trike sideways. Unable to recover his balance, he fell onto the grimy garage floor. He erupted in feral cat screams, while Letty, whose only concern was extricating her baton from beneath the trike, was matching Anthony in decibels as she yelled at him to get up. Eva, annoyed that another victory at chess was being delayed, demanded of Angie, "Why didn't you move?" Angie, fed up with Eva's unfair tactics and her screaming, fighting siblings, gave in to the urge to sweep the chess board clean with a violent swipe of her arm.

Eva stood up so quickly she bumped the table, sending the board to the floor to follow the pieces. "Clean it up," she screamed. She went over and lifted a fuming and thrashing Anthony from the grease spot and wrestled him into the house. Letty marched in after them.

Angie surveyed the disaster—the scattered chess pieces, the overturned board, the tricycle on its side like a toppled animal. She could see the dusty heat of the garage, unmoving and indifferent. Beyond the oil-stained sheen of the driveway was the street, still empty except for the slow crawl of the mail truck in the lazy hush of the afternoon. Angie turned and went inside without closing the garage door, without recovering the strewn wreckage.

She watched TV, flopped on her bed and listened to her transistor radio, leafed through *Reader's Digest* for the jokes, watched some more TV, all the while vigorously ignoring the mess in the garage. She went to the kitchen to get a snack, but there was the door to the garage right next to the refrigerator. She knew she would have to pick up the mess before her parents got home from work, which made her mad since she was responsible for only part of it—one fourth of it, if fault were to be apportioned equally. Justice as always was in short supply.

She flung open the door, ready to right the disarray with a vengeance, but before her eyes could settle on the objects of her wrath, they met the startled eyes of a black teenager. His hands went behind his back and Angie didn't want to imagine what he might be hiding. His look of surprise gave way to one of defiance as if he dared her to question his presence in her family's garage. Angie opened her mouth to say something, but nothing came out except a small gargle. She slammed the door shut and locked it.

She kept her hold on the doorknob as her hands leaked sweat and the pulse in her thumb pounded its way up her arm. She wondered what the boy was stuffing in his pockets, packing under his shirt, or throwing over his shoulder. As she imagined the contents of her family's garage being scooped up and hauled away, she became indignant at the trespass, at the bold seizure of their possessions. She flung the door open again, an *aha* gesture that was pointless since the boy was gone.

She ran to the sidewalk and looked up and down the street. She saw no one, just Mrs. Melendez watering her crab grass. Angie, emboldened now that the intruder was gone, slapped her fist into her hand, hard so that it hurt. She went back into the garage and stowed the tricycle in its proper place, kicked Letty's baton to the side, scraped up the chess pieces, folded up the chess board and gave one last look around to see if anything was missing. Something was absent. She was sure of it. She pulled the garage door down and went inside the house, her skin prickly, her breath short. She slammed the kitchen door shut behind her.

A few days later, Angie was in front of the mirror looking for signs of junior high readiness while Eva lay on her bed humming "The Impossible Dream." Their mother was in the hallway wondering aloud where her new bra was. She opened the door to Eva and Angie's bedroom, as usual without knocking, and asked them if they by accident had her new bra in their dresser drawer. Eva righted herself at the intrusion. "We would know if we had your bra, Mom."

"We would definitely know," Angie said. Their mother's breasts were unapproachable in size as far as Angie was concerned. Neither she nor Eva showed the least sign of ever approximating them. Angie's voice held a twinge of resentment as if her mother were deliberately holding back on them. Her mother took her tone for sarcasm.

"Don't get smart with me," she said. Her gaze went ceiling-ward, her tone mystified as she left the room, "Where in the heck could that bra be?"

Eva looked at Angie. "How does a bra that size disappear?"

Angie guffawed, but suddenly inhaled with a painful snort, and she slapped her forehead at the image that sailed into her brain—a trespassing black teenager looting the Rubio laundry—before shrugging it off like a chill.

* * *

At the beginning of the summer, Angie had turned twelve—the nothing year before becoming a teenager. There hadn't been a party, unless you counted Nelda and Little

Eddie coming over for cake and ice cream. Angie had endured Nelda asking her if she had wished for boobs when she blew out her candles. She thought that Little Eddie, who had performed card tricks and made quarters disappear in front of her, had been on to something when he suggested she wish for a Houdini-like escape from Kimball Park.

The days were long and hot. Boring, yet filled with anticipation. Dread, really, of what lay at the end of the summer—junior high.

In the afternoons she lay on her bed, her window open to the still air, not the slightest ripple to the dusty curtains, the buzz of flies at the screens adding to the drone of the day. She placed her transistor radio on her pillow and fell to daydreaming about balancing on a surfboard as The Beach Boys harmonized about California girls. She tried to picture herself in a French bikini, though that took too great an effort, so she had to visualize the body of someone else—Ursula Andress, Raquel Welch, Annette Funicello. Her own body had shown only faint and unpromising signs of puberty. She checked the mirror periodically, felt the pertinent parts, and while change seemed imminent, it also seemed stalled, just like the slow summer around her.

September came and the news about Watts faded. It was time to begin junior high. Angie's body had changed very little, but her mother had bought her a bra. It had hardly any cup and it seemed ridiculous to wear such a thing. The alternative, an undershirt, was even more ridiculous. So, on the first day of school, she strapped on the cupless bra. The material, thickened with padding, caused slight mounds to rise from her chest. It was a start.

Angie remembered her mother's missing bra which had yet to turn up. She didn't want to think who might be responsible for its missingness. She had other things to think about—like missing breasts to put in her own mini-bra. And though she was not missing feet to slip into the slingbacks that were the current fashion, she could not bring herself to wear that other article of clothing that was part of the costume of junior high—nylon stockings. Angie didn't want to abandon the socks that covered her bony ankles. Since socks were not a complement to slingbacks, she had no choice but to stick with her sixth-grade Hush Puppies.

"You're kidding me," Eva said when she saw Angie lacing the old oxfords.

"Leave me alone."

"Don't worry, I will."

Two years earlier, Eva had confided to Angie in a grudging but earnest way about the horrors of the new world of junior high, where school had become a baffling battery of lessons entirely apart from the textbooks the teachers assigned them to read or the problems they solved on the blackboard. Since then, Eva had adapted. Or perhaps she had accustomed herself to the misery and was leaving Angie on her own to do the same. She left for the bus stop without her.

Angie hesitated on the sidewalk in front of Silvia's house. It was clear that she and Silvia Rico were no longer best friends and, in fact, hadn't been so in a long time. Still, since they lived next door to each other, they could at least walk to the bus stop together. She knocked on the door and Junior Rico appeared. Angie was mortified. She had thought that Junior would have already left to saunter down the middle of the street with his friends, moving for traffic only when a car blasted its horn, and even then, moving in sexy slow motion.

Junior's eyes went from Angie's anklet socks and Hush Puppies upward to the notebook she held at her chest. Angie stood perfectly still, wishing she could be mistaken for a statue. She glanced ever so briefly at Junior's beautiful face and then lowered her gaze to his Adam's apple so as not to see his perfect teeth in that smile that electrified. That laughed. At Angie, who forced herself to speak.

"Is Silvia here?"

"Nope."

"Oh." Angie turned to leave.

"She rode in with Judy Wiekamp. They think they're hot stuff now that they're in junior high."

"Oh," Angie said again. She was halfway to the sidewalk.

"You don't think you're hot stuff, do you Angie?"

Angie shook her head as she hurried away.

* * *

In homeroom Mrs. Horton sat them alphabetically. Silvia Rico, who had nodded at Angie as she straggled in with the other bus riders, was seated near the front. From her seat in the back, Angie scanned the classroom. Several elementary schools fed into the junior high, and Angie was alarmed by all the kids she didn't know. Mrs. Horton passed out their class schedules and while others were comparing notes on which classes they had together, Angie stared at her schedule and wondered if she would know anyone in any of her classes, anyone at all.

Through the chatter around her, a question floated to her ear. "Can I borrow a pen?" It hung there unanswered or maybe the reply had been swamped by the tide of talk that rolled over the classroom. She stared harder at her schedule, at the list of subjects—World Geography, Algebra, English, Spanish, Art, P.E.—at the room numbers and the start and end times, and soon everything smudged together beneath her hard, hard stare, so when the black fist knocked on her desktop, her face flew up and met its owner with a vicious heat in her eyes.

Immediately, all the hotness behind her glasses seeped to her neck and down to her sweaty palms. She stared at the boy seated next to her. Why hadn't she noticed him before? She recognized now the flaw in the strategy she'd been following— that if she noticed no one, then no one would notice her, how alone she was, how her single, solitary self was left out of the junior high world.

"Um, do you have an extra pen?" the boy asked.

His face was friendly, but his manner cautious. He was lanky, but he didn't slouch in his chair and sprawl his legs into the aisle like most of the boys. Neither did he sit with an aggressive lean like the others. His posture was exactly, intentionally neutral and Angie tried to adjust her own to match his.

She hated to part with her school supplies. She unzipped the plastic case in her three-ring binder and removed a pen from her set of five. She offered it without extending her arm all the way across the aisle, her grip firm to ensure the pen would not fall to the floor.

"Thanks," he said, as she released her pen to his hand.

She nodded, not trusting herself to speak. Her pulse jittered at her throat the way it always did when a boy spoke to her. She assured herself she was neither more nor less flustered by the fact that he was black.

She turned back to study her schedule. She watched out of the corner of her eye as the boy used her pen to doodle all over his. As the classroom buzz and banter among the other kids grew, Angie felt that she and the black boy next to her doodling with her pen were the only ones not yakking it up with someone else. Angie felt a frantic need to insert herself into a conversation.

"Excuse me," she said to the girl in front of her, but the girl didn't turn around.

Before Angie could decide whether to speak again or pretend she'd never said a thing, the boy next to her tapped the girl on the shoulder. The girl whirled around at being touched.

The boy held up his hands in apology and pointed at Angie. "She wants to talk to you," he told the girl, who arched her eyebrows at them both.

Angie, speechless, shot a look at the boy next to her who went back to his doodling. With beads of sweat threatening to trickle from the roots of her bangs, she faced the girl who waited, eyebrows still cocked. But with no words apparently forthcoming from Angie's mouth, the girl turned around and resumed her conversation with three other girls.

Angie looked back down at her desk where her class schedule lay, wondering how she would get through the day. She tried to think of something to say to the boy across the aisle. Perhaps she could ask for her pen back. Should she ask if he liked Bill Cosby in *I Spy* or Sidney Poitier in *To Sir, With Love*? Should she say something about Watts? About Martin Luther King?

She quietly cleared her throat in preparation, bringing her hand to her mouth, which caught his attention because now he was looking at her, waiting.

The question that came out of her mouth surprised her because it was only after she spoke it that she realized what had been on her mind: Who was this boy and where did he come from?

"What elementary school did you go to?" She was pleased with her conversational tone. She didn't always manage that.

The boy seemed to weigh the question. Or maybe he was weighing her. Finally, he said, "Not one around here. I'm new."

She was about to ask his name and offer hers, but Mrs. Horton shushed them all so she could read the morning bulletin. When she finished reading the welcome back announcement, the cafeteria special and the do's and don'ts of lunchtime behavior, the off-limit sections of the campus during passing periods, and dress code violations, the minute hand on the clock made an audible sweep followed by the bell and an exodus to the door. It was only when she was in the hallway, caught up in the swell of junior high student bodies that she realized the boy had not returned her pen. It bothered her—that empty slot in her plastic zippered pouch.

It wasn't until third-period English that Angie puffed a sigh of relief at the sight of a familiar face. There in the front row was Frances, taller and larger all around, but still unmistakably Frances. They hadn't seen each other since third grade, but after a few awkward moments, they manufactured as best they could, if not their friendship of four years ago, at least the memory of it. Angie ate lunch with Frances and her other friend, a red-haired, fully freckled girl named Phyllis. Like Frances, Phyllis was tall with breasts in full bloom and feet that pointed outward in ballet position, though surely not as a result of dance training. These physical similarities, plus their sound-alike names made for a harmony that was broken when Angie was thrown into the mix. Despite her negligible size, she felt conspicuous there at the lunch table with them.

As Phyllis and Frances talked about how many pages of their new notebooks they had filled so far that day, Angie looked around at the other groups that had formed through some law of attraction that excluded skinny brown girls in braces, glasses, and Hush Puppies. Silvia Rico and Judy Wiekamp sat optimistically at the threshold of the popular group, which took up several tables by the windows where the sun lit their heads.

In the opposite direction, Angie noticed Wanda Garcia (whom she hadn't hung out with since fourth grade) and her group of friends: Roxy Tamayo, Mona Castro, Becky Rincón. She hardly knew them, yet she felt she should. She wondered what they laughed about so loudly. They all talked at once at full volume, as if they each had something so important to say it had to be shouted. Angie liked how they would suddenly break out in song, doing *Shindig!* dance moves in their seats. They were singing "My Girl" and she heard Wanda croon at the top of her lungs, *I've got a sweeter song than the birds and the bees.* For a reckless moment, Angie considered walking over and helpfully explaining that the lyric was actually *the birds in the trees.*

Not far from Wanda's group, she saw the boy from her homeroom sitting with the few other black students in the school. Despite their small number, they stood out, yet they went unnoticed. The brown kids outnumbered the white kids, and though the white kids ruled, both groups were more or less at ease with one another, with their insults, the sideways looks, the occasional accidental nudge against the lockers—playful with a side of intimidation. No one knew exactly how to talk or shoot the breeze or dish with the black kids, so they smiled without making eye contact, talked in all-purpose, inclusive terms when in their vicinity, and openly grooved on Motown.

The boy from homeroom looked in Angie's direction and before she could pretend she was looking elsewhere, he nodded at her. She gave a half-nod, added a half-smile in case the bob of her head had not been evident, and then turned a confused look on Frances and Phyllis as they waited for an answer to a question she hadn't heard.

That first week of school seemed to solidify the social groups. Angie was part of a trio, which was three times better than being a solo act in junior high. Still, she wasn't entirely at ease. While she was grateful for the company of Frances and Phyllis, she found herself noticing too often and with much dislike their unflattering hairdos, their high-pitched voices, and their large feet.

It was a long week during which she learned much, such as which hallways to walk to avoid the knots of popular students that owned passage in both directions, such as which bathrooms had been claimed by the smokers, such as how quickly she had to rush from the bus to homeroom to secrete herself into her back row seat before the classroom started to fill. She also learned the name of the boy who sat beside her. Several times, when Mrs. Horton took roll and called the name Calvin Simon to no answer, she looked at the empty desk next to Angie. When Calvin entered sheepish and apologetic a few minutes later, he was handed a pink tardy slip. Angie lowered her eyes so as not to witness his discomposure.

* * *

When the weekend finally came, she comforted herself in her homework. On Saturday afternoon she sat at the kitchen table labeling the rivers, deserts, and mountains of Mesopotamia on a mimeographed map. She was meticulous with her lines, precise with her lettering, and authentic in her use of colors to indicate the various geographic features. Despite the traffic in the kitchen—her mother carrying laundry in and out the door to the washing machine in the garage, Anthony making himself a peanut butter sandwich, Letty punishing cupcake batter with mad strokes of a giant wooden spoon, Eva on the phone conspiring with one of her odd friends, and her father roaming the house in search of something—Angie kept her focus. But then her father disrupted their careful indifference to each other, halting them all with an irked waggle of his hand clamped around the old, rusty screwdriver, which despite its chipped handle and gunked-up blade never managed to be lost or mercifully thrown out.

"Anybody seen my new screwdrivers?"

Every so often a leaky faucet set her father off on a home improvement mission—tightening screws, replacing washers, cleaning out plumbing traps. He had decided that day to replace the light switch plates.

They all paused briefly to look at the grungy screwdriver.

"My new set. Have you seen it?" he asked again.

It was a set he'd bought himself the previous Father's Day when the tie, socks, and World's Best Dad mug from his children apparently failed to satisfy. It was an eleven-piece set inside a clear plastic case, each piece, ranging from tweezer-size to steak-knife size, with its own cozy little slot. He prized it, though he seldom used it.

"Not me," they each said, defensively, the way they always answered such questions, as if they were bound to be disbelieved, as if some evidence would be produced to prove them guilty. Then they went back to their business. Angie resumed her careful representation of the topography of the cradle of civilization.

"Did you check the garage?" Angie's mother asked.

Angie looked up quickly.

"Of course, I checked the garage. It's not there," her father said.

"Well, a bunch of screwdrivers don't just disappear."

Angie looked down at her map. The tip of her colored pencil had gouged a hole in her paper. She stared at the pinpoint gap in the Tigris-Euphrates, and wished upon it as if it were a star, hoping that her mother would not send them all on a search mission for the missing tools because Angie was sure they had been toted off for good, stuffed inside the T-shirt of a certain garage trespasser whom Angie couldn't name, but whose face was still vivid to her.

* * *

The next day in homeroom Angie tried to read ahead in her geography book, having spent the weekend reading ahead in all of her other subjects. But the chatter around her kept imposing itself on her ears. It taunted with its reports of parties and impromptu gatherings, hanging out at Taco Bell, and missing or making curfew, which didn't exist in her household since no one ever went out.

Angie leaned her head down closer to her book. She held her hands over her ears and spread her fingertips across the sides of her skull, but concentration eluded her. Her hair hung down and she watched it brush the pages like so many long-legged insects.

A pen slid into the open spine of her book. It was her pen, the one she'd loaned to Cal the week before. He hadn't been in class when the bell rang. Now his long arm was extended across the aisle to her. He held out a mini-sized candy bar to her. "Thanks for the loan," he said.

"You're welcome," she said. "Thanks," she added, setting the candy bar at the top of her desk. No boy had ever given her candy before.

"Who do you have for geography?" he asked, twirling the Bic Flair lodged in his hair above his ear. Angie thought of her zippered pouch—how uncool and elementary-schoolish it was.

"Mrs. Redmond. Second period."

"Me, too. Third period."

"She's kind of strict, isn't she?" Angie surprised herself at her sudden fluency.

"Yeah, I like that."

"Me, too," Angie said, hoping she hadn't gushed, blushing a little at this thing they had in common.

"Righteous," Cal said.

Righteous, Angie said in her head, loving the word, tucking it away in a corner of her brain.

*   *   *

Less and less, Angie listened to what Frances and Phyllis had to say at lunchtime. More and more, she strained to hear the conversation coming from Wanda's group. Every day, she looked forward to homeroom to exchange a few words with Cal before they each read ahead in their geography books.

At home, she asked Eva, "Who's your best friend?"

Eva snorted at herself in the mirror above their dresser as she squirted Clearasil on her pimples. "Best friend?" she said, as if it were something childish, something to be outgrown.

Angie, cross-legged on her bed, tugged at her hair, considered for a moment whether the subject was worth pursuing with her sister, then sighed at her own gluttony for punishment. "The one you're closest to. Your favorite one to be around."

"I don't have favorites," she said, a claim their mother made whenever she was accused of favoring Eva.

"Everyone has favorites," Angie said, irritated at herself now.

"Who's *your* best friend?" Eva asked.

It was mean of her to ask. Eva knew she didn't have a best friend, not since elementary school when she and Silvia Rico had ridden bikes together, made collages from *Tiger Beat* magazine for their bedroom walls, styled each other's hair, and spent the night at each other's houses. Now they barely spoke.

"I guess I don't have one either."

"Why do you hang around with Frances and that other girl? Do you know what you look like?" Eva asked, turning her ointment-spotted face on Angie.

Angie locked herself in the bathroom. While she ran a bath, she studied herself in the mirror. Looks aren't everything, she told her skinny reflection, which showed no signs of believing her. She raised her arm to compare its circumference with the bar of soap she held up with her opposite hand. The soap won.

At the start of the semester in P.E. every girl was weighed and measured. One teacher, Miss Forsythe, read the measurements aloud to the other teacher, Miss Van Dorn, who repeated the numbers as she wrote them down on a chart. For some reason, they found it necessary to shout. There were some numbers that everyone seemed to listen for—those for the popular girls, those for the fat girls, and those for Angie, which respectively elicited murmurs of admiration, muffled ridicule, and outright laughter.

"Aren't you embarrassed?" they asked her. "Only eighty-five pounds? My little brother weighs more than that."

"My cocker spaniel weighs more than that."

"My mother's toy poodle weighs more than that."

And so on down to someone's little brother's guinea pig.

How dare she weigh only eighty-five pounds when this was junior high. How dare she wear ankle socks and Hush Puppies. How dare she wear that pretend bra.

Undressing, showering, and being checked off by the gym monitor for proper lathering were the worst moments of the day. Even in the rush to finish dressing in time for the next class, there was still time to consider who might be noticing the lack of this, the excess of that. Because Angie noticed. Noticed Carly Patterson's oversized breasts, Melinda del Rio's faultless ones, Lizzie Healy's asymmetrical ones, her own stuck-in-starter-mode ones.

Angie turned off the bathroom light, stepped into the tub, and slid beneath the sheath of bubbles.

That night she curled her hair in plastic snap-on rollers and slept with them pressing into her skull. The next morning she snuck a pair of nylon stockings from Eva's drawer and slid her feet into the flat-heeled slingbacks she rescued, still stiff with newness, from beneath her bed.

* * *

Cal was late again. Angie worried about the consequences of his frequent tardiness. Sometimes he was able to slide into his seat while Mrs. Horton had her back turned to the class as she wrote the daily reminders on the board before taking roll. Today was one of those days and Angie was relieved that this morning she would not see Mrs. Horton scribble out a pink tardy slip and tuck it into the clip at the door for the office monitor to retrieve.

"Everything okay?" Angie whispered. She wanted to ask why he was always late but didn't want to be rude.

Cal just shrugged. He shoved his hands in his pockets and hunched his shoulders, sweeping Angie with a glance.

"New shoes," he noted.

Angie shifted her feet, moved them farther back beneath her desk. "Why are you always late?" she blurted.

"Hey, I'm not always late, okay?" He turned away from her and looked straight ahead. When Mrs. Horton looked down each line of desks to match faces with her alphabetized roster, Cal leaned into the aisle to make sure he was seen, then bent his head into his geography book.

Angie did the same, wishing he hadn't said anything about her shoes. She had been the object of much observation on the bus, in the hallway, and as she entered the classroom. She wished it was tomorrow when her shoes would be old news. She wished it was next week or next year.

When the bell rang, she kept her face in her book until everyone had left, even Cal. Especially Cal. She walked out in her slingbacks, moving her feet quickly as if to outrun her own shoes.

Cal didn't show up for homeroom the next day. At lunch Angie looked for him at his usual table, but he wasn't there either. She gnawed at her sandwich and turned her attention back to her friends. Frances wore the same hairdo she'd worn in third grade, except today it was adorned with two clip-on bows that pinned her hair behind her ears, which were rather small for a girl of her size.

"I like your bows," Phyllis told her. Phyllis adjusted the headband in her own hair that was frizzy and the color of gravy. Headbands were a habitual part of Phyllis's wardrobe, a color for each day of the week.

Angie hadn't meant to roll her eyes, but apparently she had as both Frances and Phyllis were staring at her, harsh hurt in their large faces. "Well," Angie began, aiming for delicacy, but in the end giving in to her own harsh hurt that lay fixed in her ribcage. "Don't you think it's a little out of place in junior high?"

They both looked at her as if she had breached a secret pact, which made her all the more insistent on pushing forward. "Look around. Is anyone else wearing little bows in their hair?"

But they didn't look around. They just finished their sandwiches in silence and then Phyllis said, "Want to go to the library?" to which Frances replied yes.

They stood up, but not before Frances raked the bows from her hair with her thick fingers. She did it as if it were accidental, even making an *oops* sound as the bows fell to her lap. She brushed them from her lap to the ground where they nestled at Angie's feet. "Look around, Angie," Frances said. "We're leaving."

Angie shrugged outwardly, shrank inwardly. As they walked away, she busied herself with packing up the rest of her lunch, trying not to remember how Frances had never laughed at Angie's perm back in the third grade, ignoring the relief she had felt those first weeks of school when Frances and Phyllis had saved her from eating alone. Why couldn't they dress better, wear groovy hairstyles, be cool? Angie looked under the table at the food-soiled linoleum and watched her slingbacks push the bows away from her.

The lunchroom was starting to clear out, but down at the other end of the table Wanda's group was still gathered, snorting through straws, hurling wadded balls of Saran wrap at each other, and talking over and under each other. Angie slid down the bench closer to them, close enough for a casual observer to assume an association between her and the group. She was fiddling with the remainders in her lunch sack, when Becky called out, "Hey, Angie, what are you doing there?"

Under pretense of answering the question better, Angie moved closer so that she was actually part of the group. "Um, just finishing my lunch," she said.

No one said anything.

"Anyone want some Oreos?" Angie held out a Baggie.

"Pass 'em around," Wanda said.

Angie also shared her Fritos and orange slices, and was reveling in the rewards of her generosity—a friendly nudge to the shoulder, a half-stick of gum, a Saran wrap ball batted her way which she caught easily to the cheers of her new lunch buddies—when amid the competing conversations, she heard Wanda say Cal's name.

"What?" Angie yelled down the table, unnecessarily, since everyone else soon picked up the subject of Cal. *He got busted. Got kicked out. He lied about his address. He used to walk all the way from the other side of Division Street to come to our school. They got some mean schools over there.*

Lunch was nearly over, and Wanda's gang was starting to disperse, leaving Angie with the empty bags and even the orange peels from the bounty she had so liberally tendered.

* * *

It was October, definitely fall. The changes were subtle, but there. The days shorter, the air nippy, the light muted. Only a month of school had passed. It seemed like seventh grade would go on forever. There were things Angie liked about being in Wanda's group—the riotous energy, the jokes. And there were things she missed about being with Frances and Phyllis—the way they got their homework done. What she could not get over was Cal's absence. Though she knew it wasn't his fault, that there was something inherently unfair about his being sent to a school that didn't have the books or teachers he called righteous, she felt his departure as abandonment.

One Saturday morning, Angie was hanging laundry on the clothesline on the side of the house that abutted the dirt lot leading to the ball field. Pop Warner games were scheduled throughout the day and a steady stream of players, fans, hangers-on, and idlers passed her house in both directions. She recognized Cal by his lanky frame and long stride, though there was no longer the constraint in his posture, the folding in of his limbs she had seen at school.

Angie hesitated only a moment before she left the towel she was hanging dangling by a single clothespin. With another clothespin still tucked in her fist, she threw open the side gate and ran to catch up with Cal who was with another boy. When she was just a few feet behind, she called his name, tentatively, like a question. There was no response, and she wondered if she had been mistaken, if this boy wasn't Cal after all. But then he spun around, the way someone might who suspected he was being followed.

They stared without speaking for a moment and Angie took a step back. "Hi," she said, not saying his name, as if it were still possible she had the wrong person.

"Hi," Cal said back. He relaxed a little and looked around. "You live around here?"

The other boy looked toward the ball field. "Hey, man, let's go."

Angie looked at the boy who was diligently not looking at her.

"That's Garrett," Cal said

Garrett turned toward her, his head tilted downward in the faintest of nods, and Angie produced a strangled noise in her upper throat, a sort of reverse gasp, made on the exhale rather than with an intake of air. A tiny cough followed because Garrett had decided to look her in the face. Angie swallowed and looked back, squarely just as she had the first time she saw him. But this time she was startled into neither immobility nor flight. It was curiosity that made her stare and an uncomfortable realization that she had never even looked at Cal this straight-on and openly. She knew they were wondering about each other, who they were and what they wanted in the world and how they could possibly get it.

Garrett gave another faint nod, then muttered to Cal, "Meet you in the bleachers."

Angie stared after him.

"Sorry, he's really okay. He's cool."

No, you're cool, Angie wanted to say.

"How's geography class?" he asked.

"It's okay," she said. "I mean, it's not fabulous or anything. It's average."

He poked at a hole in his sweater and she clipped the clothespin around her pinkie.

She wanted to say more, to tell him how she felt about what had happened at school, that none of it was righteous.

She might have except that he turned away, and she barely caught his "See you around," since it was whisked into the October breeze. She watched as he hurried to catch up with the boy she was sure was the thief of screwdrivers and perhaps even a certain large-cupped bra. She turned back toward her house, the clothespin still squeezing her pinkie. She left it there until she could no longer stand it.

Nelda and Little Eddie came over for dinner that night. Nelda brought flan for dessert and after they ate, Little Eddie set up a magic show in the living room, pre-empting *The Lawrence Welk* show on TV. He made a card vanish, pulled it from thin air, made it levitate. The Rubios clapped and Nelda beamed. "¡Qué maravilloso!" she said, throwing him kisses which he pretended to collect in his magician's hat.

"Can you make my screwdrivers reappear," her father joked.

As Angie watched Little Eddie perform an encore of the vanishing card trick, she considered her life in seventh grade thus far—how elusive things could be, how she couldn't seem to grasp anything. A small lump sat there in her throat. She blinked and waited for it to disappear.

SCHOOL SPIRIT

A ngie rooted for her team. Despite its indifference to her, she was loyal to her school. She cared about winning.

It was touch football on a dirt field. The Pep Club sold popcorn and candied apples coated with the brown dust that tornadoed in the wake of the players swarming the ball. Angie didn't fully understand the game, but she knew when to cheer without being prompted by the cheerleaders thrashing their pompoms, scissor-kicking the pleats out of their short, white skirts, or thrusting outward the mascot appliquéd on their blue pullovers as they spread their arms wide in a "V." Victory belonged to the squeaky-voiced cheerleaders.

Angie and her friends chanted over them.

Kimball's got the power,
Kimball's got the heat,
Kimball's got the spirit
to knock you off your feet!

They were raucous. Being let out of classes early had triggered some riot button in them and they screamed the last line, chortling with aggression. Wanda outdid them all. She not only delivered the words, she did the motions in her seat, snapping her arms up and sideways, leaning her torso forward and back, doing can-can kicks. Her movements were precise and sassy. She was loud and funny and more attention-grabbing than the cheerleaders themselves. Kids around her chanted, "Wanda, Wanda."

Though Angie was squeezed by elbows and moved not of her own accord, but by the rocking and swaying of the kids on either side of her, she felt buoyed at her association with Wanda and her gang. Only part of Angie was rooting for her school team. The other part was rooting for herself. Junior high was a contest. Go, fight, win. Or lose.

When Angie got home from school, a jumble of voices drew her to the living room where she discovered a few of them issuing from the newly delivered color TV. The other voices belonged to her family gathered around the massive console and its cardboard shell that lay ripped and discarded on the carpet. They were exclaiming at the colors, which were indeed brilliant, almost tacky in their immediacy. A commercial for dentures was on, one they'd seen many times in black and white.

"Look, you can see her gray hair," Anthony said.

Letty snorted. "You could see gray on the black and white TV."

"But it's real gray," Anthony insisted, and their father declared him to be right and very observant. Then a promo for the next episode of *As the World Turns* came on and their father rubbed his hands together with satisfaction.

"There," he said, his arm in a voilà gesture at the TV, as if he had conjured some prize for their mother, for all of them, in fact.

"Yeah, just in time for football season," retorted their mother, who had harbored a hankering for a new sofa/love seat combo.

Their father's chuckle sputtered behind his teeth and he wandered away to the kitchen. They heard the refrigerator door open and the clink of a bottle. Their mother settled back into the old sofa to watch the next commercial in living color.

At lunch the next day Angie mentioned it casually, that her father had just bought them a color TV. Whenever she wanted to be heard, she ended up blurting some enticement that would make her friends cease for a moment their loud and rapid chatter and say, "What's that, Angie?"

But Angie's voice was as scrawny as the neck from which it originated, so Angie stuffed her mouth with a large bite of sandwich to replace the words that apparently passed into thin air without meeting a single ear.

"Wait," Wanda said, holding up her hand to halt the babble at their table. "I think Angie said something." The girls went quiet and stared at Angie.

"Color TV," Angie said through her lunchmeat sandwich. "My family has a color TV."

"Cool," they all said.

"Hey," Wanda said. "Can I come over to watch?"

"Sure." Angie said it with a mouthful in the hope that the word would be vague and unintelligible.

"Maybe I can spend the night."

"Groovy," Angie said, blinking quickly as she swallowed a blob of sandwich.

After school, it was Angie's turn to reheat the casserole her mother had made earlier that day before heading to work. She made a salad and sprinkled it with chopped green onions the way her mother liked it. She cooked broccoli to the tenderness her father could not fault. She stirred up a pitcher of iced tea.

Eva came in from pretending to do her homework and surveyed the table. "What are you asking for?"

"What do you mean?" Angie said, laying the forks and knives in neat lines.

"Whatever it is, the answer is no," Eva said, imitating their mother.

Their father was in the living room watching the nightly news in color—war in color, hippies in color, apartheid in color. The volume was on high, so he hadn't heard Eva's impersonation.

Angie sliced a lemon for the iced tea.

"What? Did you flunk a test?"

"No. Did you?" Angie asked, knowing that such a thing was quite likely, despite Eva being smart. Eva who read big, fat books and stored arcane facts in her head that hardly ever found their way out. Eva whose sharp brain was out of place at Kimball Park High.

The nightly news finished just as their mother's car pulled into the garage. The sudden absence of TV noise was the signal for dinner. Letty, who had been spending unauthorized minutes on the extension in their parents' bedroom, skipped into the kitchen smug with gossip. Anthony emerged from his own room where he had been wrestling with the accordion he had recently convinced their parents to rent for him. He had developed a sudden obsession with Myron Floren and played "Lady of Spain" on his record player while he mimed the squeezing and button-pressing of his cumbersome instrument.

It was their mother's practice to come home for dinner and then return for the rest of her sales shift at J.C. Penney. She wanted a hot meal with her family, quality time with her kids. Plus, their father had made family mealtimes a condition of her taking a full-time job.

She sank into her place at the table with a groan and a sigh, surveying with a critical eye the neatly laid table, the bubbling casserole, the salad and broccoli, and lemon-garnished iced tea.

"Well, you wouldn't believe this customer today," she said. They all dug in to fortify themselves for what Eva referred to as their mother's "Penney ante rants" about the demands and silly questions from customers which she dealt with all day, standing on aching feet, bending and lifting to retrieve merchandise. She wasn't getting any younger, you know.

Had she asked them about their day, Angie would've gladly given her own rundown: Eva had scuttled her homework in favor of writing *Mad Magazine* articles on spec, all of which were accumulating in her underwear drawer, Letty was packing wands of mascara and tubes of eye shadow in her *Girl from U.N.C.L.E.* lunch box, and Anthony was spending hours in front of the mirror preparing for a musical career for which he had no perceptible talent. And Angie herself was still harboring hope of discovering some talent in herself that would lead to fame. Who was going to burst all these bubbles?

Angie watched her mother's plate, tracking the food as it disappeared into her mouth between Penney ante rants. Her mother was patting her mouth with her napkin and soon she would be fixing her lipstick, groaning as she rose from her seat to get back in the car and drive to J.C. Penney for more adrenaline-pumping aggravation, to which Angie was convinced her mother had formed an addiction, making her less tolerant of any aggravation in her own home. But Angie was desperate to ask her question.

"Mom, can Wanda Garcia spend the night on Saturday?"

Eva coughed into her napkin.

"Oh, Angie, I don't think so."

"But, why?"

"We just don't have the space."

"But I've spent the night at her house and it's smaller than ours."

Her mother sighed into her compact as she finished touching up her lips. "Dear?" she said, looking at Angie's father for help.

"Delia?" he said back. Neither of her parents liked having overnight guests. They didn't like being parents in front of other people's children.

Her mother's sigh sent a piece of lettuce wafting off her plate. Forced to utter the verdict, she uttered a grudging "Just this once," as she snatched the stray lettuce off the table and threw it back on her plate.

"Just this once," her father echoed past the cigarette in his mouth, which he was lighting up sooner than usual.

"Can I invite Jessica?" Letty asked.

This time her mother was firm. "No," she answered quickly, giving Angie a look of blame for having started things.

* * *

It turned out that Saturday was the Miss America Pageant, broadcast for the first time in living color. They had always watched it. It had the word *America* in it. It was practically patriotic. It was a ritual Angie had never really questioned, a show that up until then had been a family-only event. But now here was Wanda joining them in their living room.

After they watched *Get Smart*, Wanda said, "Let's change it to *Mission Impossible*." She even went so far as to reach for the knob.

"No!" Letty said. "Miss America is on."

"It's a family tradition," Anthony explained, whose attachment was less to the show than to custom.

"Let's take a vote," Wanda said, not ready to concede to two kids younger than her.

"Oh, now, a vote's not necessary, Wanda. We'll just leave the TV on that channel," Angie's mother said in the voice she used for her J.C. Penney customers.

"I'm down with that," Wanda said, though Angie knew she really wasn't.

They watched the parade of states, cheering for Miss California, always tall, always blond.

"Remember when you won the California History Bee in fourth grade?" Wanda said. Angie nodded, grateful for the acknowledgement, however irrelevant it was to the pageant on TV.

Wanda didn't know the Rubio family rule of TV watching. No talking except during commercials. During the parade of states, Wanda imitated the smiles of the contestants, tapping Angie on the shoulder to make her turn and look at her, making Angie miss the actual contestants.

During the swimsuit competition, Wanda snorted, "Who wears high heels with a bathing suit?"

During the talent portion, Wanda snickered at the opera singers, howled at the ventriloquists, and yawned at the concert pianists. When one contestant twirled a baton, Wanda put her hands on her hips and wondered, "Hey, why aren't there any cheerleaders?"

"Cheerleading is not a talent," Eva informed her coolly.

"Wanna bet?" Wanda said.

Wanda began demonstrating the *Go, fight, win* cheer from her seat on the couch.

She stuck both legs out to *Kimball's got the spirit to knock you off your feet*, colliding with the backs of Letty and Anthony who were seated on the floor in front of her.

Before her parents could eject them from the room, Angie nudged Wanda and mouthed, *You wanna play records?* Wanda jumped up from the couch. "Gimme some Motown," she loud-whispered back, which earned her a giant shush from the whole family.

They missed the part of the pageant when the finalists were asked a question about current events, the part that often made Angie cringe at the sweetly pronounced idiocies from the carefully lipsticked mouths. Angie had always felt a sadness at the spectacle and was relieved now to be with Wanda, listening to The Supremes and pretending to wear glittery gowns over grown-up curves as they did Motown moves. Wanda turned clownish as she sashayed around the room like a Miss America contestant, and Angie shouted her greatest dream was to be a homemaker and a part-time brain surgeon who fought world hunger in her spare time.

* * *

All through football and basketball season, Wanda did the cheers on the bench. In the hallways at school she would do them as she walked, a seldom opened textbook tucked under one arm, the other arm snapping up and down and out and in. She would end with a kick, truncated because of the crowded hall, but so well executed that you knew if she had the space, she would outkick any of the real cheerleaders who were starting to shoot narrow-eyed glances at her.

In history class one day, Louis Burdon tossed Angie a note. Angie was seldom the recipient of such things, little social artifacts that were symbols of inclusion marking you as someone who mattered. But a note from smart, sarcastic Louis Burdon with the tinge of facial hair and more than a hint of body odor who was above such junior high behaviors? Angie unfolded the note and was relieved to find that Louis was not the author. He'd only been a bored and indifferent piece of the pipeline.

The signature on the note activated the pores in Angie's palms. Angie had known Debi Dawson since grade school when she used to spell her name D-e-b-b-i-e. Now minus a *b* and the final *e*, she dotted the *i* in her name with a heart. The note was brief, urgent, and exclamatory.

> *Angie!*
> *We need to talk! Meet me after class by the trophy case!*
> *Debi!*

Angie was discombobulated by the note. Though they had been on speaking terms back in the smaller pond of elementary school, even then, Debi (Debbie) had been a big fish and Angie a sediment-dwelling mollusk. Debi's splash had only increased in the big pool of junior high.

Angie could hardly focus on the rest of Mrs. Shipley's lecture about the Spanish exploration of the New World and the French and British claims to it. When Mrs. Shipley called on her to answer a question her brain had failed to receive, Angie sat mute until Louis nudged his notebook toward her and pointed to the answer with the chewed eraser end of his pencil.

"Sir Walter Raleigh," Angie said. "The Roanoke Colony," she added, following Louis' gnawed eraser.

Mrs. Shipley looked down her glasses at Angie. "Yes, that's correct. Louis, please sit up in your chair."

When the bell rang, Angie knew she should acknowledge Louis for the help he had given her, but she felt embarrassed about the whole incident. Had she not been distracted, she would've fired off the answer on her own. She studied. She knew her stuff. She wasn't stupid.

Debi was checking her makeup in the glass of the trophy case. She swung her head and smacked her own face with her shiny blond curtain of hair as Angie stopped in front of her.

"Oh, there you are," Debi said. She shifted her position and Angie could see that they were standing near a picture of the current cheerleaders hoisting a banner they had won at the district cheer camp the previous summer. Each of them had a grip on the banner.

"You're friends with Wanda Garcia, right?"

Angie was sure that Debi knew this already, but she answered, "Right." She felt helpful corroborating this fact. She wanted to be helpful.

"Well, if you're a real friend, you should let her know that she should leave the cheerleading to the cheerleaders."

Angie was being served a threat. Yet this knowledge could not galvanize her meek and deferential self, and she offered her pandering best. "You cheerleaders have done such a good job raising Wanda's school spirit."

"If Wanda wants to be a cheerleader, she should just wait until spring for tryouts."

"Okay, I'll let her know, Deb." Angie wasn't sure why she shortened Debi's name. She kept envisioning that unpronounceable heart above the *i*.

"It's Deb–ee."

"Deb-ee," Angie repeated. *Dotted with a heart,* she added to herself.

That night Angie delayed thinking about what she was going to tell Wanda and watched the news instead. She watched the news more often now that they had a color TV. The color made the news seem more real, more here and now and, yet, because it was contained inside the Magnavox, it and all the people in it were far outside her existence in Kimball Park. Like Ronald Reagan who had hair whipped like chocolate frosting. Or Huey Newton whose black afro circled his brown-sugar face. Or Miss America, in regular clothes but still sashed and crowned on her way to see the troops in Vietnam, who bared her teeth, large and white like gleaming, unplayed piano keys.

At lunchtime, Angie wasn't sure what she was going to tell Wanda. Luckily, Wanda and Roxy were too busy dancing the cool jerk for Wanda to perform her cheers. Only in between cool-jerking and eating a hamburger from the cafeteria's fast-service window, did her bent arms rise smartly in a V or stretch outward in a T. Angie realized Wanda did these motions without thinking.

"Wanda," Angie ventured, "if you're going to try out for cheerleader in the spring, maybe you should save all those motions for when they really count."

They all turned to look at Angie, the newest addition to their group who had never before offered advice and whose opinion was seldom considered.

"Just trying to be helpful," Angie said as she crumbled one of the cafeteria's dust-textured cookies in her hand.

Becky broke the silence first with a big guffaw. "That's funny, Angie. In case you hadn't noticed, only white girls make cheerleader."

"Marci Silva's not white."

"She looks white," Roxy said.

"Acts white," Becky said.

"Therefore," Mona said, one hand on her hip, the other waving a lecturing finger.

"But doing cheers from the bench might be seen as subversive," Angie said.

"What? Sub-what?" demanded Mona who had cornered the use of "therefore" and was annoyed whenever Angie let loose her vocabulary, which had expanded with her regular viewing of the nightly news in living color.

"Wait a minute," Wanda cried. "I don't have to just be a bench cheerleader. Who says you have to be white to be a cheerleader?"

No one says it, Angie thought. It just is. Like Miss America.

Wanda stood up and swung her arms into a V. Then she lowered one arm to her hip and formed a fist with the other, while doing a lunge. "Brown power!"

They were all moved to cheer, "Wanda, Wanda."

But then Becky threw a stink bomb when she said, "What about your grades, Wanda?"

"Not to worry," Wanda declared. "I'm sitting on a C minus average."

To Angie's relief, Wanda agreed that she should curtail her spontaneous cheers in the hallways, bathroom, lunch court, and everyplace else she had elbow room. "I'm gonna ration them out," she said, kicking both legs behind her in a jump, her heels nearly kissing her rump.

* * *

When baseball and track season started and the cheerleaders were rendered useless, signs went up around the school that shouted in neon and glitter, *Do you have school spirit? Show us your stuff. Sign up for cheerleader tryouts.*

The announcement was in the daily bulletins and the school newspaper and was broadcast over the P.A. system. Cheerleaders were given special permission to make personal pitches during class time for "every eligible girl to come out and give it a *tryout!*"

In history class, after Mrs. Shipley assigned topics for their upcoming oral book reports, she allowed Debi the floor. Debi bounced on the balls of her feet to the front of the class where she stood in the cheerleader ready stance—feet together, knees slightly bent, hands clasped at her chest and elbows at right angles. She looked on the verge of breaking into a routine, or at least on the verge of pronouncing something earth-shattering and attention-deserving. Debi basked in the anticipation and though she delivered nothing more than what she and the other cheerleaders had been repeating like a broken record, her words hypnotized rather than grated with their echo-chamber persistence. Her words made you believe that anyone could try out, that anyone could win.

At lunch time, Wanda said, "Hey, why don't we all try out together?"

Roxy laughed, but then surprised everyone by saying okay. Then Mona and Becky said okay and they all looked at Angie. The cheerleaders' propaganda had not failed to affect Angie. She could almost believe that despite her skinniness, despite her brownness, despite her questionable coordination, there was a chance that she could make the squad if she just gave it a *tryout.* So, Angie shrugged assent, making sure to show her reluctance, making sure to make it clear that she was doing this out of friendship to them.

They all showed up for the first practice session after school in their white, one-piece gym uniform, an outmoded garment with elasticized waist and legs, cap sleeves, and a pocket sewn over the left breast. It leveled the playing field only as far as making all the cheerleader prospects look equally uncheerleader-like. They numbered over fifty, all of them sucked into the dream dangled before them by the cheerleaders' advertising campaign.

Angie and her friends clustered together—she didn't want to think of themselves as huddling, but that, in fact, seemed to be what they were doing. Other groups had formed, some confident, most not.

Of the six current cheerleaders, three of them were ninth-graders and would be moving on to the high school next year, presumably to take up the megaphone there. The three other cheerleaders were eighth-graders but were still required to compete for their spots. "It's a very democratic process," was the assurance that was included in the PA announcement, the posters, and the personal declarations from the cheerleaders when they had visited the classrooms. And yet everyone knew these girls had an edge, were in fact shoo-ins. So, in effect, over fifty girls were vying for three spots. The odds were dismal, Angie knew. And yet, here they all were.

Marci Silva, one of the soon-to-be-departing ninth-graders, gave them a pep talk and a lecture about the responsibilities of a cheerleader, about being a school representative, a role model, and a goodwill ambassador. Wanda hummed the Miss America song under her breath, and Angie snorted softly through clamped lips without fear of penalty. Marci was the kind of fair-skinned, straight-nosed Mexican that appeared as the love interest in telenovelas. She was immune to the mutterings of the masses.

Marci had everyone count off, so they ended up in five groups of ten. This effectively broke up the clusters and Angie found herself in a group of girls she barely ever spoke to, the reason being they barely ever spoke to her.

"So, you're trying out," Silvia Rico, her once best friend said.

"Wanda wants me to."

"I'm just trying out for fun," Silvia said.

"You'll probably make it," Angie said.

"You too."

At the same time Angie was silently calling Silvia a liar, she knew she was storing away hope that maybe she would make it. Maybe she had an undiscovered talent for chants and cheers and cartwheels.

Except for Marci, each of the current cheerleaders took charge of teaching the signature cheer to the wanna-bes. Debi Dawson was in charge of Angie's group.

"Form two lines," Debi commanded in a manner that made Angie realize the power of pom poms.

Angie fell into the back row as was her habit in anything involving rank and file. The problem was she couldn't see clearly when Debi demonstrated the cheer and had to rely on the girl in front of her when trying to copy the moves.

Marci roamed the groups, giving tips, sometimes demonstrating a move herself, and exhorting everyone to smile. "You have to be infectious!"

"And remember, you have to make it seem as if you're making eye contact with the whole world!" Much of what Marci said came with an exclamation point.

When Marci stopped to observe her group, Angie felt scrutinized and utterly brown, her flappy movements shying from Marci's stare. Marci moved through the ranks of Angie's group, singling out a girl here for a tight-lipped comment or there for a pursed smile. She glided past Angie without a word, though not before cupping her hands around her mouth megaphone-style and yelling in her cheerleader sing-song, "If you want to be here, then really be here. Punch it up! No ragdolls!"

To which, Debi added, "If you want to learn the cheer properly, watch me. Not the girl in front of you or next to you. Watch me!" And though she said it with a smile, her voice was tight with annoyance, presumably at having to teach the unteachable. So far, Angie was discovering no latent talent for splits, kicks, jumps, or even throwing her hands up in a V.

After the first practice, Angie and her friends waited in front of the school for Becky's older brother to pick them up. They sat on the curb, except for Wanda who was practicing the cheer in the street.

"Go, Wanda!" The four of them on the curb mimicked Wanda's movements, aware that theirs didn't come close to the easy precision of hers.

"I'm quitting this," Mona said.

"Me, too," Roxy said.

"Me, three," Becky said.

Wanda stood with her hands on her hips. "Well, someone has to try out with me."

They all looked at Angie, whose every instinct told her to quit, but whose deepest desires urged her to stay in the game.

"I'll do it," she said.

They all patted her on the back at this gesture of friendship and sacrifice.

Angie and Wanda practiced every day after school—twice a week under the tutelage of Marci and the other cheerleaders, and the rest of the time at Wanda's house. Angie didn't want it to be known at home that she was trying out for cheerleader. She practiced in the bedroom when Eva wasn't around. At night in bed, she tried to visualize the movements. Sometimes she did them under the sheets, once entangling her legs and falling out of bed.

"Nightmare," she said, when Eva switched on the lamp between their beds.

It was the jump Angie couldn't get right, could hardly believe it was humanly possible. How she was supposed to kick her legs apart while wind-milling her arms up so her hands could meet in a clap was beyond her. But Wanda did it beautifully with sharp jabs of her wiry arms and the spring of her muscular legs.

No matter how many times Wanda demonstrated, Angie could not break down the moves to make sense. "Just do it your own way. Maybe they'll give you points for originality," Wanda said.

No one at home questioned her frequent afternoons at Wanda's, except for a passing remark from Eva. "Are you teaching Wanda that the rain in Spain falls mainly on the plain, professor?"

"There is tutoring involved," Angie answered, willing to let Eva believe that she was helping Wanda with homework.

But Angie was letting her own schoolwork slide. Though she managed to finish it in time, it was slapdash and shallow, and she had ceased to read ahead the way she always had. Then there was the book for her oral report in history class. She had only fifty pages to go, but time was running out for John Paul Jones whose biography she had been assigned.

* * *

Tryout day and book report day, which were one and the same, were suddenly upon her. The night before, in acknowledgement that one last evening of effort would matter very little to her chances in either endeavor, she joined her family in front of the TV.

"Out of the cave, Batgirl?" Eva said.

"No homework, tonight?" her mother asked. She asked such questions distractedly, in the tone of mothers doing their duty, but she never waited for an answer, so Angie didn't offer one.

"Somos watching *Esa Chica!*" said Eva who liked to annoy their mother with incorrect and fractured Spanish.

As they watched Marlo Thomas bat her false eyelashes around New York City, Angie imagined she herself being singled out, a spotlight upon her as the camera picked her out of a crowd, someone shouting, *That girl!*

The next day in class, Angie was one of four students scheduled to give book reports. Mrs. Shipley asked for a volunteer to go first and Angie steadfastly stared at the partially read book on her desk. Each time a student finished, Mrs. Shipley asked for a new volunteer and each time Angie stared at her book as if by some miracle its contents would be transferred to her brain, which now brimmed with the conviction that humiliation was inevitable.

When all hope was lost that class would end and her report postponed for the following day, Angie picked up the book she had failed to read to completion and her written report that lacked a conclusion and rose slowly to her feet.

"Break a leg," Louis whispered, a fate she wished would befall her on her walk to the front of the room along with a miraculous recovery for the afternoon cheerleader tryouts.

Holding the book up, title and cover illustration facing out, in one hand, Angie read from the page she held in her other hand. It was a good report, full of well-crafted sentences whose sounds Angie hoped would distract Mrs. Shipley from the missing information, specifically, what exactly happened to John Paul Jones in the last fifty pages of the book. Though Angie was a good reader, her nervousness caused a quaver in her thin voice, so when she came to Jones's signature line, saying it with much emphasis, *I have not yet begun to fight!* it sounded too loud and emphatic as if something more should follow. But Angie was done and after a millisecond of silence and expectation from the class, she began to make her way back to her seat.

"Wait a minute, Angie," Mrs. Shipley said. "The class may have questions for you."

Angie took a few steps backward, avoiding the faces of her classmates and looking instead at the clock which Angie wished with all her might would burst, shattering the glass and triggering an alarm that would scatter Mrs. Shipley's history class far and wide.

Mrs. Shipley reminded the class that an oral book report was not officially done until two questions from the class were asked and answered.

Debi Dawson's hand shot up. "What was your favorite part of the book?"

"My favorite part was when John Paul Jones said, 'I have not yet begun to fight.'"

Louis Burdon raised his hand and for a moment as Angie braced herself for a long-winded, multisyllabic, compound clause question, she felt compassion for the Miss America contestants who nervously await the make-or-break interview question. Angie's fear was unfounded since Louis lobbed her, "What do you admire most about John Paul Jones?"

"What I admire most is that he was against the slave trade," Angie practically sang and once again made for her desk.

Again, Mrs. Shipley halted her. "Angie, we still have a few minutes. Please tell us where John Paul Jones died and where he was eventually laid to rest."

Angie lifted her eyes to the ceiling as if trying to recall those facts from the last pages of the book which she hadn't read. "Um, it's been a while since I read that part, so it's kind of hard to remember the exact details."

"Um, try," was Mrs. Shipley's grim encouragement.

Angie took a stab. "Well, it could've been that he died at sea."

Mrs. Shipley frowned. "Angie, did you actually read the entire book?"

Angie knew she couldn't wait for the bell to put an end to her misery. She couldn't delay the inevitable with more flimsy dodges. She couldn't dodge the question with sweet Miss America gibberish. She exhaled a meek and remorseful "No."

"Well," Mrs. Shipley said, "I have no choice but to give you an 'F'."

Angie showed up at the gym after school still feeling the "F" tattooed to her heart. *"F" as in fight,* she told herself. *Go, fight, win.*

It turned out the tryouts were closed—no one was allowed to observe, except of course the judges, consisting of the departing cheerleaders and Miss Van Dorn, the cheerleading coach. Becky, Roxy and Mona had come to cheer on Wanda and Angie (mostly Wanda, Angie knew), but were forced to retreat beyond the handball courts.

The candidates lined up in pairs outside the gym. Angie tried not to feel scrawny and insubstantial in her gym suit. As they waited their turn, Wanda chanted the cheer under her breath *(Kimball's got the power, Kimball's got the heat)*, closed her eyes and did abbreviated arm motions and truncated lunges and kicks. Angie also closed her eyes, but all she saw was herself falling out of bed, her legs tangled in the bed clothes.

When it was their turn, Wanda slapped her on the back. "Let's get it done."

The judges sat together in the first and second rows of the center bleachers. Wanda and Angie were directed to a spot a few feet in front of them. They positioned themselves with outward poise, which immediately collapsed with a pop quiz from Marci.

"Please tell us why you want to represent Kimball Junior High as a cheerleader."

It was a Miss America question. "World peace," Angie joked, which elicited not the slightest amusement.

Wanda took over. "I've got spirit! And I've got bounce! I've got excellent coordination!"

While Angie thought Wanda sounded like a TV commercial, there was no denying the truth of her statements. Wanda's response registered only a marginally more noticeable reaction from the judges.

"Whenever you're ready, ladies."

In her eagerness to perform, Wanda forgot to give the count for them to start in unison and Angie ended up several beats behind. She skipped a movement to try to catch up, but never managed to be in step with Wanda. She was a ragged echo to Wanda's shouts of "Go, fight, win," a clumsy facsimile of Wanda's crisp, rhythmic strokes. When Wanda finished her cheer with a perfectly executed jump, Angie dispensed with her own jump, merely ending with a hop so she could finish on nearly the same beat as Wanda did. And while Wanda did a series of spontaneous post-cheer jumps, Angie waved imaginary pom poms and shouted, "Go, team," though she really meant *Go, Wanda,* because Wanda had blown it out of the water. Wanda had kicked it! And Angie, who had been a floppy, flappy mess felt as if she'd *been* kicked.

They ran out of the gym, breathless—Wanda from the excitement of her outta sight performance and Angie from the exertion of trying to escape her humiliation. They ran past the line of girls still waiting their turn to strut their stuff, but Angie knew that no one could come close to Wanda. They found Becky and Roxy and Mona leaning against the fence, sharing a bag of Cheetos.

"Wanda was fab," Angie shouted, her voice high and wobbly, her latent cheering talent still absent.

"I really was," Wanda agreed. "I felt it. It was like I wasn't even trying."

"It just came out so naturally," Angie said, seething with a muddle of feelings.

Becky tossed the bag of Cheetos in the air. Orange dust flew into their faces and hair. Becky, Roxy and Mona did ragged cheerleader jumps around Wanda who reprised her flawless routine, while Angie leaned against the fence and let herself sag into the mesh, which gave very little under her flimsy weight.

Later, Angie declined a ride home and watched her friends troop off together to wait for Becky's brother to pick them up. During the two-mile walk home, Angie tried not to think of anything. She focused instead on her feet moving steadily over cracked sidewalks and up and down littered curbs. Gradually, she took in her surroundings, the overturned carts in the grocery store parking lot, the pigeons roosting on the benches outside the taquería, the yards with plastic flamingoes.

As she passed a house whose front yard had been cemented over and ringed with miniature palm trees in giant pots, a familiar voice called to her. Amid the fronds, she located Louis Burdon slouched in a patio chair, his feet resting on the matching patio table in front of him. A fat paperback was propped open on his knees.

"This your house?" Angie asked. It was a stupid question, but Angie felt completely stupid from the day's events.

To her relief, Louis only nodded and the sarcasm that followed was directed not at her but at his surroundings. "I do sometimes feel as if a waiter will appear at any moment with a frothy drink." He gestured around him and then at the one table, one chair. "It's like some tacky outdoor café that knows its limitations."

Angie emitted a feeble laugh.

"I've never seen you come this way," Louis said.

"I usually take the bus."

Louis was the last person who needed to know why she was walking home late after school. The last person who needed to know she had made a fool of herself trying to be something she was not nor could ever be.

"What are you reading?" she asked, because her feet seemed rooted there in front of Louis's imitation outdoor café, making escape difficult.

Louis held up the book. The author was Ken Kesey. Angie had never heard of him. After her day of humiliation, she felt even worse. There was so much she didn't know.

"Oh," she said. "Is it good?"

He nodded. "You can borrow it when I'm done." He added, "Way more captivating than John Paul Jones."

Angie winced. "I have only just begun to die of embarrassment," she confessed, and because her feet seemed to have unstuck themselves from the sidewalk, she began to walk away.

"Bye," Louis called out and she turned to wave at him, slouched in his patio furniture. *Like some tacky outdoor café that knows its limitations.* The words dragged at her heels.

When she had crossed the park with its graffiti-covered tennis courts and saw at the end of the block her house where inside, the color TV was emitting its pigmented electronic signals, she felt how much the world was moving ahead, and wondered how much it would take for her to catch up to it.

That night after she watched the news with her father and listened to her mother's Penney ante rants at dinner, she went to her room and finished the book on John Paul Jones. He did not die at sea, but in his bed in Paris. His alcohol-preserved body was eventually exhumed, transported across the Atlantic, and buried on his home soil. The end. Angie closed the book.

* * *

"Second alternate?" Wanda said. "I'm second alternate?" She pronounced each word as if not knowing which to emphasize, which was the most unbelievable.

They had gathered after school at the fence again, not exactly stunned, not exactly devastated. Earlier, they had craned their necks to see past the others bunched around the list posted on the gym door. As other girls had turned away in tears of either joy or disappointment, Angie, Wanda, Becky, Mona and Roxy were left to stare at the list of the winners and two alternates. Wanda was the only brown girl on the list, and she was last.

Wanda slumped to a squat and leaned against the fence. They all slumped beside her. Together, their weight scooped a wide bowl in the mesh.

Wanda buried her face in her hands.

"You were gypped, girl," Becky said.

"You're the best in the whole school," Roxy added.

"In America," Mona finished up.

Wanda's shoulders heaved.

It was Angie's turn to say something. She cleared her throat and raised her fist at half-mast. "Brown power," she ventured.

There was silence all around as Becky, Roxy and Mona stared first at Angie and then at Wanda who was slowly lifting her head. Wanda grinned through her tears. "I'm down with that." She raised her fist too. The others did the same.

And Angie, finally finding, if not her cheerleader moves, at least her cheerleader voice, shouted, "We have only just begun to go, fight, win."

CLASS PLAY

In Home Ec class, after Angie overcame the initial fear she'd always had of machines, her penchant for order and symmetry resulted in beautifully straight seams, well-fitted sleeve caps, and covered buttons without puckers. Plump and pretty Mrs. Orville beamed at Angie. "Such quick and nimble hands," Mrs. O exclaimed. Later in gym class, when Angie let the volleyball sail past her rather than smash her fingers trying to play it, she would hear those words repeated by mocking teammates.

In English class, her penchant for order and symmetry resulted in sentences that were grammatical, properly punctuated, and pleasingly worded. Mrs. Kinney took much note of this and gushed over Angie's "bent" for the written word. In the halls at school, classmates would tip their torsos sideways when they saw her.

It was this bent for words in combination with her quick and nimble hands that led to Angie's central, if off-stage, roles in the class play. For her semester sewing project, Angie produced a lined wool skirt with hidden zipper, deftly attached hook-and-eye, precisely placed welts, and nearly invisible hand-stitched hem. The fabric was blue with muted gold specks and to match it, Angie made a vest of soft, gold sateen. Mrs. O was over the moon with delight and when it was the Home Ec Department's turn to create a display that represented its best work, she made Angie's ensemble the centerpiece along with two minor-league works—an apron and a caftan—by other students.

The display did not escape Mrs. K's eyes, which fluttered with excitement as she addressed her ninth-grade Advanced English students.

"People," she said, clapping her hands. On her lip was a bit of saltine cracker. She kept a box in her desk drawer because a continuous ration was necessary to keep her low blood-sugar in check and prevent her from falling faint across her desk or slumping in her chair. Or, as once happened, practically in the lap of big, blond Graham Lunde whom she had castigated for having written and read aloud to the class his personal essay assignment which climaxed with his death by crazed squirrels. It had produced yips of laughter from the girls and howls from the boys. Even Angie had giggled until a stone-faced Mrs. K focused a laser-searing stare on them all and elicited silence with a hatchet gesture of her hand to inform the entire class and Graham, in particular, that death was not a laughing matter. Later, when she landed unconscious and sprawled across Graham, the students realized that indeed death was not funny, though Angie thought it could be incredibly embarrassing what with Mrs. K's arms flung above her head to reveal perspiration spots, her blouse askew to expose a bra strap, and her big toe jutting like a fat worm through a hole in her stocking in the foot that had escaped from her shoe. The hair on her unshaved legs lay smashed beneath her nylons like tiny, trapped spiders.

"People," Mrs. K said again. "For our spring unit we will not only read, but we will perform for the other ninth-grade English classes *Romeo and Juliet*. And we will not only perform, but we will perform in costume. And the costumes will be created by Angie."

Someone made kissy sounds and Mrs. K's face went blotchy with outrage. It wasn't so much the innuendo about Angie's favored status that appalled Mrs. K. It was the fact of the kissing sound, that someone, a boy of course, had puckered his lips in her class. It was clear that Mrs. K hated anything that remotely hinted of sex or sexuality and that she expected the fourteen-year-olds in her class to behave as adults and not as the hormone-charged animals they were. So, she addressed them as "people" as a reminder, a reprimand, a plea.

Mrs. O and Mrs. K had confabulated, Mrs. K said, and had agreed that Angie could, along with other able students in the sewing class, use class time to produce the costumes for the play. The word "confabulate" was immediately seized upon by the students, who uttered it with sexy growls on the many occasions Mrs. O and Mrs. K were seen confabulating—walking the halls together or standing in the doorway of each other's classroom, with the tall Mrs. K bending her oily head to better catch the soft-spoken syllables from Mrs. O's kewpie-doll mouth. The picture they made was one of lovers, or so the hormone-charged adolescent animals whispered. And there was the rumor that Mrs. K was not really married, because what man would be married to a woman who didn't shave her legs, shunned high heels, and wore a faint mustache above the saltine crumbs on her lips. Such was the total grossness the students witnessed at close range every day with a kind of glee. Now Angie had become part of that spectacle.

But at least now there would be the distraction of a play about star-crossed lovers. Tryouts were democratic with classmates voting for the person who, in Mrs. K's words, "most sincerely captured the essence of the character." Angie wished she could try out for the role of Juliet. She knew she could emote, could deeply and sincerely capture the essence of

Juliet, her innocence and honesty and sorrow, though she had only proven it at home locked in the bathroom with the water running. But being brown, skinny, and bespectacled, she didn't resemble a Juliet in any way on any planet. Anyway, her role was already assigned. Roles, that is. She was the head costumer. She was the script editor. And Mrs. K had, without holding tryouts for it, bestowed the title of narrator on her. She would be in front of an audience, but without a costume and not really part of the story. More like a talking human prop.

Judy Wiekamp, Silvia Rico, and Melinda Peters all raised their hands when Mrs. K asked who was interested in trying out for Juliet. They each took turns reading from the scene in the orchard with the famous "Wherefore art thou" line and the "Tis but thy name" sonnet. Angie said the words in her head, because she knew them well, knew their cadence and inflection, felt their echo between her temples.

Judy's voice carried. It was a shout, a look-at-me insistence. Judy was confident in her high-cheek-boned, straight-nosed, middle-of-the road looks. Judy had presence. And this is what Mrs. K reminded the class of when they were ready to vote, so they would not make the mistake of voting for Silvia who, when asked to project her sweet-spoken syllables, emitted high shrieks unbecoming to a tragic heroine, or for fair-haired Melinda whose wooden, one-note delivery sent heads nodding into chests.

Out of an old loyalty, Angie considered voting for Silvia, but in the interest of art, raised her hand instead for Judy. Silvia received an embarrassingly few votes and the rest were evenly split between Judy and Melinda.

Mrs. K was grim that the class had not fully heeded her instructions in the first place. "Well, I'm afraid I must break the tie. Judy, congratulations, you are our Juliet."

After the female roles were assigned, with Silvia getting the part of Nurse, and Melinda that of Lady Capulet, anticipation swirled over who would be Romeo and kiss Judy Wiekamp. When Mrs. K asked for volunteers, no one budged.

"There are at least ten male roles in this play, which means there are plenty of parts to go around. Do you want to have a choice, or should I make the choice for you?"

To Angie's surprise, Louis Burdon raised his hand. At first, the classroom filled with snickers. However, the idea of sloppy-shirted, big-brained, fuzzy-faced Louis kissing Judy appeared too intriguing, and some of the students began to clap as if it was a done deal.

Mrs. K held up her hand to shush them. "Anyone else?" she asked, looking directly at Graham who with his Norwegian looks would pair nicely with Judy, the Veronese origins of Romeo and Juliet notwithstanding. Judy turned to smile at Graham in encouragement.

Just when it seemed that Graham was going to concede to this recruitment, another voice, one seldom heard in class, intervened. "I'll try out."

They all turned to look at Frankie Flor, a quiet Filipino who had joined the class after the winter break, bringing to three the number of brown students in Mrs. K's Advanced English class, an addition that did not go unnoticed, especially by Angie who found Frankie nice-looking and his quietness appealing.

Mrs. K was so taken aback at Frankie's announcement that she forgot about trying to wheedle Graham. "Well, why don't we have both of you read a few lines? Louis, you first."

Louis read the lines that Romeo delivers beneath Juliet's balcony. His voice was thin and nasal, yet surprisingly natural in rhythm, but Mrs. K did not remark on his audition.

She looked at Frankie, as the rest of them already had been doing even while Louis read. "Now you," she said, nodding, curious.

Frankie cleared his throat, pausing long enough to make them wonder if any words would in fact issue from him. When suddenly they did, the room went quiet and Angie's heart thumped in her ears, a backbeat to the melody of Frankie's voice. When he came to "It is my lady, O, it is my love!" there was a single sigh exhaled by all the girls in the room, and Mrs. K forgot about democracy and voting, and proclaimed, "Well, it looks like we have our Romeo."

Once the spell was broken and Frankie was again the silent, mostly unobserved, newish student, it seemed to strike everyone at once that this Filipino boy was going to kiss a semi-popular white girl in front of all the ninth-grade English classes. It's just like *Love is a Many Splendored Thing,* gushed some of the girls. Yep, agreed Angie silently, remembering how the soap opera had dared to feature an interracial couple only to be rescripted by network censors.

When it came time to block the scenes, everyone waited for the kiss. Frankie and Judy stood at the front of the class, scripts in hand, delivering their lines, Frankie in his dulcet tones.

My lips, two blushing pilgrims, ready stand
To smooth that rough touch with a tender kiss.

No one snickered when Romeo referred to his lips as blushing pilgrims, so ready were they to see those pilgrims press themselves against Judy's mouth.

Judy stumbled through her lines, her matter-of-fact enunciations breaking the spell that Frankie had cast. She held the sibilance in the last word so long it was a hiss. Angie wanted to cover her ears.

For saints have hands that pilgrims' hands do touch,
And palm to palm is holy palmers' kiss.

The students at their desks were following along in their books, fingers tracing the lines, quietly tapping the page to hurry the actors along to the action.

O, then, dear saint, let lips do what hands do.

Angie was aware that now all eyes were up front, but she stared fixedly at the stage direction in the script: *Kisses her.*

A loud clap burst her concentration and the giddy zeal of the class. Mrs. K clapped her hands again, then waved them about as if erasing something in the air and said in her theater voice, "Kiss over," thus sparing the actors and depriving the onlookers with this expediency.

Mrs. K did this with each rehearsal. It became a joke in the hallways among the couples making out against the corner lockers.

The kiss became the subject of conversation at lunchtime. The consensus of Angie's group, vocalized loudly by Wanda, was that interracial unions were a sign of social progress and that everyone should just be cool with it. She held up peace fingers with one hand and a radical fist with the other.

Others around their group glared, declaring that the issue wasn't race.

"Notice," Wanda said, instructively, "only the white people say it's not about race."

Wanda waved the rolled-up editorial page of the school newspaper and held her nose with the other. "It's a matter of maturity," she nasalized, quoting the opinion columnist, Betsy Morgan. "Are fourteen-year-olds mature enough to handle an on-stage kiss?" Betsy was the social page editor who usually wrote the spotlight column which trafficked in clichés. *At 5'2 and eyes of blue, red-haired Susie Martin is the All-American girl-next-door.*

"It's a question of art," Angie maintained. "It's the actor's job to convey in as believable manner as possible the feelings and actions of the characters. Verisimilitude."

"Easy for you to say," Judy retorted. "You're not the one on stage."

Angie pointed out with deference that even if she wasn't exactly on stage, she was still part of the play. She had a stake in it.

There was whispering among Judy and her friends and Judy's eyes widened. "Oh, I get it. You wish you were in my place, so Frankie could kiss you!"

Angie snorted feebly while acknowledging in the confounding convolutions of her heart that that was exactly what she wanted.

"Trust me, Judy, I do not want to be you." The words escaped her mouth before Angie could think.

Judy opened and snapped shut her mouth several times, little squeaks of fury springing from between her quivering lips. Finally, she inhaled deeply and then delivered her breathless, stagey response. "And why would anyone want to be you?"

Angie camouflaged her recoil with a shrug. *Fair enough,* she thought. *Just wait until I'm famous.*

For now, she was reconciled to being strangely both anonymous and infamous, aware that she numbered among the common herd, aware also that she was visible enough to be mocked. She wasn't always sure why she was being mocked.

Sometimes she would try to extract information from Letty at home. "So, what's new," she'd say breezily as if they were the best of friends. But Letty would have none of it. No small talk. No sisterly confidences. Just the straight dope.

"The rumor is that Mrs. K is a lesbian and she's in love with you."

"Ha, wrong!" Angie said, disdainfully, happy to correct her sister who traveled in social spheres far from Angie's. "The rumor is that Mrs. O and Mrs. K are lovers."

"No," Letty said, one-upping Angie's disdain. "That was last week's rumor. You, as usual, are behind the times."

"Rumors, rumors, rumors," Angie shouted. "Who cares about rumors?"

*   *   *

Angie stayed after school one afternoon to put the finishing touches on Romeo's tunic. Fingering the fabric that would touch Frankie made her wrists wobbly. She stood back to admire her work. Mrs. O had left the room to cart some supplies to storage. Angie looked around to make sure there was no one hiding under tables or behind dress forms. She lifted the tunic and held it against her puny chest and folded the arms around her bony shoulders. She closed her eyes. Footsteps in the hall made her drop the tunic, which slid like a fainting damsel to the floor.

"Is that my costume?"

Angie turned quickly, lost her balance, and when she stepped to regain her footing, she found her shoe squarely on the back of the tunic. She lifted her foot to see her sole fuzzily imprinted on the purple sateen.

"Ouch," Frankie said.

"Sorry," Angie said, slapping at the dirt. "See, good as new."

"Should I try it on?"

Angie handed him the tunic. "You can just slip it on over your shirt."

"That's what I was planning to do."

"Oh."

Beneath the tunic, his shirt bulged in the armpits. He should've taken off his shirt for the best fit.

"Perfect," he announced anyway.

"Perfect," Angie echoed.

Mrs. O came in then. "So, this is Romeo."

"That's me," Frankie said, and he launched into his lines.

> *My name, dear saint, is hateful to myself,*
> *Because it is an enemy to thee;*
> *Had I it written, I would tear the word.*

Angie couldn't help herself. The words burbled up like some esophageal response.

> *My ears have not yet drunk a hundred words*
> *Of that tongue's utterance, yet I know the sound:*
> *Art thou not Romeo and a Montague?*

She startled both Frankie and Mrs. O with her emotive muscle.

"My goodness, Angie. That is amazing. Who would've guessed?"

"Yes, who?" Frankie agreed.

Angie smiled at the floor, pleased at what she'd done and vastly irritated that anyone would be so flabbergasted at her display of such a skill.

Her irritation diminished when Frankie suggested they walk together on the way home, and it dissipated completely when they began reciting scenes together, gesturing to traffic as they stood on a corner waiting for the light to change or at a squirrel in the branch of a tree that was the height of a balcony. Their concentration was interrupted when someone from a passing car yelled, "Hey, Romeo. That's no Juliet." They walked in silence for a block.

"Too bad Judy doesn't recite as well as you do," Frankie said.

"Have you heard that rumor that Judy is a lesbian?" Angie said, the words gathering of their own accord from some tiny, dark space in her brain.

Frankie stared at her with more astonishment than he had shown when she had first recited Juliet's lines. "No," he said. "That's not what I hear."

"Oh, well, I don't believe any rumors anyway," Angie said, her forehead burning beneath her bangs.

"Well, here's where I leave you," Frankie said.

"But—why?" Angie's heart hammered with remorse.

Frankie stared at her again. "I live down this street."

"Oh."

He turned away, and Angie trudged the last half-mile home, reciting lines on her own to no one.

* * *

Angie wasn't making all the costumes. Judy's was being "conceived and created" (Judy's words) by her mother. Judy brought it in one day. It was on a hanger and protected from the elements by a see-through garment bag. Mrs. K hung it from the upper ledge of the chalkboard after Judy made a thorough sweep of the eraser over nonexistent chalk dust.

Rather than just show the costume, Judy asked for permission to wear it while they rehearsed their lines in class.

"Well, it's not a dress rehearsal," Mrs. K said.

"I just feel more in character in my costume," Judy said.

"Well, then, please change quickly."

"I'll need help with the lacings," Judy said.

Mrs. K slipped a saltine in her mouth and clutched her side. "Angie, please go with Judy."

"That's okay, Silvia can do it."

"Angie is in charge of costumes. She'll do it."

Angie followed Judy reluctantly out of the classroom, down the hall, and into the girls' room.

Judy hooked the hanger on a stall door and without modesty slipped out of her fitted dress with scooped neck and raglan sleeves. Her bra gleamed new and white, the elastic of her pink panties skirted her outie belly button.

Judy handed Angie her clothes and Angie without thinking took them. She watched as Judy wriggled into the gown, expertly zipped herself up in back, and gently tugged the bodice lacings into place—all without Angie's assistance. Angie twitched with annoyance at being Judy's audience, her maid-in-waiting. The feel of Judy's clothes draped over her arms made her twitchy.

Judy smoothed her dress, which Angie had to admit was an excellent piece of sewing.

"Let me be frank, Angie," Judy said.

"Huh?" Angie didn't want Judy to be frank. Angie didn't want her to kiss Frankie. She wanted nothing of Judy's frankness.

"Look, I just need to get this off my chest," Judy said.

Angie's eyes inadvertently went to Judy's laced up bodice. She quickly dropped her eyes downward to find herself staring at Judy's clothes in her hands.

"Here's the thing," Judy said. "Have you ever heard of a Filipino Romeo?"

Angie twisted the sleeve of Judy's dress in her grip. "Here's the thing, Judy," Angie said, "It's a play. It's acting. If you're good at it, you become the character."

"It's Shakespeare," Judy said, distracted enough by the point she was trying to make that she failed to notice Angie mangling her school clothes. "It's Shakespeare," Judy said again. "Not *Hair.*"

Judy had bragged earlier that her parents had seen *Hair* on Broadway on their recent trip to New York. Judy's description of the profanity, nudity, and racially integrated cast made it sound as if she herself had witnessed such revolutionary, hippy raunchiness, and that, in fact, she was part of the vanguard of the Age of Aquarius. She had invited some friends—Angie was not among them—to her house to listen to the soundtrack and dress as hippies. Silvia had reported to Angie that the partiers had pretended to smoke pot, but that Louis Burdon, the closest thing to a hippie any of them knew, had actually brought some actual weed, which horrified Judy.

Angie thrust Judy's clothes into her arms. "Time to rehearse," she said, pushing through the door, not bothering to hold it for Judy who soon caught up to her, paused just long enough to mutter, "Don't forget who the heroine of this play is," before she made for the classroom door to enter first.

"She dies in the end," Angie reminded her as they joined the others assembled for a scene at the front of the classroom.

Mrs. K clapped her hands for their attention. "Okay, people, we're going to deal with the kiss."

She produced a folded paper fan, spread it open and demonstrated its purpose—a shield for Judy's face and Frankie's once he leaned in to supposedly kiss her.

The students groaned and Frankie blushed behind his dark skin. Judy was all business as she took the fan from Mrs. K and practiced opening and closing it.

Graham started a low chant, "Boo, hiss, we want a real kiss."

Mrs. K whirled around and lowered her plain face toward Graham's handsome one. "You are in the ninth grade, not the second. Behave accordingly."

"Ninth-graders kiss," someone said.

"Not in my play," she said.

"It's Shakespeare's play," Louis said, mumbling something about censorship.

Not anymore, Angie thought, glum at the prospect of a sanitized rendering of a classic. Not that she really wanted Frankie to kiss Judy. She only wanted him to kiss Judy as long as Judy didn't want to be kissed by him.

* * *

They did the performance in the lunchroom. A space was cleared for them on the floor and Mrs. K had brought the Japanese screen from her living room to conceal the cafeteria service counter. At least the screen would give some context to the Japanese fan that Juliet would unfold at the end of Act 1.

Since Angie as the narrator would not be in a costume, she had for days dithered about what to wear. She would be standing in front of the audience for the entire performance, introducing the scenes and summarizing the action that they could not act out in their 50-minute class period. Just when she thought she might hit her mother up for a new outfit, Mrs. K called her aside and strongly suggested Angie wear something subdued that would not call undue attention to her. After all, she was the narrator, and she should be somewhat but not entirely invisible, Mrs. K said. Neutral, she said. Which is why Angie should wear a black skirt and a white blouse. So, Angie showed up in her colorless outfit looking like an usher.

Though they would be doing a second performance that night for the parents, Judy's mother showed up to the daytime performance with a bouquet of roses which she lay on the seat next to her, so her hands were free to snap flash photos whenever Judy was on stage.

The audience, already alerted to the non-kiss, was ready for the fakery. When the fan went up, the audience smacked its collective lips. When Juliet withdrew her fan, her face flamed while Romeo's flashed a barely detectable smirk and Angie missed her cue. From her vantage point at the side of the stage, she was the only one who saw that Frankie had kissed Judy for real.

Mrs. K's own face was blotchy with outrage at the misconduct of the other ninth-graders. The perspiration on Mrs. K's forehead was creeping downward, making a slippery slope of her nose down which her glasses skimmed and dropped to her chest. Luckily, they were attached by one of those beaded loops that allowed the glasses to hang like an absurd necklace when they weren't on her face. Mrs. K's eyes glimmered naked and helpless, and Angie was glad when Mrs. K thrust her glasses back on. But then she was glaring at Angie, who had yet to resume her narration of the play. Angie, still reeling from the illicit kiss only three people in the world knew about, cleared her throat into the microphone causing electronic feedback that made the audience cover its ears. Angie took a deep breath, which was also amplified, and then narrated in a soft and trembling voice the transition to the next scene.

When the play was over, when Romeo lay poisoned on the linoleum and Juliet had draped herself over a bench loaned from the locker room, her hands holding in place the sword that was her demise, when the families stood agape at the tragedy they had wrought, Angie wrapped up the show with "And so ends our story of young lovers and doomed love."

She had not meant to emphasize *doomed*, but it came out large and dark and somehow comical so that the audience giggled. But then, cued by the vice-principal, who had been invited as a special guest, they applauded politely at first, and then raucously because now they were performing, stealing the show from the actors, from Angie and her costumes, from Mrs. K until the vice-principal inserted himself in front of the microphone and ordered silence or mass detention.

As the audience trailed out muffling its guffaws, Angie fanned herself with the pages of her script, resisting the urge to aim her makeshift fan at her armpits where the moist fabric of her starched white blouse clung as if glued. The crew, the students without parts in the play, were gathering props to store them for the evening performance for the PTA. The actors headed to the restrooms to free themselves from gowns, tunics, and tights. Angie watched Frankie saunter left with the boys while Judy stalked off stage right with the girls, all of them riled at the reception the play had received from their classmates. "All of that fuss over a kiss that never even happened," she heard Judy say.

After threats by some of the cast to defy Mrs. K and stage a walk-out in protest of a second performance, it was Judy who rallied the nearly mutinous players by reminding them that her mother, PTA president, had arranged a pizza party after the final curtain.

After school as Angie was hurrying toward her bus, Judy caught up to her and whispered, "I know you saw. If anyone else finds out, I'll know who told." Before Angie could point out that perhaps Frankie might tell, Judy elbowed past her to board the bus and plop down dramatically in the seat Silvia had been saving for her.

* * *

The evening performance landed on her mother's day off from work, so Angie counted on getting a ride to school and not having to appeal to Silvia for a ride. What Angie didn't count on was having the whole family pile into the car. Wasn't there anything they wanted to watch on TV? Reruns, Eva said. What about homework? Done, Letty said. No tantrums to throw, she asked Anthony who shrugged. It was all due to her parents' recent agreement to do more as a family, to recapture the sense of togetherness they believed once existed.

Cramped in the family station wagon with her tensely polite parents, glumly sardonic Eva, studiously indifferent Letty, and quietly seething Anthony, Angie did her best to ignore them all. Her mind was on the play, how she would make it better with her own expressive voice clearly articulating the narrative bridges in the action. She would be the glue, not missing a cue, her composure an inspiration to the cast. In her colorless attire, rather than be neutralized, she would stand out. She could, in a sense, be considered the star, because when you counted them, most of the lines belonged to her. She would save this play. Mrs. K would thank her. The cast would thank her. Frankie would admire her. Maybe he would kiss her.

When they arrived, her father glided the station wagon into a spot next to the Rico station wagon.

"Is Silvia in the play, too?" her mother asked as they all got out of the car. "Why didn't you say so?"

Angie *had* said so. Either her mother never remembered what she told her, or she never listened in the first place. Angie had stopped caring either way, she told herself. "She's the nurse," Angie said.

"Didn't you want to be in the play?"

"Mom, I'm in the play. I'm the narrator. I'm the glue," Angie said, taming the shrill in her voice on the last syllable. "I mean isn't that why you're all here? To see me?"

Before anyone could respond, Angie dashed ahead of them to the auditorium.

Frankie was the first person she saw when she entered the rear door of the auditorium. He was wielding his sword at some invisible foe, looking graceful and comic in his purple tights and tunic. He relaxed out of his fighting stance when he saw Angie, pushed a hand through his wavy dark hair, and looked dreamily into the distance. "But, soft! What light through yonder window breaks?"

But instead of offering up the next line, Angie could only blurt, "Are you going to kiss her again?"

She'd meant it to sound nonchalant, even playful, as if it were some jokey conspiracy between them, but it came out all wrong. She could taste the bitterness in her mouth. She swallowed and pressed her lips into a smile. "I mean that was some improvisation. Your leading lady was caught off guard. Nearly had a cow." Angie made herself stop talking by scratching her nose and hovering her hand over her mouth.

Frankie grinned. "I know." He pitched his voice in Judy's near nasal register and clasped his hands, his sword clamped inside an armpit. "Romeo, why for art thou brown, Romeo?"

"Ha!" Angie laughed, feeling a sort of kinship, even an intimacy with Romeo, with Frankie. "She sure looked mad when you kissed her," she said, coming back again to that word because what she really wanted to ask was *How was it? Did you like it? Did she?*

Frankie drew invisible shapes on the floor with his sword. "Probably shouldn't have done it."

That's my line, Angie thought. She shrugged. "Judy will be prepared this time."

"What about you?"

"Huh?"

"Ready to perform for the grown-ups?"

"I'm going to knock'em dead," Angie said.

"That a girl," Frankie said, and he placed the tip of his sword on her shoulder as if knighting her.

Then Louis and Graham barged through the door and Frankie joined them in a brotherly clash of swords before Mrs. K came and rounded everyone up for a pre-curtain huddle. "Dignity, people. We must maintain dignity. Let's do Mr. Shakespeare justice."

Angie, driven by her own promise to "knock'em dead," set the tone. She opened the performance with a cordial welcome of the audience to the town of Verona, her voice clear and without wobble nor the tiniest squawk of feedback from the microphone. Angie made eye contact with the audience, even her family in the tenth row, asserting herself as their guide to the story, as someone vital to its unfolding. There were no missed cues that night and no silliness among the audience save for a snicker or two from a younger sibling, who was immediately shushed by a parent. When Juliet opened her fan to shield the non-kiss, there was a murmur of sweet appreciation from the audience and a smile of relief from Angie. When Angie spoke the final lines of her narration, "And so ends our story of young lovers and doomed love," she hit the perfect note of sadness and detached wisdom. The audience was effusive in its applause and demands for curtain calls, and Angie without hesitation took her place in line with the cast for bows.

Backstage, Mrs. K's face was pink with pride and so overcome was she with the success of the evening that she was pulling students into her for hugs. The students, themselves flushed with the thrill of victory, went willingly into Mrs. K's embrace, heavy with B.O., surreptitious cigarettes, and saggy upper arm flesh. "This tragedy was a triumph!" she declared over and over.

She spun a pirouette and clapped her hands the way she did in class, but this time there was a girlishness about it, as if she were in love, and they, her students, were the loved. "Now change out of your costumes and then go have some pizza."

Angie, who didn't have a costume to change out of, went to join her family. Her parents were still in their seats, her father with a cup of coffee and her mother with punch and a plate of cookies in the empty seat next to her. They knew few other parents and Angie was embarrassed for them sitting alone while other parents mingled around the refreshments table. The PTA ladies were unboxing pizzas that had just been delivered, designating one end of the table with a sign for *Cast Only*. Graham and Louis, already in their street clothes, were descending upon the pepperoni.

"So, what'd ya think?" she asked her parents.

"Nice," said her mother.

"Very nice," said her father.

Nice was the word of the day, Angie decided. It was as if they were sending instructions to each other on comportment. She would not expend energy on trying to extract anything more from her parents. "I'm going to get some pizza."

Her siblings had each found someone they knew to hang out with and were stuffing themselves with pizza and cookies. She caught Eva's eye and was rewarded with a thumbs-up, and Angie signaled her gratefulness with a smile. The cast pizza table was now being swarmed by the actors. Angie reached for a mushroom slice, then turned around to look for Frankie, but Louis stepped in front of her. After gulping down the giant wad of food that had occupied his mouth, he congratulated her. "You were a good narrator. You got us off to a great start. We aced it, man."

"Yeah, we did." Angie was feeling the goodwill all around her. Everyone was slapping each other on the back, shaking hands, blowing kisses. Almost everyone. "Well," she said, "I wonder where the stars are."

"Their parents were taking pictures of them and the infamous little fan backstage," Graham said, fluttering his lashes and puckering his lips behind his hand. "They're probably just getting changed now."

"I'll go tell them to hurry up before the pizza's gone," Angie said, carrying her own half-eaten slice.

When she got backstage, she saw the rear door propped open a crack and heard low voices outside. She tiptoed to the door, flattening herself against the wall.

"We have chemistry," Judy was saying, which puzzled Angie at first since chemistry wasn't offered until tenth grade.

"Since when," Frankie said, but his tone wasn't disagreeable or challenging.

"Well, we certainly had it on stage this evening." Judy was still using her Juliet voice.

"We all had chemistry this evening," Frankie said. Angie bit her cold pizza and nodded. She could take credit for that.

"I think it was in the stars," Judy said.

Angie rolled her eyes and imagined Frankie doing the same since she heard no reply from him. She wondered if this might be her cue to throw wide the door and rescue Frankie, but then Judy spoke Frankie's name in a voice both pleading and inviting.

"Why didn't you kiss me for real tonight?"

Angie nearly choked.

"I already made my point this afternoon," Frankie said.

"Make it again," Judy said.

Angie inclined her head, straining to hear Frankie's answer, but none came that she could hear, until the sound of mouths separating from each other nicked the night air followed by the long whoosh of Judy's sigh. Angie's stomach roiled with the half-digested pizza. She smashed what remained of the slice in her hand, feeling tomato sauce and mushroom bits ooze through her fingers. Her knees wobbled as if suddenly bereft of bone. She willed her body to move, but she was still rooted in place when Graham came in shouting, "Wherefore art Romeo and Juliet?"

Angie shouted back as if accused, "I haven't seen them."

Graham, seeing the door ajar, walked over and pushed it open. "Aha!" he cried. He made a magician's flourish. "Voilà, I give you the star-crossed lovers."

Judy pulled Frankie in by the hand. "We were just getting some fresh air," she giggled to Graham. She turned and saw Angie. "Oh, were you looking for us?"

Angie merely gaped, her vocal cords inoperative at the sight of Frankie's hand so compliantly in Judy's. She tightened her own hand, still gloppy with pizza, into a fist.

"Good job tonight, Angie," Frankie said, looking mildly sheepish and, Angie thought, completely like an ass.

When Angie finally moved her mouth to speak, Judy was already leading Frankie away. Angie had a momentary urge to unfold her fist and yank Frankie's other hand, to jerk him off balance and Judy with him, to tumble them both at her feet.

* * *

The next day, the ninth grade was abuzz with the news of Frankie and Judy as a couple. It was inevitable, said some. It happened all the time in Hollywood.

At lunchtime, Angie slouched next to Wanda as they watched Frankie and Judy eating together a few benches away. "I myself did not see that coming," Wanda said. "Someone should tell them the play's over."

"Let's see how well they do without a script," Angie said, studying the pair for signs of dialogue.

Judy ate an orange slice and then fed one to Frankie. She wiped his chin with a napkin. Their lip movements were all about chewing with not a hint of a syllable.

"Maybe they need a narrator," Wanda joked.

"Don't look at me," Angie said. "I just finished narrating a tragedy."

Though they were not within earshot, both Frankie and Judy turned in her direction and for a moment there was a staring match. Frankie blinked first. Then Judy.

Angie refused to blink. Someday, she promised herself, she would narrate her own story.

EXTRACURRICULAR ACTIVITIES

When Angie entered the unfun funhouse that was high school in the fall of 1968, she felt it in all the kinks and bends of her gut—change. It was in the air in the mood-altering Santa Ana winds that drove specks of dust deep into ear canals and windpipes. It was on the airwaves with The Beatles singing, "We all want to change the world" and their syllabic symmetry of "revolution", "evolution" and "solution."

Angie was down with that—eager to revolt, ready to evolve, looking to solve the problem of her and her invisibleness. It was time to reinvent herself. Junior high was history. High school was happening. A fresh start. A new groove.

"Join a club. Meet new friends," urged her mother, who had herself gained "girlfriends," as she called them, since entering the work force.

Angie had paged through Eva's yearbooks at the photos of the different clubs—drama, journalism, health careers, Latinos Unidos, speech. She wanted to join them all, to meet new friends in every one of them, to have the most friends she'd ever had in her life.

She showed up for the first meeting of the Health Careers Club even though her volunteer work as a candy striper at the local hospital had already convinced her that her future did not lie in comforting and healing the infirm. When the gray-haired club advisor welcomed the girls as future nurses and the boys as future doctors, Angie left the meeting in quiet protest.

She shied away from the Latino Club, afraid that her lack of Spanish disqualified her for membership. She longed for the journalism club, but the popular kids had commandeered it, making the school newspaper a show piece for their cars, clothes, and couplings. There was the drama club, but Angie had had her fill of theater the previous year in Mrs. K's *Romeo and Juliet* production. Her last hope was the Speech Club. She had things to say. She was sure of it.

Angie took her sack of bologna sandwich, Fritos, and apple slices to the speech room for the first meeting. There were a dozen or so students scattered about the room and Angie took a desk toward the back. The room had a stage with a curtain, and the club president sat at the edge of the stage, dangling his legs, his hands stuffed in the pockets of his letterman's jacket. Angie recognized him from a recent photo in the school newspaper. Doug Goodman was the "proud owner of a used, yet groovy, midnight-blue Mustang. When he's not pinning opponents to the wrestling mat or earning top honors at speech tournaments, he's driving to the beach, the bowling alley, or the drive-in movies with his girlfriend, Judy Wiekamp." Judy had lost no time infiltrating the ranks of the in-crowd, though she was starting modestly with the lower tier. Speech Club president was still pegs away from football quarterback.

Judy sat at Doug's feet. She turned and waved jauntily at Angie who waved back and produced a smile of her own before stuffing her mouth with Fritos to disguise the contrived action of her grin muscles.

Doug called the meeting to order. The first order of business was introductions of old and new members. They were to give their name, year in school, and the reason they were interested in the Speech Club. "I'll go first," he said, swinging himself off the stage and onto his feet. "I'm Doug Goodman. I'm a senior. I'm in the club because, well, I'm the club president."

Judy slapped his arm playfully. "And because you're a great speaker."

"That's the rumor," Doug said.

Judy introduced herself next, saying she was interested in the club because she wanted to develop her skills at self-expression.

By the time it was Angie's turn, all the good reasons were taken. Change, she thought. *Change* was in the air, on the medal podium at the Mexico City Olympics when Tommie Smith and John Carlos raised black-gloved fists just months earlier, or in the streets where radical women placed a beauty queen's tiara on a sheep. Statements without words which everyone heard.

Angie decided to say what she actually felt. "I want to have something to say and I want to be heard."

"What? Speak up," someone said, and the room reverberated with Speech Club mirth.

Angie's hands, already folded in her lap, clamped around each other in a death match.

She left the meeting having dug fingernail dents into her palm. She headed to her afternoon class—Mrs. Brimsler's tenth-grade Sex Education class where Angie was assigned to the front row.

Angie witnessed up close Mrs. Brimsler blushing at the rude sounds that erupted during her lectures, which she dealt with by passing out cough drops as if her students were merely innocent throat-clearers. Her black-framed glasses imprisoned her scared blue eyes, which flitted to the fluorescent lights overhead or the institution-green linoleum beneath her sensible pumps to avoid eye contact with the smirking adolescents in the classroom that always seemed so airless. Her thin lips pursed whenever she was not painfully articulating in a tiny voice the details of genitalia, the mechanics of menstruation (which she mispronounced as *menace*-tration), or the process of birth. It was inevitable that she would be referred to as Mrs. Primsler behind her back.

Despite the awkwardness, Angie was serious about the class. Serious about learning, serious about earning an A.

One day, after they had labeled diagrams of female and male parts and written down the function of each in objective, clinical terms, Mrs. Brimsler explained the physiological changes that occurred during intercourse, pausing every so often to dispense a cough drop.

It was October, but the weather was still summer-warm. Nevertheless, Mrs. Brimsler shut the door to the classroom. "Take out a fresh sheet of paper," she squeaked. There were groans and frantic, last-minute glances in notebooks at diagrams and vocabulary words.

"This is a quiz," Mrs. Brimsler said, holding up her hand like a stop sign to halt the complaints. "You will not turn it in," she said.

There were sighs of relief, but Angie didn't like those terms at all. What was the point of getting answers right, if no one was going to know about it, if it wasn't going to escalate her already healthy grade point average?

Mrs. Brimsler cleared her throat. "I'm going to read aloud ten questions. Write the answers on your paper."

With the door closed, the room was starting to heat up and Mrs. Brimsler's face was heating up with it.

"Hey, can we open the door?" Max Delgado asked. He was slumped in his seat, his legs stretched out into the aisle. Max never raised his hand to speak, and Mrs. Brimsler invariably chided in her child's voice that anyone wishing to speak must raise his hand and sit up straight.

This time though she folded her lips into each other, bustled to the back of the room, and turned off the overhead lights. "That should help," she said, turning redder as she returned to face the class. "You must answer each question as truthfully as you can."

Angie's hand began to sweat, making her pencil slippery, and she knew that she would fudge her answers.

Mrs. Brimsler read each question twice, her eyes blinking behind her glasses, her voice croaking with the strain of pronouncing each word. The questions were alarming to Angie. She had had no problem with the genitalia diagrams or saying *penis* or *vagina* or *scrotum*, all words that sounded wicked with their long vowels and labiodental consonants yet were proper terminology. Proper was what Angie was all about. She could say those words without giggling or blushing. She could draw them with the detachment of a scientist. But the questions issuing from Mrs. Brimsler's prim mouth were on a topic shockingly personal and humiliatingly non-applicable to Angie.

"Have you ever kissed a member of the opposite sex?" Mrs. Brimsler read from her list.

There were smirks and guffaws all around, because who in the tenth grade hadn't been kissed?

Angie stared at her blank page and then very faintly, the lead just skimming the paper, she penciled in *No*. But with the subsequent questions, what Angie feared became evident. The kiss was the least of the actions. Everything that followed was one move closer to The Act, and there was no way she could fudge the answers. No boy had ever touched her breasts (they hardly existed), her vagina, or clitoris.

Likewise, she had never fondled, kissed or sucked a penis. She had never exercised birth control, never had one, two, or more sexual partners. Answering *No* to the first question virtually guaranteed that *No* would be repeated down the page.

But wait, there was that time she and Little Eddie had collided during an illicit game of indoor hide-and-seek. It was only a few years ago when they should've long ago left such play behind. They had both ended up on the hallway floor, Angie sprawled across her cousin. Dazed, for a moment they stared at each other, before Eddie, the film buff, shouted "Burt Lancaster and Deborah Kerr in *From Here to Eternity*" and yanked Angie's mouth to his. A kiss is a kiss, no matter when it happened or under what circumstances, Angie reasoned, even when the boy who kissed her was her cousin, even when that cousin was pretending to be Deborah Kerr. Angie didn't dare take her eraser to her page. Instead, she penciled a *Yes* over her *No* to Question 1. But she couldn't in good conscience change her other answers. Usually, during quizzes, she left her paper exposed in case Wanda across the aisle from her needed to borrow a correct answer or two. Today, she covered her paper with her arm.

They were told to tally their scores. Each *Yes* answer was worth one point, each *No* worth zero. Angie looked at her measly, questionable point, happy after all that her grade point average would not be affected by her score.

"If you scored 0-2 points," Mrs. Brimsler said, reading from the score key while also trying to survey the room, "you are behind most of your peers. Be aware of pitfalls in trying to catch up."

Everyone looked around, including Angie, who did so to throw off track anyone who might suspect her score.

"If you scored 3-5 points, you're on par with most of your classmates."

There were self-congratulatory smiles and audible sighs from some of the girls.

"If you scored 6-8 points, you're above the average. Exercise caution in your decisions."

There were chuckles from some of the boys.

"If you scored 9-10," squeaked Mrs. Brimsler, whose pink cheeks looked ready to combust, "you need to seriously reconsider your actions and their potential consequences."

"I'll keep that in mind," Ricky Fernandez said in a low voice that was heard by everyone. While some girls gasped, even Angie knew Ricky's score range—the highest one, indicating flagrant, decadent sex—was no surprise. She remembered him from elementary school. He was a flirt even then, no one beneath his notice, not even Angie whom he had palmed in the small of her back perilously close to her tailbone one morning when they were both at school early in an empty hallway. No one doubted his score.

A tiny chirp of disapproval escaped Mrs. Brimsler's clamped lips. She turned on the lights and opened the door, the sudden small gust of air mocking her sigh. A crumpling of paper further heckled her composure. The bell rang and she nearly startled out of her sturdy shoes before she leaned with relief against the chalkboard to let her students herd themselves out the door. Angie found herself behind Max, whose fist squeezed a wad of paper. The veins at his wrist popped, his biceps flexed and then relaxed as he dropped the balled-up paper into the trash can on his way out. Someone nearby fished it out. Angie's own sheet of answers was tucked into her notebook, which she clutched to her chest.

By lunchtime, word had spread about the quiz. Students who wouldn't have Sex Education class until the following semester either thrilled or paled at the gossip. Though few students who took the quiz shared their scores, a number was attached to everyone. Those who didn't reveal their number were assigned one by consensus. Then there was Max Delgado. It turned out he had answered every one of Mrs. Brimsler's questions with the same two letters followed by an exclamation mark. *Ha!* Was it scorn at the idiocy of the quiz or did it denote a score on par with that of Ricky Fernandez?

And even though Angie was sure that no one's number was the undiluted truth, it was clear to her that everyone was far ahead of her. The evidence was all around her in the hallways with couples pushed up against lockers, making out, eyes closed to the looky-loos.

* * *

After school, Angie sat on her bed trying to make sense of her geometry assignment, while Eva sprawled on her own bed reading a fat book. Angie drew and labeled an isosceles triangle on her homework sheet. It looked slightly sexual. Everything looked sexual to her now.

She glanced at Eva. Had she ever been kissed? How many points would she have scored on the quiz?

Eva and Angie were in the same school once again and for the last time. Eva was a senior and Angie a sophomore. High school was yet another transition that Angie had both dreaded and anticipated. It was a chance to start over. To reinvent herself. To put her missteps and humiliations of the past behind her. She had joined the Speech Club determined to have extracurricular activities. Now, with Mrs. Brimsler's quiz, extracurricular activities had taken on a whole new meaning.

Eva hadn't had Sex Ed. The requirement had begun that year with Angie's class. "You're lucky you didn't have to have Sex Ed." Angie said.

"You're lucky you don't have to take accounting," Eva replied, not looking up from the tome that made a dent in her bed. Eva did little homework these days and spent her time reading fat biographies of famous people.

At their mother's urging, Eva had signed up for business and secretarial classes at school: accounting, business English, advanced typing, shorthand, and office helper. The last wasn't actually a class. It was helping out in the office, filing, running the mimeograph machine, and keeping the bulletin boards current. The office helper also delivered messages to the classrooms or a summons for a student to see the principal, and handed out excuse forms for absent students to obtain parental signatures, half of which were forged.

"Eva, no one's making you take it."

"It's my safety net. In case I don't make it as a concert pianist." She sighed and threw her book on Arthur Rubinstein aside. A raft of pink slips fluttered to the floor.

Angie leaned from her bed to peer at the forms—blank absence excuse forms, contraband that rogue office helpers trafficked in. Angie gasped at her sister's illicit activity.

"Relax. It's not like they're rubbers or anything."

"Like you would know anything about rubbers," Angie said, throwing down the challenge.

"I heard about your quiz. Didn't ace that one, did you?"

"Ha," Angie scoffed, imagining how Max Delgado's quiz answers might sound aloud. She busied herself with gathering some of the pink slips off the floor. Eva snatched them from her hands without thanks.

"So, where do you go when you cut class?" Angie asked.

"Cut class? All of my absences have been excused."

"Come on, Eva. Can I come next time?"

Eva snorted. "Miss A-student?"

"You used to be."

"Before I got smart and set my sights on practical goals." Eva stuck her face back in her book about a Polish piano prodigy. Angie went back to her isosceles triangle and began labeling its decidedly non-sexual parts.

Angie decided she was on her own when it came to the facts of life. It's not as though she'd had no introduction whatsoever. She'd seen *Valley of the Dolls* when she was fourteen, her mother inexplicably allowing her to go with Nelda and Eva.

Nelda and her mother had been whispering in the kitchen one Saturday afternoon when Angie walked in dressed in her candy striper uniform. The whispering stopped. Nelda looked up and grinned at Angie.

"Hey, there, Cherry Ames. Solve any hospital mysteries lately? Save any lives?"

Angie didn't answer Nelda's questions, hoping to make clear she'd never read the books about the mystery-solving nurse, that she had different literary tastes than Nelda.

"Looks like the cat's got her tongue," Nelda said. She did that often—spoke of Angie in the third person when Angie was two feet in front of her.

"I'm going for my shift," Angie said to the room and anyone in it who happened to hear her.

"Maybe I won't invite her after all," Nelda said.

Angie, hand on the doorknob, stopped. "Who?" she asked. "Where?"

"Nelda's taking Eva to see *Valley of the Dolls*," her mother said.

"She's old enough," Nelda said.

"So am I," Angie said, who was dying to see the much-hyped movie about sex and drugs.

Nelda and her mother exchanged looks and shrugged. "Okay, you're in," they said together.

Angie realized later the movie was a substitute for any birds-and-bees talk her mother or even Nelda in her stead would otherwise be obliged to give. During the movie, Angie noted the morality tale about drugs, ambition, greed, and the general perils of being a woman, but what she focused on was the sex. Sex! Right there in the movie theater, sitting between Eva and Nelda, she experienced an alarmingly pleasurable warming of her body, every cell in it from her scalp to the soles of her feet prickling with ferocious awareness and a soft ruckus of waves engulfing her and lifting her out of her seat. She hadn't wanted to take her eyes off the action, yet she was tempted to glance at Nelda and Eva to see their reactions. Both were fixed on the screen, Eva's expression tight, Nelda's face in meltdown.

Later in the car, Nelda, her face only partially restored, looked at them. "Any questions, mijas?"

Eva said no. Angie, her underpants a sticky mess, shook her head. Nelda revved the engine and drove out of the parking lot.

*   *   *

Angie's plan to reinvent herself had already been shot to hell with the Sex Ed quiz. Still, she held on to the hope that she could repair the damage or divert attention from it by joining a school club.

The discussion at the Speech Club meeting focused on raising funds to help send the speech team to the regional competition. Doug pointed out that even those not on the speech team could exercise their school spirit by participating in the fundraiser, which he was calling the Improvisational Challenge. A soapbox and microphone would be set up on the lawn at lunchtime. Students would pay $1.00 each to name a topic about which the speaker would deliver a cogent, two-minute address. Humor was encouraged. Doug prepared to demonstrate. "Give me a topic," he told the assembled membership.

"Love," Judy said.

"Sex," someone else offered to a round of cheers.

"Death," Angie found herself saying, never meaning to be heard.

"What's that?" Doug asked.

"Nothing," Angie said and pretended to study the Improvisational Challenge sign-up sheet that was being passed around. She scribbled her name on a line making it as illegible as possible and greasing it with a sliver of bologna for good measure.

Doug opted for the topic of love and took the stage to deliver an off-the-cuff speech that began with the title of the sleep-inducing hit "Love is Blue." Angie took the remains of her lunch and slunk out of the room.

Angie didn't stop at her locker to get her book for her next class. She walked right past it, down the hallway, through the restricted access parking lot and off campus. She'd never cut class before, had always hated being absent, fearful that something (like life) would happen without her. Now she understood that life was happening without her no matter where she happened to be. She walked past the Catholic school and crossed the street to the park and sat under a tree on the slope just below the public library. A squirrel darted and froze, darted and froze, darted and froze on a nearby tree as if trying to gauge Angie's reflexes. Angie extracted a remnant of bread crust from her lunch sack and placed it on the ground near her. The squirrel zigzagged down from its perch, skittered toward her, snatched up the bread crust and galloped away.

"You're welcome," Angie said, tossing another shred of crust at the retreating rodent. She got up and went inside the library, which was full of toddlers and their mothers and old people. Angie went to the children's section where she hadn't been since elementary school, where now as a high schooler who failed a sex quiz and was not a member of any club, she could see over the tops of the shelves. She pulled a few books off and opened them, checking to see if her name was on any of the check-out pockets. She looked for the biographies she'd read back then—Marie Curie, Nellie Bly, Amelia Earhart, Helen Keller—but negotiating the aisles scattered with toddlers proved irritating and when Angie heaved a big sigh, the librarian looked her way, which Angie interpreted as an eviction notice.

She left the library, exiting the little building that had once felt like home. As she stood at the corner waiting for the green light, a car slowed down to make a turn and Angie sensed the driver's eyes upon her. She caught a glimpse of Max Delgado behind the wheel before the black Trans Am accelerated around the corner.

Max Delgado cutting class was no surprise. She seldom saw him in Sex Ed. Everyone talked about how certain kids could teach the class. Max by all accounts was one of them. He had fulfilled the bad-boy promise he had shown in fifth grade, which was the last time Angie had exchanged words with him. He was a regular in detention, had been suspended a few times, and was given a wide berth in the halls where he sauntered, hands in pockets where who knew what was hidden. Angie decided to cut through the shopping center to avoid another sighting of Max. At Montgomery Ward, she tried on lingerie that drooped off her body and perused the makeup counter full of objects whose purpose confounded her until it was nearly time for her to be home from school. She arrived at her doorstep just after Eva, who lowered her glasses at Angie. "Didn't see you on the bus."

"Nobody sees me on the bus," Angie replied.

Eva held the door open. "After you, Invisible Girl."

On the nightly news, they watched John Lennon and Yoko Ono's bed-in. Angie's mother, who had stayed home from work with a headache, pronounced it disgraceful and silly. It was about peace, her father said. "What's so silly about that?"

The rest of them were quiet as their mother fumed silently on the couch at being contradicted.

Finally, Letty said, "I think they look gross."

"Looks don't matter," Eva chided.

It's what their mother had always said to them, all the while telling them which clothes did or didn't suit them, how they should wear their hair, and *wouldn't a dab of makeup add a little improvement to their faces?*

The sight of John and Yoko naked in bed was a stark contrast to the image Angie had kept hidden in the recesses of her brain of Jennifer and Tony in *Valley of the Dolls*—the image that Angie imagined sex should look like: A blond woman with a killer body garlanded in lacy pink lingerie and a handsome man driven wild by it. But shaggy-haired, bespectacled Lennon and the equally shaggy-haired and square-jawed Ono had also spoiled sex for Angie, or at least complicated its meaning with social and political messages.

The next day she turned in a forged absence excuse slip, one that she had hoarded while picking up Eva's scattered stash from the floor a few nights ago. Maybe she had seemed overly nonchalant or not nonchalant enough when turning in the illegitimate pass. She was summoned to the office during second period by none other than office helper Eva who walked her back to the office like a warden.

"What'dja do?"

Angie shrugged, though she wanted to throw herself at Eva's mercy and beg her for some kind of intervention. But they walked the halls in silence. When they reached the office door, Eva whispered, "Honor among thieves."

* * *

When Angie entered the detention room after school, she ignored the stares from the other detainees. She was an anomaly among the regular offenders. She had acquitted herself well under the cross-examination of the vice-principal, maintaining ignorance of any purloined caches of blank passes. The only discomfort she felt about being in the detention room now was that, as a first offender, she had no idea of the protocol. The detention monitor that day was the ancient English teacher who made his students memorize endless, tedious stanzas by dead poets. Angie hoped she would be in his class one day. She wanted to fill her head with unusable words so as to crowd out all the bewilderment in her adolescent brain.

Mr. Devine told Angie to write on the board her name and the time she entered detention. When an hour had passed, she could erase her name and be released to the free world. She wrote her name underneath the last person who had signed in—Max Delgado. She turned around and there he was in the front row. He gave her the smallest of nods and she did the same, a wave of heat creeping up the back of her neck. At her desk, she opened her geometry book and busied herself by copying theorems into her notebook where they remained as incomprehensible as ever.

When Max got up to erase his name from the board, Angie didn't look up, not even when Mr. Devine said, "See you again soon, Mr. Delgado."

Five minutes later, Angie went to the board and erased her name, then left without a word of acknowledgement from Mr. Devine.

Around the corner from the classroom, Max Delgado slouched against a support beam. "Need a ride?"

The thought of herself in the bucket seat next to Max sent her heart accelerating. "Okay," she said, holding her books across her chest to cover the surely obvious throb.

He led the way to the parking lot and his Trans Am. He didn't open the door for her, and she was glad for that. She was capable of opening her own doors, at least in the most literal sense.

She waited to see if he would buckle his seat belt before she buckled hers. "You like to live dangerously?" he asked.

She shrugged. "I live across from the park," she said as he started the engine.

He shifted into gear. "I know."

She looked at him.

"Elementary school," he said. "Your house is below the schoolyard. I used to see your mother hanging laundry."

"Where do you live?" she asked, feeling she had a right to know.

"I'll show you."

He drove with his left hand on the steering wheel, his elbow resting on the open window. His right hand wrapped around the gearshift knob, and Angie stared straight ahead to avoid thinking about the proximity of his big-knuckled hand to her knee. She didn't even attempt conversation. She had no clue where to begin. She remembered how in fifth grade he wasn't much of a talker. She hardly knew him then and nothing had changed, except that now he had full-fledged acne, his hair on his head was greasier, the hair above his lip more pronounced, and his hands were as big as plates.

They were a few blocks from her house when he turned west past the liquor store and gas station and down a dead-end street rutted and worn to its stony underlayer. He pointed to a faded blue stucco house with white trim and matching white bars on the windows.

"We're not that far from each other," Angie said.

He started the car again and drove past their old elementary school then pulled into a side road hidden from car and foot traffic. He parked near a retaining wall that was shielded by untamed shrubs.

"What are we doing here?" Angie asked, her voice deliberately loud to avoid sounding as small as she felt in Max's muscle car.

"Wanna talk?"

"Okay."

They were both silent. Angie waited for him to begin. *So, talk,* she thought, pressing her hands into the upholstery of the bucket seat to rub the sweat from her palms.

"Why were you in detention?" he asked.

"I cut classes. You saw me."

"Why'd you cut? You're one of the smart kids."

"I'm not." To Angie's dismay, tears fell from her cheeks into her lap.

"Hey," Max whispered, and suddenly his hand that had been caressing the gearshift was now around her skinny shoulder. It was massive and gentle, and Angie's skin prickled with a longing that went beyond the physical delight of Max's touch.

Max leaned in closer. "Angie, I'm going to kiss you."

In the seconds before Max's mouth with its scrubby mustache touched down on hers, Angie wondered why Max wanted to kiss her, wondered if her lips would know what to do.

"Work the muscles in your lips," he told her as he pulled his mouth away briefly.

Angie found it easy to follow Max's instructions.

"You learn fast," he said, which pleased her because, except for geometry, she had always caught on quickly.

"Do you want to do more?" he asked.

"Like what?"

"Touching."

"I don't know," she said, but Max's hand moved hers across the gearbox and between his legs. She was shocked by the very idea of her hand on a penis—"engorged" was the term they had had to say out loud in Mrs. Brimsler's class. She had barely time to process this new sensation when Max's hand went to her chest and her very tiny breasts. She drew back, embarrassed, but he pulled her back in.

"It's okay," he assured her, so she relaxed and she let his hand travel the narrow width of her chest making her nipples beneath her padded bra flood with current and when he pushed his hand past her stomach and between her legs she lost any sense of spatial relations she possessed, which was little given her trouble with geometry. She did not attach words to what Max was doing. There was only sensation and the recollection of what she had felt with *Valley of the Dolls*. And now here it was again, and she let it fill her until it was over, and she looked in astonishment at Max who grinned at her.

They sat in silence for a few minutes, Angie at a loss for words and Max seemingly lost in thought. He drummed on the steering wheel a few times and then turned to her.

"This was a one-time thing, you know."

Angie swallowed hard. "I know," she said, though she didn't know. She just could think of nothing else to say, except maybe *Wonder what my Sex Ed score would be now?* because she couldn't help but feel experienced and knowing and in on something that had previously been a mystery to her.

"Why even this one time?" she asked.

"I've liked you since fifth grade."

"Then why—?"

He shook his head, so she stopped talking.

"Will you say hi to me in the hallway at school?"

"Yeah," he said. "But not detention."

She looked at him.

"Just kidding," he said. "But I doubt if I'll see you in detention again."

"What? Turning over a new leaf, Delgado?" she said. It annoyed her just a bit that he would think that one little detention session had set her back on the straight and narrow. That she had learned her lesson, that her small act of revolt was a tiny blip in the scheme of infractions that she was incapable of committing.

"I'm just me. You're just you." Max shrugged, opening his burrito-wrapper-sized hands to indicate something obvious and incontestable.

He started up the engine, but she opened her door. "I'll just walk from here."

"Suit yourself," he said, but he reached for her hand and squeezed it. "Adios, muñequita."

She got out and pushed the door shut and watched the Trans Am raise a fan of dust as it pulled away.

* * *

As promised, at school the next day, Max said hi to her in the hallway, which was really just a nod, but it was acknowledgment enough, and Angie continued on her unmerry but reasonably content way to meet Wanda for lunch until she was accosted by Judy Wiekamp.

"Where've you been? We're about ready to start."

Before Angie could answer, her elbow was inside Judy's bossy grasp and she was being tugged to the grassy quad near the outdoor lunch tables. Doug from the Speech Club was testing a microphone next to a music stand. A banner stretched between two poles planted in the lawn announced the Improvisational Challenge.

"You signed up," Judy reminded her.

"But I'm not really in the club," Angie protested.

"You're third on the list. Right after me. Stand right there."

A crowd began to gather around them, and Angie considered the consequences of running away. Her escape would have many witnesses. Her improvised speech would have just as many. Angie decided she would rather be humiliated for saying something than nothing at all.

Doug was explaining the rules of the challenge. Anybody could pay a dollar to propose a topic for a speech. Then others could vote with their quarters for their choice. The speaker would deliver an entertaining, enlightening, or educational speech on the topic garnering the most quarters. After all the speeches, the crowd could further cast their quarters for their favorite speaker.

Sex was the winning topic for Doug, and he accepted the challenge with a mature tolerance for the antics of the masses. He spoke ostensibly about the sex lives of camels, which he claimed to have firsthand knowledge of because his family was hosting the Saudi exchange student whose uncle was a camel trader. Aside from sharing that camels have sex while sitting down, his speech, though articulate, was lacking in graphic descriptions of the particulars. Doug rose above the *boos* with a polite bow.

The winning topic for Judy was sex. She marched to the microphone and orated about the importance of sex education to help teens make responsible decisions about their lives, sparking make-out sessions by the couples in the crowd.

By the time it was Angie's turn to speak, she was prepared. Sex. Yeah, she could talk about it. She stepped up to the microphone.

The crowd had grown. Wanda was pushing her way to the front. Max stood off to the side, leaning against a garbage can. Angie took a deep breath and the intake of air was amplified across the quad. It sounded sexy, which stirred the audience to hoots and shouts. But it also sounded like a gasp of comprehension, which stirred her to the kind of if-then reasoning that eluded her in geometry. She accepted the challenge with a newfound sense of purpose.

"Sex," she said to get their attention and to signal her intent to abide by her assigned topic. "Sex," she said again to give her brain time to scour its crannies for something to say on the subject. It was beginning to sound like a cheer. Gimme an S!

"Camels do it," she said to jeers. "People do it," she said to cheers. "Even Sex Ed teachers do it. Presumably," she added. Angie was on a roll. The crowd was with her.

"We all want to change the world," she said, though what she really wanted was to start small. She wanted to change her little world of being Angie Rubio. She wasn't sure how to go about doing such a thing. Somehow, she knew that her classmates wanted the same for themselves, even the pretty, popular kids. They wanted to know what would happen to them beyond their lives of making out in the hallways, or petting in the front seat of a Trans Am.

"Is the solution in a fist?" she asked, raising her own the way she'd longed to when she watched Tommie Smith and John Carlos. "Is it in tossing a beauty pageant crown in the trash can?" She wasn't sure if the audience was following her logic or questioning whether she had any, but apparently they appreciated the gesture because fists emerged above heads and for a moment Angie understood the meaning of solidarity.

She blathered on, but her words mattered little since her audience, which was now a large crowd, simply delighted in its own self-expression. She raised her voice above the burbling throng and seethed with passion about whatever surged to the front of her brain and the core of her heart. She was a passionate person! What did it matter if her two-minute harangue jumbled references to black-gloved fists, crowned sheep, and televised bed-ins? What did it matter that her heart beat wildly as she watched the principal rushing down the corridor to restore order?

She leaned more closely into the microphone and turned up the volume.

Guided Tours in Living Color

The Blue Boy. Angie stared at the painting, understanding it was a masterpiece, feeling the weight of its history, feeling also the weight of all she didn't know about art and history and the world, feeling as if the weight could squeeze her heart.

In the Huntington Gallery, she and her classmates stood before Gainsborough's opus fittingly awed as they knew they should be. Some felt required to chorus their worship or at least their own hip assessment of a pompous boy in blue glad rags. "Cool," they said, nodding, heads tilted. "Mod," someone snickered. But in the echo chamber of the hushed gallery, only the "ooh" and "ah" sounds were picked up by the walls and ceiling to be shot back into the air and in their ears, its tenor changed to something ghostly and disturbing as if contesting their sincerity. Some of the students giggled and moved on to the next painting. Other visitors glided in to fill their spots, prepared to appreciate art better than a bunch of high school kids, despite their being Kimball Park High's best as Mr. Otto often told them, even if at times, it sounded like a plea.

Mr. Otto's tradition was to take his Advanced Language Arts and Literature class to Los Angeles for a weekend to be exposed to its cultural and historical sights. All year, Angie had looked forward to this trip, her first real trip away from Kimball Park and into a world of big ideas, expansive buildings, and exalted accomplishments that made her feel ridiculously small and under-schooled and impatient to catch up. She was anxious too about her procrastination of the assignment due in just a few days.

"Consider this your magnum opus," Mr. Otto had weeks ago told Angie's class, referring to the eleventh-grade English requirement to write an autobiography. The meeting of his bushy eyebrows signaled his uncompromising seriousness, which required Angie to hide her eye-roll behind her book. When Mr. Otto caught an eye-roll or a smirk from one of his students, his hurt was so apparent it made them all squirm. It seemed that a grown-up should be able to suffer adolescent eye-rolls with greater self-possession. If Angie had any goal in life, it was that.

When she thought of her life thus far, the last thing Angie wanted to do was commit it to paper for Mr. Otto to read and grade. What experiences worthy of inclusion in a form as self-important as autobiography did a sixteen-year-old in Kimball Park have? Especially the sixteen-year-old that was her—Angie Rubio. It's not as if she hadn't tried to have experiences. They just seemed elusive or inconclusive. And now she was expected to package them in a neatly inked, three-hole-punched narrative. She wondered now if she was meant to include something about Blue Boy in her autobiography, with whom, at the moment, she was utterly baffled.

Nudged aside by the newcomers, she studied the painting from the periphery. It was European, so it was supposed to be important. She looked at the question on the mimeographed sheet Mr. Otto had passed out on the bus. "What can you say about the light and color in Gainsborough's most famous painting?"

She stood like a spy off to the side of the knot of people and listened to them murmur about the painting in knowing, assertive terms which wrapped themselves around the nib of her pen as she scribbled in her notebook. "The background is dark except for the patches of yellow at his back so that the blue boy appears to emerge from the painting with wings. The different hues of blue give the richness to his clothes. The light on his forehead and cheek warm the sullen mouth."

It didn't matter that the words weren't exactly hers. She believed she might have been thinking them. They were just buried deep inside her or floating around in a random sea of inklings and ideas that were waiting to coalesce. She wandered past other paintings, her eye registering them only fleetingly, her mind still occupied with the color blue, with the seemingly winged boy, with the push and pull of dark and light, near and far, balance and asymmetry, and with the looming deadline for her autobiography. She settled herself on a hard, low bench and scribbled and scratched out and scribbled again until she was satisfied that, among the blots and do-overs, there were sentences that combined to make sense, maybe even a story.

Blue

The summer I turned five I watched my father remove the training wheels from my bike, thinking how forlorn they looked tossed on the grass. I straddled the bike, my feet planted on the sidewalk. My father held the bike while I moved my feet to the pedals and lifted my bottom onto the seat. I was balanced only because of my father's grasp.

"Pedal," he said.

I pedaled and the bike wobbled.

I remember my father's hand on the back of my

*bike seat, a cigarette in his other hand. His sandals
thwacked the sidewalk as he jogged alongside me,
the bike still wobbling. I knew he would let go and I
waited for it, waited for the fall. I didn't expect that
tiny moment when I was balanced on my own and I
felt something close to flight, but also abandonment.*

*When I crashed to the earth and lay on my back,
my head just scraping the trunk of a tree, I listened
to the wheels of my bike spin on their own, humming
without a care. I stared at the blank, blue sky, then
watched a bruise blot my elbow. My father came and
picked my bike up and held it for me again. Sullen, I
picked myself up and pretended to limp. He pretended
not to notice. This time I pedaled hard and away from
him—for just a moment longer than the last time.*

When the students had been asked to raise money for
their trip to L.A. by selling chocolates, they groaned at the
intrusion on their time. Angie hated selling things, though
she did manage to coax Nelda into buying most of her allotted
inventory for her clients. Nelda had found her calling as a
real estate agent and her sudden and undisputed success had
allowed her and Little Eddie to move to a charming house
near the beach within bicycling distance to a private school.

Angie's trip to L.A. was measly compared to the trips Little
Eddie took with his class (botany tours on the Baja Peninsula,
Broadway samplers in New York City, New Orleans blues
festivals) which didn't require selling boxes of mixed chocolates
with gooey insides when most people preferred nuts.

When the class failed to sell the requisite number of
chocolates, putting the trip in jeopardy, jelly-hearted Mr.
Otto came through with his personal funds to make up

for the students' shortfall. Although his generosity was met without overt graciousness, Angie for one, was grateful, if also embarrassed at Mr. Otto's softness for his students, his weak desire to give them something they hadn't entirely earned.

The Huntington was the third stop on their tour that first day. They had begun with the Farmer's Market and its famous clock tower inscribed with "An Idea," under which they took turns posing for photographs. Angie was the last to take her place under the sign, by which time everyone else was wandering off to another part of the market. She was embarrassed when Mr. Otto offered to snap the photo. She handed over her camera and stood pigeon-toed, one hand clasping an elbow behind her back, looking past Mr. Otto's ear, not wanting to look directly into the camera, but also hoping to achieve a faraway look suitable to the caption that would appear above her head. After Mr. Otto clicked the shutter, she mumbled a thanks and took back her camera, trying not to make contact with his furry hand.

Then came a quick visit to Grauman's Chinese Theater where they measured their feet against those of Elizabeth Taylor and Rock Hudson. The students briefly acknowledged the authentic Ming Dynasty Heaven Dogs guarding the main entrance, only because they were the subject of the question on Mr. Otto's History and Culture of L.A. worksheet.

After the students completed their worksheets of the Huntington art gallery, they scattered like marbles through the various gardens on the property. They played a rowdy game of hide-and-seek, concealing themselves in or behind trees, statuary, or copious-leaved shrubs. Angie had not been invited to play and so walked the gardens alone as squeals of discovery burst alongside a path or in the distance across a bridge or a pond. It was time to get back to the bus, but

Angie, seeing no-one else heading in the direction of the parking lot, continued to stroll the manicured paths. Her last sighting of a chaperone was of Mrs. Wiekamp in the gift shop being rung up for items that Judy had plonked on the counter. Before that, she'd seen Mr. Otto heading into a men's room. She'd last observed the other chaperone staring into the depths of a gargantuan tropical plant. It was *Ms.* Otto, Mr. Otto's sister. She insisted on Ms. rather than Miss, which made the students snigger at the made-up word. Even Angie, who believed in the reason behind the new abbreviation, felt unsure at the sound that came from the back of her throat, a deep hum that itself felt rebellious. Of course, Mr. Otto called her Bernadette. She called him Billy.

Angie was in the Shakespeare Garden at the pomegranate tree from *Romeo and Juliet*, whose lines she could still recite from ninth-grade English when she saw Mr. Otto darting down the path toward her. Even from a distance she could see the pitch of his eyebrows making a steep climb toward his hairline. He was like the White Rabbit, checking the time and muttering, *Oh, dear.*

"Angie, where are the others?" he asked, panting. She could tell he was working hard to contain his irritation. She wished he would just explode in anger. Sometimes she feared for his heart. Feared the mess that would result from his ruptured insides.

"I don't know," Angie said. "All around."

Just then Ms. Otto strode up. She was robustly built like him but imposing not so much for her size but for her no-nonsense manner, which contrasted with her brother's shy dithering. Lacking enough parent volunteers, Mr. Otto had recruited her to help shepherd the students from place to place and to keep them out of mischief, which she did by appearing suddenly out of nowhere to gesture them back to the fold or send a searing glance into their midst or lasso them with a whistle, which she did now by putting two fingers to her mouth and piercing the air.

"Really, Bernadette," Mr. Otto said.

A moment later Angie's classmates began materializing on the paths that intersected with the one where Angie stood with Bernadette and Billy Otto. The Ottos herded them all back to the bus, its engine idling with Judy and Mrs. Wiekamp and Silvia Rico already aboard with packages on their laps.

"Goodness, we thought we'd lost you all," Mrs. Wiekamp said.

When they were settled in their seats, Mr. Otto remained standing as the bus made its way through the parking lot. His face was grim, his hair wild from all his herding and scurrying and stumbling. They waited for his lecture, a proper dressing-down. They watched his mouth open and snap closed. They listened to him sigh as he surrendered to their stares and sat down without a word.

* * *

They ate at Bob's Big Boy for dinner. When their stomachs were heavy with fried and creamy foods and hunks of pie for dessert, they checked into a motel where they split into pre-arranged groups for room sharing.

While Angie hadn't necessarily looked forward to sharing a hotel room with Judy, Silvia, and Judy's mother, she had convinced herself that it would be an opportunity to reestablish if not a friendship, perhaps a comradeship. At least goodwill. Or what she really wanted—acceptance. But when Angie lined up behind Judy and Silvia as Mrs. Wiekamp fitted the key into the lock, Ms. Otto popped her head out of the room next door. "Say, I have an empty bed in here. Send one of your girls over so you're not so crowded in there."

Angie waited for Mrs. Wiekamp or even Judy or Silvia to say *four in a room was not a crowd, they were just fine, thank you.* But Mrs. Wiekamp, having finally jiggled the key enough to unlock the door, called out, "Thank you, Bernadette!" and went inside, followed by Judy and Silvia and the closing of the door.

Angie picked up her overnight bag and shuffled next door. She stood at the doorway, not knowing where to put her bag, wondering if she should claim a bed. Ms. Otto had disappeared inside the bathroom, so Angie waited through the noisy swivel of the toilet paper dispenser, the flush of the toilet, and the running of the faucet. When the bathroom door opened and Ms. Otto emerged, Angie studiously absorbed herself in the watercolor on one of the walls.

"What do you think?" Ms. Otto asked.

"Oh, the painting?" Angie said, feeling stupid at having been caught pretending interest in motel art. "Well, it's not Gainsborough."

Ms. Otto hooted. "Pick your bed."

Angie dropped her bag on the one nearest her, though she would've preferred the one nearest the bathroom.

"Well, I'm going to read before lights out. You're welcome to the TV. It won't bother me." She stretched out on the other bed and rested a fat book on her stomach, which rose with each breath just audible above the street noise.

Angie didn't want to watch TV with Ms. Otto in the room reading some important book. Anyway, she needed to work on her autobiography. She sat at the little table under the big globe of light that hung on a chain from the ceiling like a misplaced moon. Unsettled by the idea of "lights out," she wished she could let it shine through the night, imagining that somehow Ms. Otto would be able to discern her thoughts in the dark, see through the black curtain of her dreams and find them lacking. The way she herself found her words lacking as she intermittently and with great effort scratched some onto the page. Through her start-and-stop scribble she heard the occasional turn of the page by Ms. Otto's index finger. The anticipation of that soft flick stalled her thoughts, so that amid the many inked-out lines, only a few survived intact.

Black

At my First Communion party, I received a child's prayer book, a scapular, and a rosary. I used these piously for a while, the way I was taught by the nuns in their black, floor-skimming robes. I went to confession regularly, the way I was made to, in that airless, darkened closet. I recited my penance and fasted before communion, my hunger a perfect, round pit. But I told nobody about the giant black hole that was opening up between what I said and did, and what I actually and truly believed.

At ten, Ms. Otto took her tall, large-boned self to do a bed-check of the other rooms. *As if that would guarantee anything,* Angie thought. She wondered what the other kids had been doing in their motel rooms—watching TV, telling dirty jokes, sneaking a beer or a joint, carving their names on the underside of the table, already stuffing the tiny shampoo bottles in their luggage. Whatever they were doing, they would continue to do after Ms. Otto's curfew check.

With Ms. Otto out of the room, Angie peed, changed into her pajamas, and brushed her teeth, skimping a bit on her molars in her hurry to finish her personal hygiene while she was alone. By the time she heard the key in the door, she was in bed with the covers up to her ears pretending to be asleep. It would've been too embarrassing to exchange goodnights with Bernadette, which is how Angie had given herself permission to refer to her roommate.

The next morning, while Bernadette tidied her side of the room and hummed "Do You Know the Way to San Jose," Angie dressed in the bathroom. Angie's mother had bought her some new outfits for the trip. They were ill-fitting as were most clothes Angie wore, sagging off her shoulders, bagging around her waist, drooping at the crotch. And while not exactly ugly, neither were they mod or hip or cool. Angie knew her mother meant well and she did appreciate the gesture, but her mother's taste in clothes was not her own, though she had yet to determine what her own taste was. She only knew it did not include striped pantsuits. Nevertheless, they were folded neatly in her overnight bag. Her mother had laid them out on Angie's bed the night before the trip and Angie had packed them, liking the idea of new clothes to match the new vistas Mr. Otto promised awaited them on this trip.

In a sudden fit of optimism about the day, Angie had decided to wear one of the pantsuits. She chose the navy blue with red pinstripes. The pants were loose at the waist and slack in the butt, but not excessively so. The jacket covered or at least camouflaged a bit the failings of the pants. Or was it the failings of her butt? Either way, Angie thought she had adequately addressed the hitch in her wardrobe. She raised herself on her tiptoes to try to see the full effect of her outfit in the mirror above the sink. Navy-Blue Girl, she pronounced herself. With red pinstripes, she added, as she offered the mirror a sullen smile.

"That's a very fine ensemble," Bernadette commented when Angie came out of the bathroom.

"My mother bought it," Angie said, wanting to dissociate herself from any responsibility. Even with the few steps she had taken across the bathroom threshold, Angie felt the roominess of her pants at her waist and her bottom. Loose was better than tight, she assured herself. Though she did have to wonder why pants didn't exist that fit her just right.

"Well, ready for another big day in the big city?"

Angie nodded, hoping it *would* be a big day, mind-blowing and revelatory even. She followed Bernadette out of the room, feeling the slouch of her pants with each step.

The problem with not being in a room with any of the other students, aside from the obvious one of being left out of any unchaperoned shenanigans, was Angie couldn't see what the other kids were wearing. Now as they gathered for breakfast at the nearest Bob's Big Boy, she could see that with the exception of Judy and Silvia, all the other kids were casually dressed, not even school-clothes casual, but play casual. Nobody else was wearing an ensemble. Judy and Silvia were wearing A-line shifts and lightweight cardigans. Angie hung back so as not to be noticed. She realized she would have gone unnoticed had she worn something they'd all seen before. Sure, they would've seen her. They just wouldn't have noticed her the way they did now with smirks and sidelong glances. She was glad when they were all seated in the restaurant and most of her was hidden by the table. She wished she could sit there all day, except that she found herself sitting next to Bernadette as if they had overnight formed a club of two.

"Well, Angie, you were quite industrious last evening."

"Yes," Angie answered. She could not let on to her teacher's sister that she was furiously trying to finish a class assignment.

She put a forkful of scrambled egg in her mouth to discourage further expectations of conversation from her.

"And you make a very agreeable roommate."

Angie nodded. "You, too," she mumbled through a mouthful of egg.

* * *

On the bus Angie, still feeling conspicuous in her pantsuit, sat alone, though she wasn't the only one. Some of the kids who had stayed up late despite bed checks and lights-out curfew had eaten breakfast with their heads in their plates and were now spread across the bus seats catching some winks. Mr. Otto, his eyebrows in a panic, nevertheless pretended not to notice, while Bernadette every so often would exclaim in an operatic pitch at some landmark or attraction (look, another Bob's Big Boy!), startling them out of their snooze. They were headed to Occidental College for a tour. None of them had ever heard of it.

"Looks like a bunch of museum buildings," someone said when the bus pulled up.

Mr. Otto stood at the front of the bus. "You'll be applying to college soon. Think about what you want in a college experience. Here's your chance to ask questions."

"Where's the bathroom?" someone asked, inducing guffaws from the bus and a pained what's-the-use shrug from Mr. Otto.

Really, what's the use, Angie thought. Most kids at their school who went to college ended up at the local state or junior colleges. This college was a million miles away.

Mr. Otto had them count off into two groups for the campus tour. There would be no freely roaming students here, no need for Bernadette to whistle them back, no need for Mr. Otto's face to bulge with suppressed fury. Before he released them to the tour guides, Mr. Otto warned them in his deep, beseeching baritone, "Remember who you are. Be good representatives of your school. Make your parents proud." He watched them file off the bus, his eyebrows slanted toward each other as if grasping for reassurance, his eyes bulging with hope and encouragement at the students who slid past him, indifferent to his clenched face. Angie found herself mincing her steps to minimize the distraction of her waistband that hovered rather nonchalantly above her nearly nonexistent hips.

Mr. Otto trailed one group and Bernadette trailed the other, which was Angie's group. Despite the discomfort caused by her outfit and the snickering that followed her, Angie moved to the front of the line where Judy Wiekamp and her mother were already swamping the guide with questions while managing to insert casual mentions of Judy's GPA, extracurricular activities, and leadership potential.

Jessica, the guide and herself a student, bobbed her blond head and smiled, her teeth a perfect complement to the gleaming white buildings of the campus.

Angie wanted to casually drop her own GPA into the conversation, though any references to her extracurricular activities would consist of her attempts at figuring out how to have extracurricular activities. As for leadership potential, she could always claim to be a leader in the follower department. Though when it came down to it, she was rather bad at following as well. She was a drifter, she decided. Like tumbleweeds or dandruff. Propelled by wind or gravity, or someone else's momentum.

They visited the library, a dorm, the commons, and an empty classroom where they were invited to have a seat. Angie slid into one of the chairs, thankful for a moment to partially conceal herself and her pantsuit beneath the desk. She tried to imagine herself studying here in one of these gleaming buildings amid gleaming students like Jessica.

Bernadette sat down beside her. "Does it feel like a fit?"

Angie straightened, then slumped, then straightened again, her pants sliding around her waist as she did so. "It's just a chair."

"True."

"I mean, all colleges have chairs."

"True again."

"Bernadette," Angie said, and then blushed. "Ms. Otto," she began again, "which college did you go to?"

"Wellesley. In Boston. A women's college."

Angie nodded at these three facts as if they meant something to her, though, really, they were as familiar to her as the white porticoed buildings with red tiled roofs that surrounded them, the kind seen on picture calendars of the Italian Riviera.

The tour guide was leading them out of the room. Angie waited until the others left, then hitched up her pants and drifted after them, turning back once to look at the empty seats, trying to imagine herself there, a college student amid other college students, but the empty seats refused to be populated.

The two groups reconvened at the bus, and while there were no stray students to round up, even the orderly arrangement of the tour took its toll on Mr. Otto, who seemed ready at any moment for a rubber snake to detonate from the bushes or a dead bird to drop from the sky, or a furry, brown tarantula to crawl out of his shirt collar.

* * *

On the bus, Angie stripped off her jacket, freeing herself from her ensemble. She whipped out her notebook and scrawled another installment of her autobiography.

Brown

In the third grade, I was one of three brown
children in my school. The other two were my sisters.
Phonics lessons and storybooks reminded everyone that
brown is an animal.

How now, brown cow.

The quick, brown fox jumps over the lazy dog.

The little brown monkey—the story of a monkey
and his jungle friends.

These lessons found their way to the playground
where they were chanted on the swings and jungle gym
and accompanied by Tarzan yells on the monkey bars.
They fired up my limbs. I outlasted every kid on the
monkey bars. Outlasted my own blisters and stretched-
to-the-limit armpits.

* * *

In the afternoon, they visited Griffith Observatory, where it was not possible to traipse through the exhibits in a large group and Mr. Otto had to resign himself to allowing the students to scatter like billiard balls. "You have ninety minutes. Use them well. Ten questions on your work sheet pertain to the exhibits here," Mr. Otto said. "And remember, the chaperones will be circulating."

Everyone went off in small groups or pairs, but Angie no longer cared that she was alone. Jacketless, she felt some relief that she no longer resembled a flag or holiday decoration or a giant roll of wrapping paper.

She went off in search of illumination. Angie's mind had always resisted science, especially things like astronomy and chemistry, things that dealt with the invisible because they were either too small or too far away, things that involved sizes or distances or numbers of multiple zeroes that were hard to fathom, things that required either a scientific brain or great leaps of trust.

Angie watched the mesmerizing swing of the Foucault pendulum. What does it demonstrate, asked Mr. Otto's worksheet. The rotation of the earth, wrote Angie and she spun off like a minor planet to the next display, bumping as she did so into Bernadette.

"Sorry," Angie mumbled.

"Hey, we're cool," Bernadette said, sidestepping Angie to trail after some other students.

"You wish," Angie said under her breath as she headed to the Hall of the Sky.

Angie answered questions on her sheet about day and night, the paths of the sun and the stars, the phases of the moon, tides, and eclipses. The room was dark and even though it was crowded, there still seemed to be a hush all around as if everyone were awed by the universe.

She finished her worksheet and wandered into the gift shop where a number of other students were already browsing the key chains, snow globes, and mugs. Mrs. Wiekamp and Judy were there, their hands full of souvenirs. Silvia was rotating a rack of key chains engraved with names. "Here's your name," Judy said.

"Yeah," Silvia said, "but that's not how I spell my name."

"It's the American spelling," Mrs. Wiekamp said. "Well, English," she amended. "Oh, but that shouldn't matter. Here, let me buy that for you."

Angie found her name on the rack exactly the way she spelled it. After she paid for it, Mrs. Wiekamp drew her aside and whispered, "Angie, dear, here's a little safety pin to help keep your pants in place."

Mrs. Wiekamp slipped the safety pin into Angie's hand, a move at once secretive and blatant. It was also, she understood, a move a mother would make, and Angie clasped the pin in her palm and hurried off to the ladies' room. Safely within a stall, Angie dabbed behind her glasses with a wad of toilet paper and took a deep breath. When she exhaled, her pants sagged. She pinched the waistband at her navel and fastened it with the safety pin. It made a slight knob beneath her shirt, but at least her pants felt more secure.

Even though the ill-fitting pants came from her mother, Angie for a moment missed her mother. Angie's mother would never chaperone a school trip, especially one that was out of town and lasted an entire weekend. Not that Angie wanted her mother to be a chaperone. Angie knew her mother would've felt as out of place as she herself usually did. She wondered what her mother would've thought of Blue Boy or a college that looked like a museum, or an observatory that struck you silent with wonder, or another student's mother who rescued you with a safety pin.

Angie went outside and sat facing the Hollywood sign. Then she changed her mind and relocated to a view of the Pacific Ocean. The glare of day made her eyes smart after the dark interior of the observatory exhibits. She had felt the majesty of the cosmos, the smallness of her place in it. Now, looking at the ocean, its blue vastness seemed less daunting. She stared, unblinking, at the horizon. Then she squeezed shut her eyes and opened them to see orange starbursts bounce upon the water. When the effect subsided, she could see Bernadette motioning at her to board the bus.

That evening after another dinner at Bob's Big Boy, they all retired to their motel rooms worn out from two days of sightseeing and traffic in L.A. Hijinks were at a minimum. Even indefatigable Bernadette was showing signs of wear and tear, her shoulders a little less square, her jaw less rigid. Angie changed into her pajamas early, anxious to shed her safety-pinned pants, which she rolled up and shoved into her overnight bag.

"Maybe a little TV tonight, Angie?" Bernadette asked.

"If you want," Angie said, getting her notebook out. "I'm going to work on something."

"Your autobiography?"

Angie stopped turning pages. "Um."

"Billy told me about the assignment. I'm sure you're not the only one scrambling to finish up."

Anytime Bernadette referred to Mr. Otto as Billy, Angie wanted to both laugh out loud and cover her ears.

"I think it's a stupid assignment," Angie said.

"You don't think it's valuable to review your life experiences?"

"We're teenagers," Angie said.

"I'm sure you have something to say."

"I'm looking deep in my soul,"

"That a girl."

Angie squeezed her eyes shut as she had earlier that afternoon when she had detonated tiny orange explosions through her eyelids.

Orange

*Fourth grade was the year of my orthodontia. I wore
headgear at night which made me scary to look at. Yet, I
was drawn to mirrors, fascinated by my scary self.*

*I got food stuck in my braces. The tiny rubber
bands I had to wear in my mouth sometimes came
loose and shot out from my teeth or else were sucked to
the back of my tongue on an inhale. Kids teased me.
My parents just told me to ignore them. That really
solved the problem.*

*For Halloween, I chose a tiger outfit that came
with an orange-and-black-striped mask. The eyes were
green, which I liked, even though my ordinary brown
eyes were visible through the cut-outs. Long black
whiskers were painted on either side of the mouth
which was wide with bared fangs and a menacing
tongue. I took some scissors and punctured the plastic
and traced around the inner border of the gaping
mouth until the teeth and tongue of the tiger were
completely cut away. When I put the mask on, my own
mouth with its disorderly row of silver-bound teeth
was visible in all its exquisite awfulness.*

* * *

Breakfast had to be rushed. It was their last day in the City
of Angels and everyone had overslept. There had been a power
outage in the middle of the night and the clocks had stopped.
When the power was restored the clocks just blinked zeroes.
Mr. Otto was in a tizzy, and Angie watched Bernadette buck
him up with a firm slap between the shoulders. While Mrs.
Wiekamp rounded up kids and overnight bags for the waiting
bus, Mr. Otto and Bernadette went across the street to order

breakfast sandwiches at McDonald's. They returned with the goods just as everyone and everything had been loaded onto the bus and were welcomed with cheers. Mr. Otto beamed, and Angie had to admit that at such times, he did resemble a Billy.

They had one last attraction to visit before the ride home to Kimball Park and none of them except Judy Wiekamp had ever heard of it. It sounded vaguely gimmicky or like an ecological oddity: Forest Lawn. Did forests have lawns?

"It's a cemetery," Judy said. "Famous people are buried there."

"Like who?" Angie asked.

"Walt Disney, for one," Judy said.

"Sam Cooke," Bernadette said.

Angie looked at her. "Are we allowed to see their graves?"

"Graves are private things, not sight-seeing attractions," Mrs. Wiekamp said to Judy, though Angie knew the words were meant for her.

Mr. Otto shushed everyone to give them a rundown of the day's schedule. He had a piece of egg in the cleft of his chin, but before anyone could snigger or roll their eyes, Bernadette signaled to him and he took his handkerchief from his pocket and wiped his lower face, taking a swipe at his forehead while he was at it. He explained that because they were a bit behind schedule, they would have time to view only a few features of the park.

"Park?" someone asked. "Like where people have picnics?"

"I want to eat my lunch next to Walt Disney's grave."

Mr. Otto waved his hand as if their comments were flies. "We have just over an hour. The bus will make a tour of the grounds and we'll see some of the statuary, many of them replicas of Michelangelo's famous works. Then you'll have some time to visit the museum. This means you will not have to answer questions 47 through 50 on your work sheet. After our visit, we'll head back to Kimball Park and get you home to your parents."

There was such relief in his voice as he uttered the last sentence that the students booed and hissed without reservation. Their time out of the classroom had emboldened them all weekend. Even Angie voiced aloud a testiness that had been accumulating like an extra layer of skin. "Never thought I'd look forward to that," she said, just as the boos subsided so that her remark echoed in the vacuum.

The boos had been a chorus, while Angie's remark had been a solo and Mr. Otto trained his disappointment on her. She met his eyes for just a moment before she turned away to look out the window. A docent boarded their bus, which then began to roll slowly through the grounds. The docent was a pant-suited lady with expensive, beauty-shop hair, and a telephone operator voice. She pointed out the sights with choreographed gestures of jeweled hands and rouged face. They looked out their windows bored and listless, too tired even to snicker or snort or yawn. For her part, Angie knew she was forever through with pant suits.

Angie was also tired of seeing art. There was something antiseptic and bland about the place, this intrusion on the dead, as if the whole place, the sweeping lawns, the copycat statues, the elaborate fountains, and the ornate architecture were Disneyland without the rides.

When they pulled up to the museum, the docent thanked them for their attention and with a crisp wave was off the bus. Mr. Otto stood up and loomed extra-large as he grabbed the ledges of the overhead storage racks and lifted himself onto his toes. His eyes reached everywhere, seeking each of them out to place blame.

Because they had limited time and because Mr. Otto did not want to spend time chasing down straying students, they were parceled out to one of the three chaperones. They descended upon each exhibit in tight knots, with the chaperons guarding the rear like herding sheepdogs. Angie more than once wanted to make a break for it. Dressed today in denim pants and the same white shirt she wore yesterday, Angie felt less inhibited than she had all weekend. She also felt as if their weekend of cultural and historical enlightenment was coming to a close without offering much closure in the way of revelation. Wasn't this supposed to be a game-changer, an eye-opener, a soul-barer?

In the museum they dragged their feet, their scuffling reverberating in the zigzag of the galleries. They openly shared answers among themselves to the worksheet questions, even though many were deliberately wrong and full of sarcasm. They'd had enough art. They wanted low-brow: comic books, gossip magazines, celebrity graves.

By this time, Angie was fed up with the worksheet. She knew that Mr. Otto would collect them once they were on the bus. She felt her answers to all the other questions had been thoughtful and well-articulated. Whatever points she lost on this assignment, surely, she could make up with her autobiography which was coming along slowly but surely and with great conviction.

When they had finished viewing the museum art that had begun to look like all the other art they'd seen that weekend, there were still twenty minutes before departure time and the end of the bus driver's required break.

"Would this be a good time to visit the gift shop?" Mrs. Wiekamp asked.

Mr. Otto's eyebrows vetoed the suggestion, but his shoulders surrendered to Mrs. Wiekamp's promise that she would supervise five students at a time, with the others lining up outside to rotate in at five-minute intervals.

"We'll see you in twenty minutes and no later," Mrs. Wiekamp said, crossing her heart.

Angie followed a dozen or so other students behind Mrs. Wiekamp. She wasn't particularly interested in seeing another gift ship. What could they possible sell at a cemetery gift shop? But she was antsy to see something remarkable at this final stop of their weekend in L.A. and the gift shop was the last hope.

Angie waited impatiently outside the shop with a half dozen other antsy students until Mrs. Wiekamp could rotate them in. When ten minutes had passed without any action, Angie began tapping her foot and checking her watch, the second hand sweeping away precious seconds that could be spent browsing key chains, magnets, and coffee mugs emblazoned with the Forest Lawn logo. Not that she wanted any of those things. She was hoping for some unexpected little find that would serve as a memento of the trip, something meaningful and profound.

Angie decided she would go in and politely remind Mrs. Wiekamp that there were students waiting their turn for the gift shop and time was running out. She failed to explain her intent to the others, who upon seeing her jump the line, were incited to defy the rotation rule and pushed their way into the narrow shop congested with goods and now with themselves. There was so little room to maneuver that elbows and shoulders began to clash with the metal, plastic, and glass souvenirs producing not so much a noisy jangle as an inharmonious vibration that could only signal collapse. Mrs. Wiekamp, who was with the cashier, had not yet noticed the swell of students in the shop, despite being jostled as she pulled out bills from her purse to pay for a bag load of merchandise. Angie, confined to one spot by the customer overflow, busied herself by shaking the snow domes on the shelf in front of her until inside each one, glitter floated over miniature statuary and graves. Perhaps she would buy one. Perhaps this would be her souvenir from the cultural awareness weekend.

But just then Mrs. Wiekamp turned around and gasped at the sight of unauthorized students in the gift shop. She started trying to herd the students closest to her toward the exit, but some of those were among the newcomers and resisted her corralling gestures. Anyway, there was so little room to move, bodies seemed only to rebound off each other, especially since there was a counterforce coming from the door. Mr. Otto, red-faced and sweaty-haired, had somehow wedged himself inside. He opened his mouth and as he shouted Mrs. Wiekamp's name his voice shook as he was jostled by gift shop customers attempting either escape or a stubborn insistence on a souvenir.

"I'm doing my best, Mr. Otto," Mrs. Wiekamp called back, gathering her packages and positioning Judy and Silvia ahead of her like shields, trying to prod them forward through the congested aisle, but making little headway.

"Mr. Otto, maybe if you moved away from the door, we could all get out a little faster."

The students' eyes moved from Mrs. Wiekamp's flushed cheeks and fluttering eyelids to Mr. Otto's winched eyebrows. Even the non-students paused in their souvenir-searching, aware of something on the verge of escalation. It was a stand-off between the career PTA president, a woman who looked like the Brady Bunch mom, and the wild-eyed teacher with caterpillar brows where all his frustrations were stored.

Angie realized that this is what they had been waiting for all weekend. They had, purposefully or not, pushed Mr. Otto to the brink and now they would all have to witness the mess. Unless someone stopped them. Angie looked around, but no one seemed inclined to intervene. All that was needed was for someone to say something, anything, to stop Mr. Otto's visibly expanding forehead from bursting. But Angie was not a shouter. She closed her eyes the way she did at the movies when she refused to watch the scary parts. She could sense the tension in the air, the leaning of torsos and craning of necks, the raising on tiptoe of the people around her. She opened her eyes. The scary part wouldn't happen without her, she realized. *She* was the scary part. She picked up one of the snow globes on the shelf next to her, shook it furiously and set it back down. She watched the chaos of the miniature snowstorm and when the snow had settled, she pushed a line of snow globes off the display to bounce off the backs and rear ends of those standing nearby before they clattered to the floor.

Heads turned in Angie's direction where people started to move away to distance themselves from blame. A security guard suddenly appeared and began dispersing the crowd, exposing the fallen snow globes, some dented, a few shattered, near Angie's feet. Mrs. Wiekamp, having recovered from her temporary discombobulation, was sending commands with her eyes to any students still remaining in the shop, but her eyes skipped over Angie. From outside came the screech of Bernadette's whistle. As the others exited, Angie bent down to gather the wreckage. She was interrupted by one of the shop employees who arrived with a broom and dustpan. Rendered useless, Angie rose to face Mr. Otto or at least his shirt pocket behind which she imagined his heart thumping angrily. She looked up expecting to see his eyebrows pushed as far as his receding hairline, but they were resting caterpillars, and his eyes were calm, his shoulders unhunched.

"Sorry," Angie said.

Mr. Otto nodded. "Go get on the bus, Angie," he said.

As she left, she knew he was pulling out his wallet to cover the damages. Whatever they were, she knew they would have been greater had Mr. Otto gone berserk in the gift shop. Angie had saved him. Was it apparent to no one but her?

Bernadette was standing at the front of the bus doing a head count when Angie boarded.

The ride home was quiet. For a while, Angie stared out the window at the homes and businesses pushed up against the sides of the freeway, but her thoughts were still back at the cemetery, its rolling green hills, the dust and bones of rich and famous people beneath them, and nimble statuary, flowing fountains, and souvenir shops above them. Eventually, Angie took out her notebook. She was still pages away from a complete rendering of her life.

Green

The Sound of Music *came out the year I was in seventh grade. My sister Eva and I saw the movie approximately a zillion times. Those green hills, alive with the sound of Julie Andrews, beckoned to us. We wanted to spread our arms and sing above Salzburg. We imagined ourselves as one of the Von Trapp children with fake English accents despite being Austrian. We longed for a plucky, never-to-be-a-nun governess to rescue our family from estrangement. We listened to the soundtrack over and over, memorized the songs, and recited the movie dialogue which had implanted itself*

*into our voice boxes. We fell in love with Julie Andrews,
her bobbed hair, her long nose, her slightly bowed
legs—always with the green hills in the background.
We wished for soprano voices. To be named Maria. Or
maybe to be the subject of a song. "How Do You Solve
a Problem Like Angie?" And like in the song, Angie is
not really a problem. She's just Angie.*

* * *

When her parents asked her how her weekend in L.A.
went, she answered fine.

"Did you wear the new pantsuits?" her mother asked.

"Take any pictures?" her father asked.

"Buy any souvenirs?" Eva asked.

"Yes," she snapped, excusing herself to unpack.

The next day at school, it was business as usual in Mr.
Otto's class. No debriefing of the trip, not a single reference.
He allowed them class time to put the finishing touches on
their autobiographies, which were due in two days. He sat
at his desk bent over some papers, his wild shock of hair
suddenly grayer than the previous week. Even though it was a
long time off, Angie didn't want to grow old.

Gray

*Gray is the color of my life now. Gray like the color
of the lockers in the hallways. Even the slamming
of the metal doors during passing periods has a gray
sound, sort of drab and indifferent. Books and papers
and lunches are stored in lockers. Other things, too.
Makeup (not in mine). Drugs (not in mine). A poem
(not in mine anymore). I wrote it in chemistry class*

*while Mr. Dembrowski was prattling away about
metals and noble gases, inserting jokes about the
periodic table of elephants.*

*I'm not a poet and don't aspire to be one.
Nevertheless, I wrote a poem. And despite my lack of
poetic sensibility, I believe the poem I wrote, this one
and only poem I will ever write in my life, was a good
one. It had molecules and atoms in it. Atomic weight
and bonds. It had metaphorical heft. It had a punch
line, not like a joke that made you laugh, but a line
that knocked the breath out of you because it was so
true, and it was the kind of truth that could only be
said in figurative language.*

*But in that long, gray hallway of lockers, someone
spun the combination on mine and, along with
some loose change and my page of conjugations of the
Spanish verb "to be," took my poem. My words. Me.*

Angie worked steadily in class, looping sentences across the
lines, slowly filling a sheet, front and back, but when the bell
rang, she was still pages away from finishing. For the first time,
she felt a twinge of panic at the possibility of not meeting a
homework deadline. Judy Wiekamp, who had assumed the
role of homework hostage negotiator, had already asked on
behalf of the class for an extension, assuring Mr. Otto that
better quality work would be delivered safely into his hands if
only he would give in to this one request. But after the L.A.
weekend, Mr. Otto seemed determined not to cave—not to
wheedling, complaint, or even bogus negotiation. Secretly,
Angie thought Mr. Otto owed her for preventing him from
a cataclysmic tantrum at the Forest Lawn gift shop. Secretly,
she thought he should grant her special dispensation. But she
would not ask.

The next day she claimed a sore throat and sat up in bed with pen and paper, once in a while remembering to cough loud enough for her mother to hear before she drove off to work. Angie worked all day and that night stayed up late to finish her opus. Her handwriting became larger and loopier. It slanted more steeply so that the last sentence practically collapsed on the standard-rule blue line. She fell asleep with the pen cradled in her hand. She dozed through her alarm and later watched through the kitchen window as her school bus drove away while she tossed dry cornflakes straight from the box into her mouth.

Angie had never turned in an assignment late for English class. She changed her clothes and put on sneakers and hoofed the two miles to school. She would be late for class, but she would arrive before it was over. She grew sweaty at the neck and armpits. A pebble found its way into one of her shoes, but she trudged on without stopping. Her bangs, damp and limp, clung to her forehead, but she did not push them to the side. When she got to campus, she walked the empty halls, the soles of her sneakers thumping softly. She was tired from the trek, from the lack of sleep, from thinking and writing about her life. She stumbled into the classroom, barely aware of her classmates, and offered her opus, her Blue Boy, with both hands to Mr. Otto. She saw the relief in his eyes as his burly, furry hands received it with fifteen minutes to spare before the end of class, for which he found it necessary to mark her tardy.

Most Likely to Succeed

Over the summer, as her family began to unravel at the seams, Angie had kept two words close to her like cards up her sleeve or buffalo nickels in her pocket— "provocative" and "bold." She had decided to become these things.

She arrived at school early one morning at the beginning of her senior year, hoping to catch Mr. Otto alone in the journalism room. Angie had never taken any of the journalism classes whose students produced the school newspaper. The paper had always been the province of the popular kids. Besides, she hadn't wanted to do profiles of cheerleaders, homecoming queens, or football heroes. She hadn't wanted to do feature stories on students' cars or whether clogs were appropriate footwear for school. Which is why she was seeking to put forth her proposal to Mr. Otto.

He was sitting at his desk with a pile of typewritten sheets in front of him. That was another reason Angie had avoided journalism class. In direct rebellion to her mother's decree that every girl should know how to type, Angie had each semester since seventh grade refused to sign up. Angie paused in the doorway when she noticed Judy was sitting at another teacher-sized desk, shuffling stacks of papers. Silvia was standing nearby as assistant shuffler.

"May I help you?" Judy asked.

"No, thanks," Angie said politely, reminding herself that polite and provocative were not mutually exclusive. "I actually have a question for Mr. Otto."

"Mr. Otto, Angie has a question for you," Judy announced as if heralding visitors were part of her job as newspaper editor.

Angie went to sit in a chair next to Mr. Otto's desk. He gave her his full attention, but so did Judy and Silvia, though they pretended to be occupied with their paper shuffling.

"I have an idea," Angie said. "A suggestion based on what you said about my autobiography last year." Angie's voice was at its usual small volume, but in the near empty classroom, her words might as well have been broadcast over the P.A. system.

"If it's about the newspaper, you can tell the editors," Judy called from her teacher desk.

"Go ahead," Mr. Otto said. "Whatcha got?" He lifted his bushy eyebrows in encouragement.

"Well, remember you said the approach to my autobiography was provocative?"

Angie waited for Mr. Otto to acknowledge with a nod that he had indeed used the word. Not exactly what he'd had in mind, he had said about her autobiography, but provocative, nonetheless. Bold, even. He'd given her an A minus.

Mr. Otto bent his head slightly as he inched his eyebrows closer together.

"Well," Angie continued, "my idea is to add a regular column, monthly maybe, to the paper about some topic that's, well, provocative." She was really becoming fond of the word.

"Provocative in what sense?" Judy asked. "I hope you don't mean X-rated. We have to abide by the journalistic standards for high school newspapers. All of our reporters are aware of that."

Angie decided to let that one pass—the jab at her not being a reporter. "I mean provocative in the sense of meaningful issues of the day. Civil rights, women's lib, the environment. But at a micro level—the school campus." Angie was pleased that the words fell so comfortably from her, as if they had been incubated and nurtured from a few stray notes to a full-throated melody.

"We already have a column like that. It's called Opinion. Besides this is the '70s. All the important stuff happened in the '60s," Judy said.

"What?" Angie said. "What?" she said again, unable to cough up more and better words. She turned to Mr. Otto, waited for him to correct Judy in her ignorance, her stupidity, her utter, utter witlessness.

But Mr. Otto merely said to Angie, "How would your pieces be different from the Opinion column?" His eyebrows twitched as if to shape a question mark.

While Angie tried to compose herself, she stared at a photo pinned to the bulletin board behind Mr. Otto's desk, recognition and curiosity distracting her for a moment from her mission.

Mr. Otto unpinned the photo and handed it to her. "You remember Bernadette?"

Of course, she remembered Bernadette. Who wouldn't remember Bernadette?

"Where is she? What's she doing there?"

"She's a magazine writer. She's on assignment. Somewhere in Ecuador, I think."

"Wow," Angie said, her scalp pricking with shame at never having asked or even wondered what Bernadette did for a living. And there she was amid the locals at an outdoor market, the cobbled streets, the colorful facades, a mountain in the distance. Angie marveled at the far-away-ness of it all, the possibilities of the world beyond Kimball Park.

"How would they be different, Angie?" Mr. Otto asked, taking back the photo, which Angie let go of with reluctance. "Your pieces?"

Angie wasn't exactly sure how they would be different. She just knew they would be. She bit her lip.

"Why don't you write something on spec. Show us what you mean. We'll see if we can use it. How does that sound?"

"Yes," added Judy, "we'll see if we can use it."

"Okay," Angie said. Her little two-syllable response had all the force of two decibels, well below the noise of shuffled papers.

She hadn't wanted to ask Mr. Otto what writing something *on spec* meant. Not in front of Judy and Silvia. After school, she stopped at Eva's apartment, a one-room unit in a shabby duplex not far from the Kimball Park shopping mall. Eva was saving her money for an apartment in a modern building with air conditioning and automatic dishwasher.

"So, how's senior year going?" Eva asked. Having ditched most of her senior year, she had given up on the notion of college, always emphasizing the word *notion* to underscore that it was a whim, a fancy, something not meant for the likes of them. "We're the worker class," she would say. "Someone has to drone. Someone has to cog."

"What does writing something on spec mean?" Angie asked.

"On speculation." Eva was changing out of her work clothes—dark slacks, button-up blouse, slip-on flats. Angie thought of the times she had watched Eva shed one or another costume—junior high pencil skirts and nylons, senior high A-lines and Peter pan collars, and now what amounted to funeral clothes.

"Which means what?"

"I thought you were the smart one."

Angie knew that Eva was really the smart one. Angie was the one silly enough to be believe that if she colored between the lines, she could make art, that if she got As, she would go to college.

"I'm speculating that..." Angie paused to allow Eva to fill in the blank.

"...whatever you write will be deemed worthy of being published," Eva obliged. "So, will it?"

Angie picked up the funeral slacks that had slipped off the chair. "Yes," she said. "It will."

*   *   *

The world at large was breaking apart, so why not her family. Diana Ross and the Supremes had performed together for the last time earlier that year, and Paul McCartney had announced his split from The Beatles not long after. Chet Huntley retired that summer and David Brinkley would report solo on the quagmire of Vietnam, riots in the streets and college campuses, and thermonuclear testing. Change— to put it mildly—was the name of the game. It was all around her. Yet she seemed to be spinning slowly like a Ferris wheel, stalling occasionally, rocking in the breeze and watching life go on in the distance. But things were also happening right under her nose.

Eva had dropped out of junior college to take a full-time office job. Letty was checking off a daring list of to-dos in preparation for the infamous sophomore year Sex Ed quiz. Anthony at age twelve had reached an improbable 6'2" and was busy learning to corral his limbs. He had outgrown his tantrums. The longer his bones had grown, the less able he seemed to sustain any intense emotion, though he did have a habit of silently expressing his displeasure at the world by offering his middle finger to the TV, his homework, the loud music from a passing low-rider outside while they ate dinner in silence. "That's enough of that," her parents would say each time, at first sternly, then resignedly, and finally absent-mindedly. "Well, at least he's not directing his finger at anyone," her mother said. "Right," said her father. "Just the world at large. I get that."

Angie's father had taken up and dropped one hobby after another, only to return to the TV—first the evening news and then a cop or western show. Angie always joined him for *High Chaparral* to inwardly sigh over Henry Darrow, who portrayed Manolito Montoya, a name Angie often murmured, enjoying how her lips squeezed together with the *m*'s and rounded multiple times with the *o*'s. Angie suspected her father had a crush on Linda Cristal who played the fiery and fiercely loyal Victoria Montoya Cannon who, given the option, would anachronistically decline a night of bowling to stay by her husband's side. Unlike Angie's mother, who had joined the bowling team at work.

Once, her father sent her to the bowling alley to make sure her mother had enough money to rent bowling shoes. Angie knew she was being sent on a bogus mission but dutifully spied on her mother from the far end of the bowling alley. Her mother was actually good, easily swinging the ball backward and hurling it forward to careen into the pins with an echoing rattle. She was with three other women, all in polyester slacks and blouses, coiffed hair, and lipstick. They squealed and jumped at the sound of a satisfying crash of pins and giggled at gutter balls. Angie watched her mother having fun and thought about her father at home. She walked over to her mother who looked at her with surprise and a little suspicion. Angie withdrew the ten dollars from her pocket. "Dad thought you might need a little extra spending money."

Her mother's friends smiled at her and Angie wondered if they suspected her secret mission, wondered if their husbands were scared that their wives were having fun without them, wondered if her mother was being bold and provocative with her bowling nights and her girlfriends and spending money, wondered why she'd never really noticed what her mother wanted. Or her father for that matter.

For once Angie was paying attention. How they all wanted—something.

*   *   *

There were three highlights of the year for seniors: homecoming and all the hoopla around crowning a queen and king; senior standout selections with all its superlative-laden titles (though Most Provocative was not among the categories, Angie resolved to vie for the title anyway); and prom with all its suspense over who would ask whom.

Angie could guess the kinds of stories that would be printed in the *Kimball High Clarion* about these events. They would be overstuffed with adjectives such as *fabulous*, *stylish*, and *groovy*, and studded with exclamation marks. Angie's stories, on the other hand, would provoke without look-at-me punctuation, without overworked popular expressions, and with blow-your-mind content.

Angie's first provocative piece appeared a week before homecoming.

*Homecoming. It's the first major happening of
the school year. It demands your attention, your
participation, and your school spirit! It comes with
plenty of exclamation points on posters and banners
that spirited students paint in spirit colors at spirit
parties. It involves football, cheerleaders, crowns and
sashes, bouquets of roses, borrowed Cadillacs, a semi-
formal dance in a balloon-and-crepe-paper decorated
gym and low lights for slow dancing and, if you're
smooth, some clandestine smokes and flasks. (Don't
tell the chaperones!) There's something in the air that
makes us giddy for this tradition. Tradition is sacred
and lofty and unbreakable. Unless, of course, it's not.
Tradition has history and permanence. But what if
that history is flawed or irrelevant to today's values.
What if the idea of a king and queen of homecoming
were seen as anachronistic, or even ridiculous?
Tradition comes from the word* trade *which means
to transmit or hand something over. So, what are
we handing over? Undeserved pomp and inflated
circumstance? And that homecoming theme? "Close to
You." Not at all sentimental. Just a sappy preview of
the nostalgia to come when we look back on these days
and wonder, what was that all about?*

In truth, Angie liked the song "Close to You," liked the
pining, hopeful vocals of Karen Carpenter, the electronic
yearning of Richard's keyboard. But it was the kind of thing
she kept to herself, like her crush on Manolito Montoya.

Mr. Otto asked if she was sure she wanted the piece to run,
but Judy Wiekamp lobbied ferociously for it. Later, when the
fallout rained down on Angie—when a sash with LOSER in
gold glitter was taped to her locker, when a whistled chorus of

"Close to You" followed her down the hall, when notes were passed to her in class that contained nothing but exclamation marks—Judy Wiekamp could be heard repeatedly in the hallways that, as editor, it was her job to ensure free speech, no matter how stupid. "It was Angie's idea to call them Provocative Pieces. Can you imagine? More like rants. Sore-loser rants. Just where does she get off calling a school tradition practiced all over the country, all over the world even (did you know they have homecoming in parts of Mongolia?) superficial?"

Whereas before, Angie had been a more or less anonymous outcast, she was now a notorious one, and she did not regret it—much. She met the looks of disdain with indifference. She ignored the remarks and asides in the hallways. *Wow, somebody's jealous. Commie! Women's libber!* When she got home, she cried in her room. It was a different kind of crying. A different kind of aloneness than she'd felt before. This was an aloneness she had created. A deliberate aloneness. One that felt right. Or was it righteous? She wasn't quite sure what exactly the word was.

When Letty complained to their mother that Angie was ruining her social life, Angie stood her ground.

"Why are you behaving like this?" her mother asked. "Do you want kids at school to dislike you?"

Angie excavated a line from her childhood, which sometimes seemed very far in the past and other times seemed as if it were a minute ago. "Popularity isn't everything."

She wondered if her mother remembered having said that. Words of wisdom that perhaps were not so much about wisdom but about resignation and acceptance.

Wanda and her gang tried to support her. They even agreed with her on the points she made about popularity, but they couldn't reconcile their love of spectacle with Angie's derision of a homecoming queen and princesses and their escorts and scepters and crowns all on display in convertibles that circled the football field.

"But Wanda," Angie reasoned, "remember how you felt about Miss America? How you thought the whole pageant was stupid? Remember?"

Wanda thought a moment. "Not exactly the same thing," she said.

"How not exactly?"

Wanda shrugged. "Just not. Besides, it's fun. Angie, lighten up. We're only young once."

Then Wanda and the others headed to the art room to make spirit banners.

At lunchtime, rather than hide her friendless self in the library, she sat by herself on the senior lawn, putting herself on display, a book open in front of her, a few lines of which she managed to read when she wasn't intent on whispering to herself, *Be bold, be heard, be provocative.* All the years behind her of her so-called education had just been the simmer before the boil, the taxiing before takeoff, the warm-up before the performance. Known all through her school life as a skinny, shy, small-voiced girl who was not very interesting, in her senior year of high school, Angie decided she would become a skinny, bold, provocative, loud-enough-to-be-heard girl.

And then. And then. And then. It was a stutter Angie could not get past, which was why she seldom said the word out loud. College. She wanted to go. Far away on the East Coast. She remembered Bernadette's college. She wanted that one. Wellesley. A women's college. She'd sent away for a brochure. It had photos of graceful brick and stone buildings amid woods and a lake. Young women bound for glory contemplatively strolled the grounds, studied in the vaulted-ceiling library, bonded with one another in the commons. She kept the brochure paper-clipped to the inside of her school notebook. Mooned over it as if it were a secret crush. As for boys, she had ceased having crushes on them. She was going to have a crush on life. And Manolito Montoya. That is, Henry Darrow. Him.

Angie made an appointment with her school counselor, a small man with black-rimmed glasses, a fine film of dark blond hair, and crowded little teeth. She sat in the straight-back wooden chair across from his desk, behind which he swiveled in a large chair, a fist propping his pessimistic chin.

"It's a long way to go for college," he told her.

Of course that was the point. To get away as far as she could. From this school, from this city, from this life.

"What do your parents think?"

Angie shrugged. She hadn't talked to them about it. She had come to him for answers. How does one go about getting into such a college, she wanted to ask him.

"What exactly would you like me to do?" he asked her.

Tell me what to do, she said to herself.

He looked at her, waiting. She waited back.

"There's a fine college close by and any number of community colleges. You don't have to leave your comfort zone."

Comfort zone? Where was that? Her life was a discomfort zone which she desperately wanted to escape.

"Okay, thanks," Angie said and left, having utterly failed at being provocative. Not once had he removed his fist from under his chin or ceased the quiet swiveling of his chair.

* * *

The isolation brought on by Angie's first provocative piece just made her more committed to writing her next one whose target was the Senior Favorites selection. She had to pull out her old biology notes for this one.

I have no real bone to pick about the categories: Best Looking, Best Dressed, Best Personality, Best Build and Shape, Prettiest Hair, Prettiest Eyes, Most Athletic, and Most Likely to Succeed. Well, hardly a bone to pick. Everyone has an opinion about such things anyway. Might as well certify them with a vote, a spread in the school newspaper, and a special page in the yearbook. Satisfy the general curiosity. Formalize the prevailing sentiment. But has anyone noticed that so many of the categories focus on a physical characteristic? Shouldn't we as questioning, rebellious adolescents demand something more than artificial assessments of our peers? Besides, how much of an accomplishment is having pretty hair or good looks? Remember biology class? Gregor Mendel and his pea plants? Shouldn't the award be called the Luckiest Gene Award? The Best Random Act of Genetic Recombination?

And why not add more categories in the vein of Most Likely to Succeed? But, wait, what do we mean by succeed? And on what do we base our predictions. Is one's status in high school an indicator of one's status in the bigger world? Will the invisibles, fringe actors, and conspicuous dorks remain on the far-flung margins into the unforeseeable future? Or will the late bloomers finally bloom? Will today's best be tomorrow's mess? Will today's most be tomorrow's roast?

Whenever Angie finished a provocative piece, she felt out of breath, as if she'd been shouting.

After the Senior Favorites piece was published, Letty, who had had enough of Angie's public self-destruction that was causing collateral damage to innocent bystanders, namely, her, offered up another category: Most Obnoxious

"That would degrade the intent," Angie said. "I'm not out to destroy this tradition. Just evolve it."

"God, you're so—so—obnoxious!"

That was close enough to provocative. Angie decided to give the finger to that, but so unpracticed were her fingers that her index finger inadvertently sprung up with her middle finger, negating her attempt. She looked at her two raised fingers. "Peace," she said.

*   *   *

"We're not made of money, you know," her mother said when Angie broached the idea of college. Her father was apologetic and tried to soften the blow. "You can get a good job without going to college. Look at your sister."

"You should've learned to type," her mother said, who herself regretted never having acquired the skill. She believed it had limited her choices in life. She might've been a secretary in an office wearing business suits and matching pumps. She would have had her own desk and a telephone with a line of buttons that lit up and she would've known just which one to push. She would've known the secret language of shorthand.

"What is it you want to study in college?" her parents asked her.

Angie didn't know, couldn't say exactly. She would figure it out when she got there.

That made no sense to her parents. Until she knew what she wanted to study, she should find a job, get some experience, make some money, they said. Once she started making money like Eva, able to save for trips to Hawaii and Las Vegas, or purchase a dinette set, she would forget about college.

* * *

In the spring, Angie got a letter from Wellesley. She showed it to no one. She carried it around in her binder. One afternoon when classes were over and she had dropped off her final provocative piece to Mr. Otto, she was shuffling down the hallway, feeling weary of high school.

She heard footsteps behind her but didn't turn around. There were taps on the soles. They were gaining on her, accelerating. Her locker was just ahead. She would stop and let him pass her. As she spun the lock, the footsteps ceased. She looked up into Max Delgado's acne-scarred face. They hadn't really spoken since tenth grade when he had belatedly raised her score on the Sex Ed self-assessment.

"You stayed after school?" he asked.

Angie couldn't bring herself to be sarcastic. "I turned in my last provocative piece to Mr. Otto."

"Need a ride home?"

Angie hesitated.

"Don't worry. I won't make a move on you."

"I'm not worried," Angie said. "Let's go."

They walked the hallway together. She liked the sound of her soft-soled shoes inside the rhythm of his taps. They exchanged no words until Max said, "I like your provocative pieces."

Angie smiled and thanked him. It made her happy to know that Max had read them.

In the car, they didn't say much, but Angie was not at all uncomfortable with the lack of conversation. Carlos Santana played on the radio, Max kept the beat with his knuckles against the steering wheel, and Angie tapped her foot. Max stopped the car at the park across the street from her house and killed the engine but waited until Santana's last chord faded before he switched off the radio.

She opened her binder. "Can I show you something?"

"Show me anything," he said. He blushed. "You know what I mean."

"I know," she said, feeling suddenly tender toward him. She took the Wellesley letter from the pocket of her binder and handed it to him.

She watched him read it, was touched by how gently he held the paper by the edges. He moved his finger down the side as he read the two short paragraphs which she had memorized.

He handed the letter back to her. "There are other colleges," he said.

"Yes," she agreed, though there weren't. She had only applied to one.

"What about you?" Angie asked. "What happens after graduation?"

"I've got my job at the warehouse. I might take a few classes at the junior college."

"Really?" Angie said, pleased, but also embarrassed that she sounded surprised. "What kind of classes?"

Max shrugged. "Maybe psychology. Something like that."

"Cool," Angie said. It was more than cool. Excellent, really, but Angie didn't want to gush and reveal how truly pleased she was. Then she was seized with an impulse. *Be bold*, she told herself.

"Max," she said, "Are you, um, by any chance, you know, going to the prom?"

Max shifted in his seat, scratched his head, cleared his throat. "Yeah."

While Angie waited to see if he would reveal who his prom date was, she had flashbacks to the fifth grade when Max had spoken to her for the first time and little flickers of hope had bounced around inside her chest only to dissolve when she saw Judy Wiekamp's hand in his a few days later.

"You don't know her," Max said. "She goes to another school."

Angie was relieved that she didn't know Max's date. "I hope you have fun."

"You going?" Max asked.

"Not likely," she said as she thought about her final provocative post that was due to go to press. "Not likely at all."

She gathered her books and opened the car door. "Thanks for the ride, Max."

She waited until he pulled away before she crossed the street to the house that no longer seemed like home.

Silvia Rico was in her front yard next door. They hardly ever spoke these days, so Angie just waved and moved toward her own front door.

"Hi," Silvia called out. "Guess what?"

Angie stopped, but didn't answer, so Silvia crossed the unmarked border between their yards. "I voted for you for Most Likely to Succeed."

Angie stared at Silvia, whose sweet, likable face she had always envied, whose demure demeanor made her an agreeable addition to any group, whose friendship shied from Angie's self-sabotage. "But why," she asked. "Why me?"

Silvia shrugged. "I don't know exactly. It just seemed right."

"Thanks," Angie said. "You know I won't win."

"I know," Silvia said.

*   *   *

Prom—it was a tradition that Angie would not have minded honoring. More than graduation, it seemed to be the capstone to the year, in fact, to all the years of school. But the chances of Angie being invited to the prom were miniscule, invisible as an atom. Which is why she had taken the chance of asking Max. She was glad he was going. She just wished she could see him there, dressed in a tuxedo, his mystery date on his arm.

Angie slapped her forehead at the idea that suddenly invaded it. No one knew her cousin Eddie, formerly Little Eddie until he grew past six feet. He was only fifteen, a ninth-grader, but who would know? Aunt Nelda kept him sequestered in a Catholic school across town and Eddie was dutifully biding his time until he could declare his independence. She called Eddie who accepted her invitation to crash her prom.

Securing a date for the big event didn't stop her from writing her final provocative piece: Prom in a Progressive World.

> *Prom. The final hurrah. The dance of dances. The*
> *capstone to our social lives in our three high-adventure*
> *years of high school—our academic preparation,*
> *our sanctioned and unsanctioned extracurricular*
> *activities, our bosom buddies, our rivals, our coupling*

and uncoupling, our secret crushes. And now we've come to the giddy moment when the males among us will decide whom to ask as his date to the prom, perhaps bracing himself for rejection, perhaps secure in the belief that he will be accepted. And what do the females among us do? Wait to be asked. As if we have no ability to ask for something ourselves. Why should a girl wait to be asked by a guy? But more to the point, why is a date even required? Is it impossible to think that someone might want to be untethered from another? Can we not dance alone? Can't a person enjoy an event liberated from social conventions? And why do fashions imprison females in princess outfits? What would Gloria Steinem wear?

It was, she admitted, self-serving, but it had application beyond her personal situation. It had social implications.

Her piece was largely ignored, so busy were her classmates readying themselves for the prom, their dates having been acquired through the traditional boy-ask-girl method.

At first, she tried to keep her own plans for the prom a secret, but that proved impossible. Her mother eyed her suspiciously at dinner, while watching TV, while emptying the clothes hamper of dirty laundry. Angie had resurrected from the garage rafters the sewing machine her parents had bought her when she had demonstrated a flair for straight seams and sharp collar points in junior high school. Maybe they thought she would have a career on a factory line. But in the end, Angie was not much interested in clothes except as sociological markers and as a study in gender roles.

For the prom she would have no ruffles or puffed sleeves, no empire waisted, round-necked bodice. She would not be dressed like a princess. When her mother discovered her laying out the pattern on black sateen after opening Angie's bedroom door without knocking, she inquired casually, "Oh, are you making a dress?"

"Yes," Angie replied.

"What for?"

Angie considered not telling and weighed what that would mean. She would have to arrange all the logistical requirements such as transportation and funds on her own as against having her mother offering advice on everything from her dress to her date's choice of corsage. Angie realized what an opportunity this was to aggravate and horrify her poor mother, especially given that her date would be her fifteen-year-old cousin.

"Oh, you know, the prom."

When Angie saw the light in her mother's face at the news, she almost regretted her decision to torment her mother with her prom plans. Eva had refused to consider the prom, though no one had asked her as far as Angie knew. Her mother's only real hope for a traditional prom experience was Letty. Until then, she would have to settle for an unreasonable facsimile.

Angie's mother fingered the fabric. "Black, huh?"

"Yes, black."

"It's so—adult."

"Yep." Angie continued to pin the pattern to the fabric.

"You don't think it's a little—Morticia Addams?"

"Nope."

"Who's your date?"

"Eddie."

"Eddie who?"

"Eddie, my cousin."

"Eddie, your cousin?"

They had repeated Eddie's name so many times, it began to sound like a nonsense word. Angie was afraid if she heard it one more time, she would have to bang her head on the floor.

"Eddie can't even drive." There it was—Eddie's name once again. Angie clasped her hands together to avoid clutching her skull. She realized her hands were in beseeching mode.

"So, can I borrow the car that night?"

"I suppose you'll have to. Or your father could drive you."

"No, mom, he couldn't."

Her mother gave one last glance at the black fabric before heading out the door. "Well, at least you're going to the prom," she muttered.

Because her mother was so relieved and happy that Angie was going to the prom, she slipped her a wad of bills one day as she was passing her in the hallway—a furtive gesture that made Angie wonder if her mother had lifted money from the J.C. Penney till. Angie later found out it was money that had been tucked away originally for Eva's prom expenses. Even accounting for inflation, it was a generous sum, and Angie was touched and a little saddened at how much this event meant to her mother.

"You can get your hair done," her mother said. "Get new shoes, buy a boutonniere, pay for a professional photo, go to dinner before the prom, and, of course, pay for your prom tickets."

Angie was stunned by her mother's recitation, as if she'd been preparing for years. Perhaps she had been. Angie thought back to the Toni home perm in third grade, her mother's money-saving attempt at urging them toward cuteness. And there'd been her plea for a salon hairdo for her sixth-grade graduation, which her mother had coldly and summarily denied. But for prom—the apex of Angie's eighteen years, the fancy dress-up, celebratory culmination of her education, the transformation for one night of her awkward, ugly-duckling self—her mother had saved for this day. Banked on it. A salon do, which Angie did not want. She compromised with a trim of the ends and gentle layers. It was Eddie who wanted his hair professionally shampooed and shaped, so Angie paid for it out of her legacy prom fund.

* * *

On the evening of the prom, Aunt Nelda drove Eddie to the Rubio house where Angie's father stood at the ready with his Instamatic. Eddie and Angie bore endless flashbulbs with good humor as they were directed to vary their poses with Eddie's hand on Angie's shoulder, elbow, forearm, hand. They obliged since their plan was to mug cross-eyed for the professional photographer at the prom site. Both Angie's mother and Aunt Nelda had dressed for the occasion, each wearing a J.C. Penney caftan accessorized with hoop earrings for Nelda and pukka shells for Angie's mother. They had their arms around each other. "Somos gemelas," Nelda said. While her mother and Nelda did resemble twins, Angie sensed the distance that had opened up between them since Nelda's move both in her career and in her address. It occurred to her that she heard less Spanish now that Nelda's visits were fewer. *!Qué lástima!* Angie thought, recalling the bit of dialogue she remembered from junior high Spanish class.

Angie invited her mother and Nelda to join her and Eddie in the photo shoot. Angie could smell Nelda's perfume and her mother's bath beads. She breathed in both fragrances and wondered if her body would absorb and carry them to the prom. After several clicks of the shutter, Angie's father thrust the camera at Eddie, and Angie stood between her parents. Together they blinked at the flash.

Eva had declined an invitation to the photo shoot, but Letty and Anthony occupied the peanut gallery. Letty cringed with each pose, and Anthony grinned and cued the subjects. "Say 'cheesy'."

"Please don't tell anyone that you're cousins," Letty pleaded.

To show her unconcern, Angie made a stab at raising her middle finger, but this time her fingers stayed put and her thumb stuck itself in the air. A thumbs up. A-OK. Roger that. Angie sighed at her uncooperative hand.

When they were settled in the Rubio family station wagon, Angie, behind the wheel, turned to Eddie in the passenger seat, his turquoise jacket flashy against the brown plaid upholstery. "Where to?"

She had left it up to him to choose a restaurant and he navigated her to a small French bistro tucked in a side street in the fashion district up north. While they ate creamy, squishy, garlicky unpronounceable delicacies, Angie marveled at her young cousin's aplomb.

"Where have you been all my life? Does savoir faire come with eating French food, or do you acquire this as a result of a Catholic education?"

Eddie dabbed at the sauce on his wisp of a mustache. He put a finger to his lip as he divulged his secret. Nelda paid for etiquette lessons. They toasted Nelda with their iced tea glasses.

The prom was an hour underway when they arrived. Angie hadn't planned on making an entrance, but she had underestimated the effect a tall, handsome young man could have on a crowd dressed in their best and eager to make comparisons.

Angie was sure that the first surprise to her classmates was her appearance at the event she had so thoroughly deplored in her final provocative piece. The greater wonder though was surely her date. Tall, handsome cousin Eddie.

Few people greeted them outright. Most tried hard not to stare. Some smiled little half-smiles. Mr. Otto, one of the chaperones, waved his big hand. The gym was transformed by streamers and balloons. Dimmed lights hid acne and softened hairspray-stiffened updos, gave everyone an aura, sheltered them in the cavernous gym. On the dance floor, strobe lights played on shimmery gowns and satin-trimmed tuxedos.

Eddie was a good dancer and though Angie was not, she didn't feel self-conscious about her disobliging limbs since she knew no one was really watching her. All eyes were on Eddie. Suave, fifteen-year-old Eddie. Angie interrupted her dancing so she could plant a kiss on his cheek. He returned the favor amid all the eyes that were trying so hard not to watch.

At one point, Eddie and Angie traded partners with Max Delgado and his date, a petite, gentle-faced girl with her hair teased high on her head and bangs like cake frosting sweeping her eyebrows. She had long, silver-painted fingernails that she stretched to Eddie's biceps when they danced. He looked like he could hoist her with the crook of his arm without effort. Angie was glad she had brought Eddie. He was having an excellent time. They all danced to Marvin Gaye, and Angie let loose some moves as she appreciated the rhythm in Max's hips. Then a slow song came on and Angie was ready to head for the sidelines for a break, but Max held onto her.

She remembered the last time his hands were on her and she felt her neck go hot. He seemed at ease though and he brought her closer so they could talk through the music.

"Glad you made it."

"Me, too."

"Your date seems nice."

"He is. And he's my cousin. He's fifteen." Angie said all this into Max's ear. Even so, she had to raise her voice above the music. Still, she reveled in the telling, in this joke she was pulling off under the noses of the righteous who clung to tradition and its dusty conventions.

"He looks like he's having fun."

"He is. And so am I."

The music ended, and Max gave her hand a squeeze before she went off to reclaim Eddie. He was surrounded by a group of girls who had separated from their own partners and had formed a posse, which seemed to be interrogating him. She stood outside the circle for a moment to listen. She thought of how many times and in how many circumstances she had stood outside the circle. She didn't feel at all left out. She knew the girls were simultaneously trying to impress him and pump him for information about who he was and why on earth he was at the prom with Angie Rubio. Angie knew there was the possibility that Eddie, as smooth as he was, would let something slip and all would be undone.

She wandered off to the restroom where girls were freshening makeup and repairing droopy curls. Judy Wiekamp, whose eyeball was kissing the mirror as she skimmed mascara onto her lashes, widened her eyes even further as she caught sight of Angie.

"Nice dress, Angie," Judy said, pulling back from the mirror, but not facing Angie, just talking to her reflection.

"Thanks," Angie said. She thought it best not to return the compliment since she loathed Judy's dress—ivory, like the soap, ruffled, and princess-y. She glanced down at Judy's shoes. No, she hated those, too. She searched Judy's whole person for something she honestly liked. Surely, there was something. She knew there had to be. Suddenly, it was important for Angie to find it. All of her life she had been perceived a certain way, a way that was not the whole of who she was. She stood staring at the back of Judy's dress, studying its ivory gleam as if the threads might reveal a clue in their weave, into the inner workings of Judy.

Judy turned around to stare back at Angie. "Is something wrong?" She held her mascara wand in the air, twirled it impatiently.

In the harsh light of the restroom, everyone looked gaudy—the colors of their gowns lurid, faces flushed from dancing, sweat beading at the lip and hairline, pimples showing through makeup, eyes bloodshot from whatever drug or drink they'd ingested before passing inspection at the gym door.

"What's your problem?" Judy asked.

Angie heard the rise in Judy's voice, and was overcome by an urge. She grabbed Judy by the shoulders. Girls around them gasped. Angie's fingers dug into Judy's ruffles, pulled her to her, their faces inches apart so that Angie could see small clumps of mascara at the corner of Judy's brown eyes, which blazed with—what? Fury, fear, regret. Angie drew her in and hugged her hard. It was a momentary embrace.

Angie stepped back, the faces around her a blur, and spun into a free stall, behind which she could hear the stifled exclamations and murmured mystification and pique as Judy and her friends debated the meaning of her action. She sat on the toilet, her black sateen, homemade prom dress bunched up at her waist, and relieved herself of punch.

She heard someone burst through the restroom door, someone breathless with laughter and news who sang, "Guess who Angie's date is!"

Before anyone could guess, the messenger shouted, "Her cousin!"

Angie flushed the toilet, adjusted her dress, opened her stall door, washed her hands, and gave a perfect finger as she pushed through the swinging door.

She found Eddie at the punch bowl. "Your cover's blown," she informed him.

He lifted a well-shaped eyebrow. "Do we make a run for it?"

Angie poured herself some punch. "No, we stay."

They clinked glasses and threw back a swallow. They stayed until the last dance, by which time they had ceased being an attraction. As the night wore on, the sentimentality smothered them all like a blanket. The giddiness that had infused the early part of the dance had turned heavy with sap. Now with the last song, they swayed to the Carpenters and sang along, "We've Only Just Begun." The lights went up and the weary chaperones began ushering them out the door.

While other couples headed to the after-prom at the bowling alley, Angie drove Eddie home to meet his curfew. When she pulled up to the house, the lights were still on and they could see the flicker of the TV through the living room window. Angie kept the engine running

"Mom's asleep in front of the TV. She'll want to hear about the prom."

"You go," Angie said. "I'm kind of tired."

"Thanks for the date," he said, sliding out of the car.

"Thanks for being my date."

He leaned on the car door. "Who would you've picked instead of me?"

"Henry Darrow."

"Yeah, me, too," Eddie said, grinning before closing the door.

Angie watched him lope up the steps. When she saw Nelda peek through the curtains, she drove away, but not directly home. She drove the quiet streets of Kimball Park. She drove past the high school gym, dark now, and mostly deserted with just a few stragglers heading to their cars, lit joints tiny flares in the night. She drove down Viewlands Avenue with its parade of fast-food and family-style restaurants, pharmacies and five-and-dime stores. She drove past her junior high school which looked strangely small and then past her elementary school, which looked ridiculously smaller.

She kept driving around Kimball Park, tracing its boundaries to the west where beyond the industrial parks lay the bay and somewhere beyond that the ocean, to the north where all the rest of California stretched, to the east where the mountains gave way to desert and the whole rest of the country where on the opposite end the only college she had applied to had turned her down, to the south beyond the border with Mexico a mere ten miles away, where her last name and the Spanish she didn't know how to speak came from. As she drove home, she knew that somehow, some way, she would leave by one of these directions.

ACKNOWLEDGEMENTS

I wrote these Angie Rubio stories over a period of fifteen years, often between other projects or sometimes as a distraction from them. I'm grateful for the residencies that provided space for me to work, not just a desk and a chair, not just a room of my own, but a place of nurture and inspiration where I could imagine Angie Rubio into being. Profound appreciation for Hedgebrook, its cozy cottages and the woods that surround them; Artsmith in all its hominess in the atmospheric Orcas Island winter; Virginia Center for the Creative Arts with its splendid view of the Blue Ridge Mountains and the cows on the front lawn as muses; Centrum with its pelagic breezes and resident ghosts; and Mineral School, where fittingly I put the finishing touches on the manuscript in an elementary school classroom turned writing studio, also equipped with ghosts.

Grants and fellowships from 4Culture, Artist Trust, and Seattle Office of Arts and Culture helped fund travel to residencies, time away from my job, and recompense for the undervalued work of writing.

Alma Garcia, Allison Green, Jennifer Munro, and Lily Yu read some or all of these stories with care and insight.

These journals gave Angie Rubio her first public presence: *Adirondack Review,* which published "Help," and the *Santa Ana Review,* which published "First Confession."

James Cameron has for years assumed the household and family functions that involve spreadsheets, bureaucracies, and patience so that I can write, and he always has my back.

My sibs, Rose, Sandy, Joe, and Diana, with whom I shared a childhood in a place much like Angie Rubio's Kimball Park, boost me with their delight in and support of my work.

My English teachers from so many years ago, intentionally or not, planted tiny seeds in my then oblivious young brain, where they lay dormant until my mid-life. Though most of these teachers of my formative years are no longer of this world, they remain vivid to me. In fourth grade at El Toyon Elementary, I wrote a story about a cat and a poem about the wind, and aside from the approval in Miss McDaniel's face and a gold star on my paper, I understood the rewards that words can bring. At Granger Junior High, Mrs. Runyon picked me, who was seldom picked for anything, to create scripts and costumes for our eighth-grade class production of *Romeo and Juliet*. At Sweetwater Union High, in tenth grade, I strove for A's to be worthy of Mrs. Brassey's wit and wryness. And in eleventh grade, Mr. Niemuth's praise of my mind and my words in a short exclamatory sentence inked on the front page of the assignment I had dreaded most—the autobiography required in all junior English classes—made me feel seen.

Deepest thanks to Jaded Ibis Press for publishing this book about a character who means so much to me.